Some of the very ni

Dr. Ned ... troubled
women w ... once too
often.

Emmett and ... **May**—famous actor and
actress whose ... demanding roles are those of
happy husband and wife.

Enid Keys—a divorcee for whom one man is
never enough. She walks the tightwire between
honest lust and self-destructive nymphomania.

Avery Morrison—distinguished senator and
statesman, whose personal problems make a
mockery of his public image.

Jane Bonner—a fantastically beautiful young
girl who is willing to give herself to any man for
the right price.

Arthur Slater—the high-school teacher accused
of intercourse with his students, but whose
shame goes far beyond that sin.

SECRETS
was originally published by Simon and Schuster.

Books by Burt Hirschfeld

Generation of Victors
Secrets

Published by POCKET BOOK

 Are there paperbound books you want
but cannot find in your retail stores?

SECRETS

Burt Hirschfeld

PUBLISHED BY POCKET BOOKS NEW YORK

SECRETS

Simon and Schuster edition published 1975

POCKET BOOK edition published May, 1976

This POCKET BOOK edition includes every word contained in
the original, higher-priced edition. It is printed from brand-
new plates made from completely reset, clear, easy-to-read type.
POCKET BOOK editions are published by
POCKET BOOKS,
a division of Simon & Schuster, Inc.,
A GULF+WESTERN COMPANY
630 Fifth Avenue,
New York, N.Y. 10020.
Trademarks registered in the United States
and other countries.

Standard Book Number: 671-80445-6.
Library of Congress Catalog Card Number: 75-15691.

Printed in the U.S.A.

PROLOGUE

THERE WAS NOTHING STATIC about Treysa Horn. Even asleep she seemed poised to spring into action. Her legs were drawn up, set to launch her into the middle of things, arms reaching for whatever the breaking day might offer.

In repose, her small, cheerful features appeared to pull up in a smile. Her neat round head sprouted honey-colored curls, adding to the impish look. A dog fancier had once likened her to a terrier—feisty.

The alarm went off. She sat up, feet reaching for slippers. A chenille robe went over the pajama tops she wore. She looked affectionately at her husband, who was sleeping face down on the far side of the double bed, then went downstairs.

The kitchen had been designed to Treysa's specifications. Butcher-block counter tops, scrubbed clean the night before. A gleaming stainless-steel double sink. Utensils hanging from pegboard. The red light of the General Electric coffee maker glowed, triggered by a timer at precisely the same moment the alarm clock went off.

She took milk and eggs from a pale-yellow refrigerator, cracked the eggs into a plastic bowl, added salt, and beat them enthusiastically. She squeezed oranges and filled three tall glasses and cut six thick slices from the whole-wheat bread she had baked the previous afternoon. She set the table in the breakfast nook, now bathed in sunlight. Alongside each glass of orange juice went a vitamin C tablet and a multivitamin.

Treysa assessed her work. Everything in place. Everything perfect. So very different from the way she had been brought up. Her father had been an itinerant evangelical preacher—Baptist, of course—and the family had roamed across West Texas, Oklahoma, New Mexico, wherever his calling led. They traveled in a battered Chevrolet, slept and ate in an old trailer that badly needed new springs. A hot plate served her mother as a stove and water was always in short supply. At night, Treysa slept in a sleeping bag on the back seat of the Chevrolet, her parents in the trailer.

It was a disjointed life, with few rewards. No regular school to attend. No friends. No sense of belonging. She came to crave a stationary existence, stability, a permanent home of her own. It seemed to be more than she would ever achieve, until Leon Horn came along. He had provided it all. Turned fantasy into reality. Given her more than she was entitled to. And she cherished him for doing so.

She went back up to the bedroom and woke her husband with a gentle kiss. He drew her down, held her.

"A new week," she said. "A new day."

He moved his middle against her. "If I had the time," he muttered.

Her laugh was bright, full of pleasure. "Seems to me I've heard that song before. . . . Come on, breakfast's almost ready. I'll lay out your things."

She arranged clean socks, T-shirt, jockey shorts on the foot of the bed. Her father had worn white cotton boxer shorts. And he would sit around in them on those hot Texas nights, engrossed in his Bible, the fly gaping. In later years, men who wore boxer shorts had found Treysa to be a reluctant lover. All that before Leon, of course.

She went into her son's room. At ten, Daniel was very much like his father; Daniel, too, slept face down into his pillow. How, Treysa wondered, did they manage to get enough air? She touched the boy's shoulder.

"Time to get up, Daniel. Your papa's shaving."

The boy rolled onto his back, eyes clenched. "Maybe I won't go to school today."

"Maybe you will."

"I feel something coming over me, a terrible sickness."

"Ten minutes to get washed, dressed, and down to the table."

His protest trailed her downstairs. In the guest powder room, Treysa kept an extra set of toilet articles. She brushed her teeth vigorously, finding pleasure in the act. She washed, brushed her hair quickly, applied lipstick. Her husband was at the table when she returned to the kitchen.

"You look great," he said.

"Take your vitamins."

"Since you inflicted this regimen on me, I get progressively weaker every day. Not to mention poorer. These pills cost a fortune."

She ignored the complaint, brought coffee to the table. "Always wear colored shirts, Leon. You look very nice."

He slapped her bottom and she squealed on her way back to the counter.

Breakfast over, Leon helped clear the table. "Let's move it," he said.

Treysa stood at the kitchen window, looking out. "Leon, something's the matter."

He came up behind her. "What is it?"

"The water's gone away. The pond's dry."

Simon's Pond, named in honor of Jeremiah Simon, who had settled most of the land around it one hundred years earlier. The pond, one hundred and ten feet across by eighty-seven feet, was fed by what members of the Pond Association were fond of calling The River. In fact, The River was a shallow stream no more than two yards across at its widest point. On the down side, The River carried off the excess water. Twenty years before, a stone dam had been erected to keep the water from draining too rapidly, enlarging the pond to its present size.

Here, in winter, residents of the area ice-skated. Now, in early autumn, wild ducks floated on the water, and a few years ago there had been a family of swans. But now the pond was empty of water, its bottom shining, a dark and unappealing mudhole.

Leon shot his brows. "I don't get it."

Daniel squeezed between them. "The water's not there!" He bounced up and down, as if the alteration pleased him.

"Sensabaugh," Treysa said with suddent ferocity.

"Maybe not," Leon said.

"Oh, Leon, you're too nice. Sensabaugh opened the sluice gates during the night."

"We don't know that for sure."

"I'm sure."

Daniel gazed up at his parents. "Why would Mr. Sensabaugh do that?" Daniel and Terry Sensabaugh were schoolmates and often played together.

"I have never trusted that man," Treysa said.

"Let's make certain. I'll call him when I get to my office."

"Pious men," Treysa said, rolling her eyes to heaven. "Lord save me from pious men."

"I'll talk to him," Leon said. "We'd better get going. I don't want to miss my train."

Treysa turned away from the window, put on a raincoat over her robe, and they all climbed into the Toyota wagon. Treysa drove with a cheerful abandon, slightly faster than seemed prudent to her husband. But he never criticized. Leon Horn loved his wife just as she was. He felt no need to change her. Not even a little.

Commuters from Arcadia had to travel over to nearby Westport in order to ride the New Haven railroad into Grand Central. At the station, Leon climbed out of the car, went around to the driver's side and kissed his wife on the cheek.

"I'll try to get home early," he said.

"You speak to Sensabaugh, hear!"

"I will."

"Maybe I should call him."

"I'll handle it, Treysa. Have a good day, Daniel."

"See you tonight, Papa."

Treysa turned the Toyota and headed along Riverside Avenue toward the Post Road and Washington Academy, the private school Daniel attended, promising to pick him up at the end of the school day.

"If I'm a little late, it's because I'm playing paddle tennis this afternoon."

"Are you any good, Mama?"

"The Mickey Mantle of my set."

Back home she draped the raincoat over the banister and ran upstairs. She dropped the robe and the pajama tops on the bed, decided to phone Luellyn Case. Together they might come up with an effective scheme for shackling Sensabaugh once and for all. Like the Horns, the Cases had bought their house—nearly two years earlier—because of its location on the pond. In Arcadia, water views were a high-priority item and resulted in higher property values. She dialed, got no answer. Luellyn was an early starter.

Treysa examined her naked body in the mirror on the bathroom door. Her skin glowed with good health. She was proud of the way she looked, intended to remain beautiful for herself and for Leon.

She dressed with swift efficiency. Matching bra and panties. Plaid skirt, black cotton blouse. She fingered her curly hair into place and went downstairs. Through the laundry room, into the garage, mind ranging to the day ahead.

Less than nine minutes later, she was dead.

Part One

CHAPTER ONE

I

LOUKAS DROVE EASILY without thinking about it, eyes automatically registering the road ahead. On Watson Place, four potholes that seemed to have become a permanent fixture caused him to move the faded blue Valiant into the oncoming lane. He swung into Judge's Lane and climbed the hill rapidly past shedding maples and oaks, and a variety of evergreens, fenced on either side by dry stone walls hand made by some early Connecticut farmers.

Driving came easy for Loukas. But not much else. It had become increasing difficult to sleep, and to get out of bed in the morning. Once life had been something to explore and revel in, a glittering package full of surprises and promise. No more.

There had been no dramatic moment of change. Just a gradual erosion of motive and commitment, of satisfaction and reward. A bitter fact, established even before it was recognized. A twinge brought Loukas' hand to his middle. Ulcer symptoms, Dr. Dubin had warned. Stop worrying.

Let it all hang out, Dubin had suggested.

Why not? It had become that kind of a world. Public confession rivaled baseball as the national pastime. On television, in the newspapers, in magazines, in books. People took spiritual nourishment from the guilty revelations of their betters—or at least those who dared to give up their most private acts for public entertainment and enlightenment.

9

Loukas rubbed his middle until the gnawing pain was gone. Ulcers were an affliction of driven men who lived in terror that all they'd gained would one day be wiped out. Loukas had little to lose and so felt betrayed by his body.

He turned the Valiant into Pond Ridge Road, stopped behind the green-and-white patrol car parked there, and got out, buttoning the jacket of his gray suit. There was a tight, drawn set to his body, as if all moisture had been squeezed out of him, the flesh pared down to the minimum. His head was long and large, the hair thick and graying, cut close to his head. His eyes were brown and slow to move; he had an ample Greek nose, a wide mouth, a lean hard jaw. His skin was weathered and lined.

His stride was long, carrying him effortlessly along. Bony hands dropped out of his sleeves, the broad wrists scored by thick veins. He might have been a construction worker or a commercial fisherman or a truck driver. He was a cop.

Loukas inspected the house set back fifty feet from the road. It was without style, without distinction, centered around the inevitable family room. Even so, the house was easily worth one hundred thousand on today's market. More and more such houses were being erected in Arcadia; they sheltered people Loukas seldom encountered, except in the line of duty.

Burglary victims mostly. They would show up at Headquarters to identify a bicycle that had been stolen. Or ski boots. Or golf clubs. Or to describe a stolen car. Almost always a Porsche or a Mercedes or a Jaguar. Only the station wagons were domestic—Fords and Chevys.

Sometimes they came to get their sons, picked up for drunken driving. Or with an ounce of grass in their jeans. Or for fighting in a bar.

Rich and successful people. The men smooth and confident. The women sleek and beautiful. All part of a strange world that seemed vaguely threatening to Loukas.

It hadn't been that way when Loukas was a boy.

Arcadia had changed considerably since then. One of those towns that dotted the Connecticut shoreline of Long Island Sound, it had been settled originally by Portuguese, Italians, and a few Greeks. Later the Norwegians moved in and some Irish. They fished and they farmed and life unfolded slowly and peacefully.

The year before the start of the second World War, artists and writers discovered the little village. It was quiet, pretty, a place to escape to from the heat of New York's summers without being too far from that world so central to their lives. By the end of the war, a number of creative people had established themselves permanently in Arcadia.

Artists' colony. The word spread and drew to town a generation of advertising and communications executives. The bright boys of their college classes who intended one day to paint great pictures and write great plays and compose stirring poems.

Instead, the bright boys made a great deal of money and came to speak of the dichotomy of their lives, the division between their ingrained love of Art and the pragmatic need for material gain.

The schools in Arcadia were excellent. The citizens demanded that they be so. Taxes were reasonable. Crime was minimal. Zoning provided plenty of space for a man to breathe in and houses rose in value every year. The reputation of the town spread.

Soon the transient managers came, employees of the great national and international companies. Moving at the command of their firms every two or three years. Shifted around by a hierarchy no less remote and efficient than the military. But paid better.

NewComers, Inc., was formed to introduce these strangers to their own kind. Young mothers collected at morning coffees. They bowled on Thursday afternoons, visited museums, went to the theater in New York. Epicurean suppers. Fall dances. Historical tours and lectures. Charity work. The new people dedicated themselves to the good life. To maintaining standards.

Most of the six thousand people who lived in Arcadia

were affluent, educated, gifted, sophisticated. The others —the shopkeepers, the mechanics, the carpenters, the firemen—they were leftovers from the past.

Loukas exhaled sadly; he, too, was one of the leftovers.

He stepped over the rope that closed off the driveway and went down the slope to where Sam Barker was standing. Barker was heavy, a plodding man with a flat face and tiny dull eyes. The kind of cop who always did exactly as he was told. Eyeing Loukas, he arranged his cap squarely on his big round head and snapped off a clumsy salute.

Loukas lifted a hand.

"Morning, Sergeant."

"You sealed off the area," Loukas said, giving the small recognition Barker needed.

"Yes, sir. Nobody's been allowed to tramp over the place, inside or out."

"Good work."

"It's a homicide, Sergeant. Yes, sir, that's what it is, all right."

Loukas made a sound back in his throat.

"Nice-looking lady, too. Shame."

"Any witnesses, Sam?"

"None that I know of, Sergeant. Just the lady who found the deceased."

"Where is she?"

"In the house. In the living room."

Loukas gazed steadily at the unformed man and Barker flushed.

"She was very upset, Sergeant. I told her to just sit there. Not to touch anything. She was pretty upset."

"Next time let 'em cry in the fresh air, Sam. What's her name?"

Barker opened his notebook. "Name of Sandra Felton."

"Where's the body?"

"Down by the pool."

It was a blue plastic tank set down on the ground with a redwood frame and deck. A flagstone path led Loukas behind it, to Treysa Horn. He placed himself carefully at her feet, forced himself to look down. Her face was bruised, blood seeping from her nose and mouth. Her throat was laced with purple welts and her still eyes were glazed with terror. A plaid skirt curled up around her waist. Her panties lay off to one side, as if flung away in haste. One leg went off at a right angle to her torso, the knee bent; the other leg was stretched out flat on the ground.

Bile rose up in Loukas' throat and he was afraid he was going to be sick. He fought against it and soon he felt better. He crouched down. Treysa Horn had been a pretty woman with a fine figure. But lying there, brown pubic patch exposed, skin graying, she appeared slightly offensive. Loukas emptied his lungs and went up to the house.

Sandra Felton was in the living room. She wore a flame-red warm-up suit and sneakers, sat hunched over on the couch, face concealed in her hands. She was a tall woman. Her shoulders were big, her back broad, her hands finely shaped and strong.

"Mrs. Felton," Loukas said.

She made a muffled sound behind her hands.

"I'm Sergeant Loukas, Mrs. Felton. I have to make some phone calls, then I'll want to ask you a few questions."

She nodded.

He used the wall phone in the kitchen. A man's voice answered. "Abner," Loukas said, "this is Theo. I've got a corpse on my hands. Number eight Pond Ridge Road. A raised ranch. Get over here right away."

"I've got appointments this morning."

"Cancel them." Loukas hung up, dialed again.

"Police Headquarters. Officer Hale speaking."

"This is Loukas."

"Yes, Sergeant?"

"On the Horn killing. Get the specialists out here right away."

"Yes, sir."

Loukas went back into the living room. Sandra Felton hadn't moved. He sat in a comfortable chair opposite and studied her. She gave no sign that she was aware of him. "We're going to have to talk now, Mrs. Felton."

She shook her head as if in protest. "How can people do such things to each other?"

Loukas decided the question required no answer. "You found the body?" he said. The year before he'd attended an eight-hour seminar given by the FBI in Hartford. It had been called The Criminal Investigation—A Logical Process.

Sandra Felton looked up. Her face had the same look of health and strength as her body. Her skin was smooth, her eyes large and bright, her features regular, almost handsome. She hadn't been crying, and that surprised Loukas. Most women would have been reduced to tears. He wondered about that.

"You discovered Mrs. Horn?" he said.

"Yes." Then, almost in challenge: "I was out running."

"A jogger. We've got lots of joggers in Arcadia."

"I *run*," she corrected. "As fast as I can go."

"I see."

"I live on the other hide of the hill. Sometimes I come this way."

"You run every morning?"

"No. Only when I have to get rid of—" She broke off.

"Get rid of what, Mrs. Felton?"

She shrugged and the loose-fitting sweat shirt failed to conceal the movement of her full breasts. Loukas lifted his eyes quickly. "Excess poison," she said. "It collects in the system. Or wouldn't you know about that, Sergeant?"

Loukas grew annoyed. This fine-looking woman with, he supposed, an equally fine-looking husband, probably pulling down seventy-five big ones a year, did not have to condescend.

"Okay," he said, and the soft voice took on a biting edge. "You were taking your morning constitutional. You come this way all the time?"

She searched his face as if expecting to find there the

reason for his antagonism. "There's no set pattern," she replied. "I never have had enough discipline."

"Did you see anybody?"

"No."

"No other runners?"

"Just the Richmond's poodles."

"Poodles?"

"Peggy Richmond owns two poodles, big black jobs. They were here. As if they were guarding poor Treysa. When they saw me, they ran away."

"Did you see anything besides the black dogs?" Loukas said. "Anything at all?"

"No. At least I don't think I did."

"You're not sure?"

"The dogs were barking. I could hear them before I made it this far. Sound carries through the woods this time of the year. When you're out by yourself, there's only the sound of your footsteps crunching the leaves. Anything else cuts right through. Maybe I did hear something. Somebody else running. I though it was an echo. Maybe it wasn't."

"So you didn't actually see anybody."

"I can't be sure. Maybe there was somebody. Going through the woods."

"A man?"

"Could be."

"Toward the road? Toward Judge's Lane?"

"No. Angling away. Heading toward Tudor Place, that cul-de-sac east of here."

"Did you hear a car?"

"A car!"

"The sound of a motor."

The handsome face frowned as if puzzling over a problem. "I can't be sure. The road isn't that far away. There were cars, there always are at that time of the morning."

"Try to remember. Loud? Soft?"

"I don't know."

"How did it sound? Like a Cadillac, for example? Or maybe a Volkswagen?"

"I don't know."

"Okay, let's get back to the man."

"I can't be certain it was a man."

"Describe what you saw."

"Maybe it was just a shadow. The early-morning sun does funny things when you're moving through the trees."

"Think about it. Any kind of a description. It would be a great help."

"I want to help."

"What can you tell me about Mr. Horn?"

"Not much. He's an engineer, I think. Something like that. He works in New York."

"Do you have a phone number?"

"No. I knew her, Treysa, but not very well. They have a boy. His name's Daniel. He's at Washington Academy."

Loukas knew he would have to inform the husband that his wife was dead. But he would leave the boy to his father. "Is there anything else you can add, Mrs. Felton?" he said.

"I'm afraid not."

He nodded amiably. "I may have some more questions for you later on."

II

Abner Posner was crouched over the body of Treysa Horn when Loukas came along. He spoke without looking up.

"Nice-looking piece," he said. "Hate like the devil to see good stuff go to waste."

"You prepared to say it's a homicide, Abner?"

"Now, Theo, after the autopsy I'll go on record. Not before."

"You will admit she's dead?"

"Oh, she's dead all right."

"Not pretty, is it?"

"Somebody beat the hell out of her. Why would a man do that to a woman? Look at those bruises. Mighty rough."

"Beaten to death, Abner? You're the M.E. Take a wild guess. That's all I want."

"Nope. See her throat, those welts. That's a strangler's work. Got her with his thumbs around the carotid artery. With her air cut off, she couldn't've lasted long. No blood to the brain, either. Give you odds the larynx is broken."

"You mean the voice box?"

Posner almost smiled. "The voice box. It's just cartilage, you know. Can't withstand much pressure. Might be the trachea is crushed. We'll just have to wait and see," he ended professionally.

"Would you say the man who did this was exceptionally strong, Abner?"

"Not necessarily. Anybody could do it. Even you or me, Theo." This time he did grin, but briefly. "This was done from the front. That is, he was over her, on his knees, between her legs. Worked his thumbs up against the jugular and bore down. Look at her expression. Poor sucker knew she'd had it."

"Was it rape, Abner?"

Posner pointed. "There's some viscous material seeping out of her. Semen most likely. We can assume we'll find torn tissue in there, some bleeding. I prefer my pussy a little less hairy than this one."

"Jesus," Loukas said.

"You haven't had many homicides, have you, Theo?"

"This is number one. In all my time on the force there've been only two or three others. About a dozen years back I covered a traffic fatality over on Route Thirty-two. A bloody mess. Carter Lawrence got all the killings, whenever they came up."

"Well," Posner said, "you get used to them after a while."

Loukas grimaced. "I hope not."

III

Ralph Burleigh sat on the old oak bench across the room from the Desk Officer, huddled over the clipboard,

pencil poised. His brow was furrowed and his mouth was
pursed as he studied the X's and O's on the paper in
front of him.

A well-proportioned young man, with good shoulders
and large hands, he was a familiar figure at Police Headquarters. He had been a substitute halfback on the
Arcadia High School team almost a decade earlier and
now coached the football team sponsored by the Police
Athletic League for kids under twelve. When Loukas
entered the building, Burleigh began talking at once.

"Theo! Hey, Theo, give this play a look, will you? A
variation on the old Statue of Liberty. In my version, the
quarterback hands off to the deep back so it looks like
an ordinary off-tackle slant. The halfback gives the ball
to the tight end coming back, going against the flow.
What do you think, Theo?"

Loukas examined the diagram. He remembered his
own days as a high-school athlete; he had waged a
continuous battle to conceal his fear, to pretend to be
braver and tougher than he was. He returned the clipboard to Ralp Burleigh.

"It's a little complicated for kids, isn't it?"

"Maybe you're right," Burleigh said. "I guess so. Tell
you what, Theo, come on out and watch practice some
time. We're having the first of the season this afternoon.
You've got a feeling for the game; you could help. And
I need all the help I can get." He shook his head.
"Nobody takes little leagues seriously. I don't understand it. The game is good for the kids. Teaches them
self-reliance, courage, perseverance, things like that."

"Arcadia's never been a football town," Loukas said,
moving off.

"You're right. All they know is tennis. Don't people
realize that contact sports build character? Tennis is a
girl's game—" He broke off as Loukas disappeared into
the corridor leading to the command offices. Shaking his
head, Burleigh returned to his place on the oak bench,
laboring over his clipboard.

CHAPTER TWO

I

AT ABOUT THE SAME TIME that Treysa Horn was being killed, Leo Diamond edged his long legs cautiously toward the rim of the Westport railroad station. He had been a resident of Arcadia for more than a year and a half and commuted to his office in Manhattan five days a week. He disliked the train ride, found it tedious and boring. Reading was difficult for him, the lurching and rocking of the cars tended to make his eyes tired. And he had yet to strike up a conversation with a fellow commuter that was worth the effort.

Diamond's washed-blue eyes were never still. He expected life to thrust difficulties, problems, and threats in his path and he had trained himself to be alert to their coming, to avoid them whenever possible. Protective skepticism was his spiritual armor as he effectively shielded body and soul from all dangers.

Peering down the right of way, he saw nothing but iron rails gleaming in the morning sunlight. He took it as a personal affront. He beat a hurried retreat to the sanctuary of the middle of the platform before inspecting his wristwatch. "Ah," he said in despair.

"What's wrong?" Ruth, his wife, said automatically. The train was late, she knew, and lateness drove Leo Diamond wild. He would be composing a letter of complaint to the *Times* in his head. Plotting bloody revenge against the Lords of the New Haven. Crying out in silent despair—*Why are they doing this to me?*

Only recently had Ruth Diamond come to enjoy

her husband's frequent periods of despair and dismay. So much that happened, or failed to happen, bothered Leo Diamond. The cogs and gears of his world simply refused to work right. A man seeking precision and perfection, Diamond everywhere encountered sloth, laxity, and corruption in increasing amounts.

"Ah," he said.

"What is it?" Ruth said, keeping her finely etched features immobile.

"Seven minutes late," Diamond answered. "On time, the ticket agent said when I called. No consideration for the riding public. Dissemblers, all of them."

"It'll be here," Ruth said, feeling only a small guilt over her new-found pleasure.

"When? When?"

"Your watch could be fast, Leo."

Diamond lifted his face to heaven. "This watch, it's an Accutron. Accurate to the thousandth part of a second. Bulova guarantees it. Lateness is endemic with this rotten railroad. Nobody's punctual anymore. I've got a girl coming in at eleven. The railroads should be nationalized."

"I thought you were against socialism."

"Who said anything about socialism?"

"Nationalization," she said in answer.

"Don't confuse the issue. Something's got to be done. My God in heaven, do you believe for a second that I want the government getting its grubby hands on the railroads? What kind of a fool do you take me for? Absolute chaos would result. The government can't even get a letter to Philadelphia in under a week." He pushed back his wiry red hair.

"From where?"

"What?"

"A letter to Philadelphia from where in under a week, Leo?"

He stared at her. "What are you talking about, Ruth?"

"You said—"

"I know what I said. From New York, naturally, where else?"

"Does it really take a week?"

"The point is it doesn't get there with dispatch. Are you trying to provoke me?" he added warily.

"Why would I do that?"

"I'm going to give it up, the train. Drive into the city."

"All that traffic makes you nervous."

"It doesn't make me nervous, Ruth. I just don't like it. I hate city driving. What's wrong with that?"

The train swung around the bend and commuters jockeyed for position, trying to place themselves opposite the doors. The train drew to a halt and Diamond found himself confronting the middle of a car. He never got it right.

"Not in a smoker," he cried as Ruth turned into a car. "Is this a smoker?"

"There are seats here," she answered.

"Cigarette smoke gives me a headache."

"The other cars are full," she warned.

"Ruth, you're upsetting me."

She followed him the other way. They were unable to locate two empty seats together. Back to the smoker, where they found two seats, one behind the other. Diamond motioned Ruth into one, then sat, closed his eyes, and gave his mind to the day ahead.

II

A neatly lettered sign at the side of the road: Avery Morrison. Shining brass on black iron, polished, dignified, expensive. Behind a low stone wall were twelve hundred acres that belonged to Avery Morrison. Or more rightly, land that had been entrusted to his care by his forebears. Land held for those Morrisons who would follow.

Avery Morrison had been born into a family that knew its place. Had carved that place out of the rocky New England soil. A family that judged everyone else by its own position in society. It was a family with roots in English nobility, a family aware of its responsibilities, its obligations to those less fortunate; a family of pride, of duty, of honor.

Thus Avery Morrison was raised, to embark on significant endeavors. For more than two centuries, Morrisons had worked to enlarge the family fortune, giving their spare time to charitable efforts and laboring also for the general good of the nation. Morrisons had been governors and generals, congressmen and mayors, Presidential advisers. Avery Morrison had been governor of the state and was serving his second term in the United States Senate. He was a credit to his family and intended to be one forever.

In the Morrison house, breakfast was always served in a bright and cheerful room off the center hall, from which one could look across the brick veranda past the pool and the tennis court to the neatly tailored gardens.

A wrought-iron table topped with pale-green marble stood in the center of the breakfast room. Potted plants lined the walls and a huge Saint Bernard dozed in a patch of sunlight. A young black girl served the morning meal. The Morrisons dined off hand-decorated china that had been in the family for generations, using silver that was believed to have been fashioned by Paul Revere—a family myth that Avery Morrison gave little credence to.

The Morrisons ate without haste, speaking in modulated tones about subjects of common interest. Over his second cup of coffee, Avery Morrison lit his first cigarette of the day. His last smoke would come over brandy after dinner, ten cigarettes in all, no more, no less.

Dressed in a soft gray suit with a chalk stripe, Avery emanated the confidence of a man who knew he belonged wherever he happened to be. He turned to his son, Willy. Like his father, Willy was tall, his face finely constructed, his body solid and strong.

"The plane will be here soon," he said.

Willy gazed ingenuously at his father. "Maybe you could drop me off at school, Father. How about that, being set down right in front of the Administration Building in a helicopter. That'd be neat."

Morrison kept his face still. "It would be even neater if you raised the level of your school work, Willy."

"I do okay, Father."

"Okay has never been enough for a Morrison. You have certain responsibilities. We, your mother and I, expect more of you."

"I do my best, Father."

"I would like to believe that."

Clarice Morrison spoke. She was a slender woman with brown hair that fell in gentle waves to frame her delicate face. "Willy will do better when he gets to Princeton, Avery. He's promised me that."

"Perhaps. But is may take some doing to get Princeton to accept Willy. The competition increases every year."

Willy grinned. "I'm depending on you, Father, to get me in."

Avery made a sound in his throat. "There is a limit to everything, Willy. Even a father's forbearance. Remember that."

"Yes, sir," Willy said. He studied his plate.

Avery stood up. "I must collect my things. Wouldn't want to miss the flight from Kennedy."

"Are you going to accept the appointment, Avery?" his wife asked.

"First let them offer it officially. Much depends on the station they have in mind."

"It could be Mexico," Clarice said. "I understand a change is in order there. I'd like Mexico."

"We'll see. Do you think you'd enjoy that, Willy? Summers in Mexico. It's a fine country."

"As long as I don't have to address you as Mr. Ambassador." He laughed.

Avery left the room without any response.

III

At precisely three minutes before the hour on the battery-driven clock on the wall, Ned Bookman entered his office, an addition to his house. Bookman had personally supervised its design and construction. He had furnished it with expensive care, anxious to create a calm and reassuring atmosphere, all for the benefit of his patients. At the same time, Bookman was a man who took considerable pleasure in the esthetics of his surroundings, and his personal comfort.

Edward Michael Bookman, M.D., F.A.P.A., Diplomate in Psychiatry, had trained at the Menninger clinic and at Bellevue, and then spent two years in Vietnam as a medical officer. Later, he opened an office in Manhattan before transferring his practice to Arcadia. It was a move he had never regretted; an abundance of unhappy wives of wealthy executives in the area could easily afford to pay fifty dollars for a forty-five minute hour of his time. He sometimes consulted with their husbands, sometimes with couples, and was expanding his services to include their frequently troubled and troublesome children.

Bookman checked his calendar in a reflex action. He knew without looking which name was first on the list. Keyes. Mrs. Enid Keyes. A tall woman with a voluptuous body, with mocking eyes and a plump, inviting mouth. Enid Keyes, twice married to men who were homosexuals, and a third time to a man much younger than herself, a near-boy who had been impotent. She had divorced the first two; the boy killed himself.

Sex for Enid Keyes was a constant prod beneath her pale skin, her body a temple of pleasure to be tenderly cared for and worshiped, displayed always to good advantage. Enid craved the attention of any man who happened into her path, wanted to be wanted by every one of them. She fantasized the seduction of men in pairs, in squads, in battalions. She imagined herself penetrated by a multiplicity of penises, all outsized organs throbbing with love for her. She sought opportunities to provoke, to entice, to submit. Her aim in life was to be known as one of the world's best lays. If only she could have an orgasm.

Three times a week she presented herself to Ned Bookman. Carefully turned out. Lately given to going without a brassiere, her large nipples directed accusingly at the therapist.

Enid Keyes caused Bookman to lose his professional objectivity for one of the few times in his life. He failed to view her other than as a sexual object. He yearned to heave himself upon her, to tear the clothes from her body, to revel in the lush flesh, squirm into those damp and hot holes. To taste, to smell, to fuck.

She was, he acknowledged sadly, a major hazard. Such a woman was a test for a therapist. It was vital that he resist her. That he might tumble off his psychiatric pedestal alarmed Bookman and he vowed to stand firm. He would cure her and so make himself more perfect.

The door to his outer office opened and closed. Enid Keyes had arrived. A dazzling smile lit her way as she settled into her usual seat and crossed her legs with what Bookman took to be an unnecessary flourish. His eyes were drawn to the soft press of thigh against thigh. He blinked himself back up to her face.

Her lips puckered. "You are positively aglow with well-being this morning, Dr. Bookman. Did you have a special night?" She was demure.

He steeled himself. "We're here to talk about you."

"Shall I tell you what happened to me last night?"

He inclined his head.

"Nothing is what happened. I was alone in my bed all night. What could be worse?" She was tempting.

He was silently supportive.

She leaned forward, breasts outlined against the thin blouse she wore. "I did a lot of thinking last night. I was thinking about you." He made no answer. "Does that please you? Or does it disgust you?"

"No judgments here, Mrs. Keyes. I want to help you."

"I know a way for you to help me."

He made a point of saying nothing, of letting nothing show on his face. But he was aware of a sudden rush of desire and apprehension.

"We could talk just as easily in bed. Naked. Touching each other. That would really help me."

"If we went to bed, I would be just another man, another conquest, another body."

"Who's complaining?"

"Oh, but you would. Eventually it would be another disappointment, another person who failed you."

She sat back. "You're a bastard, just like all of them."

"All?"

"I've never known a man who treated me well."

"Not one?"

"Not one."

"Tell me about your first husband. You were married to him for nearly five years. There must have been some good times?"

"That one, a homosexual. He walked out on me. Men are never around when you need them. Never."

IV

The strain of the exercise ridged Emmett May's stomach muscles. Flat on the slant board, he gave a soft grunt of approval. He sucked air between his perfect white teeth and exhaled a bit before driving his torso up from the waist, reaching for his toes, reveling in the exertion, the stretch of muscle, the smooth articulation of his joints.

Emmett May was proud of his body. Every morning, twenty minutes on the stationary bicycle, fifty push-ups, fifty sit-ups. The jump rope for ten minutes and then ten minutes on the light bag. It all showed in the finely honed body, lean and taut as a teen-ager's. A superb piece of work.

With face to match. Angular and bony, with a wide, mobile mouth and sea-green eyes that rarely blinked. A neat round head was capped with curly brown hair, just beginning to glint silver.

Only the most perceptive people recognized that Emmett May had lived for half a century. His skin was clear, his eyes shining, his hands steady. Natural foods, vitamins by the dozen, and controlled physical activity.

That's what did it. Middle age dragged down other men, not Emmett May.

When the exercises were done, he examined himself in the glass that covered one wall of his small gymnasium. Wearing only a jock, he might have been taken for a high-school football player, which once he'd been. And a good one, too. Hard-hitting, aggressive, with speed and moves to match. Had he been thirty pounds heavier, three inches taller, he might have turned pro. Instead he'd offered his God-given talents of face and body, that manly voice, to the theater.

And done damned well, too.

Better than anyone he'd been in high school with back in Indianapolis. Shopkeepers, used-car salesmen, a dentist, one or two lawyers, that's what his classmates had become. None of them made the money Emmett May did, none of them had earned equal status in the world, none could possibly have remained as youthful and vibrant and charged with life.

Emmett showered. Under steaming water, he scrubbed briskly. Then shaved. Next, deodorant, powder, aftershave lotion. He fingered his hair into place, dressed rapidly. Sweat socks, jeans, a soft sweater. A final glance in the mirror convinced him that he could have passed for one of his sons.

In the hallway that ran the length of the house, he stopped in front of the door to Judith's suite, hesitated, then knocked. No answer. He pushed open the door. Judith's queen-sized bed was turned down but had not been slept in. Moving rapidly, Emmett rumpled the sheets, tossed the pillows to one side. In the bathroom, he splashed water on the floor and dampened a bath towel, left it fall into the tub. Judith was not known for neatness. Satisfied, he went downstairs.

In the huge kitchen, Mrs. Nordstrom, the cook, acknowledged his arrival by pouring coffee into a ceramic jug. "Eggs?" she asked.

"Poached. Three, please."

"Toast?" she said without hope.

"Got to watch my weight."

Mrs. Nordstrom went to get the eggs. Emmett assembled the various vitamin pills with which he began each day and washed them down with coffee. Black, of course.

V

Donnelly, in jeans and an old black sweater, torn at the elbow, fraying at the cuffs, went through the house as if seeking something he knew he would never find.

The house was a mysterious place to him still. Full of its own secrets and sounds. Go round a corner and there was a new vista, and still strange. This was his fourth day in the house and he felt like an outsider, not yet accepted.

The spaces everywhere were good. High ceilings set atop rough white walls. Windows tall and plentiful. Dark polished wood floors. Wide doorways. He needed lots of room around himself.

His studio, the reason he had bought this particular house, was a massive chamber with exposed beams, a soaring slope of a ceiling, and twin skylights. It was a place he could move around in, pace from one end to the other, a place to keep materials and look at half-finished work. Here he would be able to think, to allow his emotions to simmer and finally break out, to work.

A heavy table had been put down in the center of the studio and on it rested a dozen of his smaller sculptures. Wood, stone, clay, metal; he worked in all of them. An emotion, an idea, wedded to the correct material, molded by his hands, shaped by his tools, hammered by his strength into something beautiful. There was a sensual satisfaction in the act of creation and in the pure joy of looking at the finished product. That was why he sculpted, why he had to sculpt. All the energy in his stocky body and fine mind had been devoted to this purpose for twenty-five of his forty-odd years.

He looked out of the window. The trees and shrubbery would soon be bare, skeletons that promised a green spring after the winter. Dead leaves were already blanketing the uneven terrain and he vowed not to disturb them, not to cut the grass. In no way would he alter the natural order of things.

Why had he come to Arcadia? No sure answer surfaced. But he was finished with city living, with the pressure, the mechanical noises of life there, the falseness of being a part of the Art World, of being an Artist. He believed artists should be treated as craftsmen, not lionized, not made important and given rewards out of line with their efforts. He had always been wary of becoming a celebrity; perhaps that was why he was here.

The community would allow him the privacy he needed in order to work, in order to become the man he wanted to be. At the same time, it would provide enough social activity to fulfill his needs. People were still vital to him. He needed to talk, to argue, to learn. He felt like a vessel overflowing with ideas, visions, questions, creative impulses.

The night before, alone in his bed, unable to sleep, he lay in the dark, smoking, letting his mind leapfrog about. Through the undraped window, he had sighted a single bright star. He fixed its position, aligning it on the crossbars of the window. He squinted and waited. And the star abruptly shifted to another angle. The earth had moved under it. Under Donnelly. Under the new house. He became a wanderer in space, drifting, knowing that he had no special destination.

He had attempted to visualize the universe, that incredible void, exploding outward, expanding forever. Into what? Was there anything alive out there? Some form of life that no earthling could imagine? If so, it would be hostile. Life, he knew, was a terrible and endless struggle to achieve—what? Life, he supposed.

Or death.

At once he yearned for a woman. Any woman would do. A receptacle for his desire. Nothing could compare with that first powerful thrust that took him inside a female body. To feel those damp hot lips close on his throbbing flesh. Terrifying, and reassuring. Proof of life, and the closeness of death. And when the spasm came, that almost always surprising spurt of anguish and relief, he was inevitably left chilled and weak and more than a little afraid.

VI

He was a child again. Picking his way through the thick woods. Placing each foot gently on the forest bed so as not to alert his enemies. Step by silent step he advanced, keeping to the shadows, using the foliage to shield and conceal himself. Often he had been an Indian on the look for hostiles, ready to give battle. Or sound the alarm. Seeking adventure. A chance to prove himself. To be accepted as a man.

The feelings were the same now. His breathing was short and sibilant. His heartbeat a heavy thump. His muscles drawn up, excitement rising as he advanced. The anticipation of what was known and the thrill of what remained secret to him.

Dry powder lined his throat and his hands were clammy. He was on his knees now, moving forward like some ungainly beast, seeking the familiar path through the brush. He came out on the rock ledge and looked around. No one had spotted him. Very carefully he took up his usual position with his back against the wide trunk of the old sugar maple tree, shaded by branches still heavy with withered leaves.

He slowed his breathing, felt his heart resume its normal beat. Here he was safe, strangely comfortable, at home with his isolation.

The house was set on a low knoll, a house of many rooms, overbuilt, overpriced, the house of a man who had more money than was decent. A successful man. A man on whom the world unfairly lavished its rewards.

Why not me?

He was ignored, mocked, left out. Always it had been so. But no longer. Already the world knew of his fury, his power and cunning, and it feared him. It would fear him even more.

Without looking at his watch, he knew it was time. Time for her to appear in front of the picture window in her bedroom, to display herself for him alone.

And as if his desire were a control to which she moved, she came into view. A woman of maturing beauty, free in her movements, comfortable in her gleaming skin. *His* wife, *his* woman. A woman who invariably failed to close the draperies in her bedroom window.

Why should she? The window opened on to the privacy of her rear lawn and the almost vertical hill behind. It was too steep to climb and no one would just *happen* onto the rock ledge above. Getting there took too much effort, too much time, and a man had to know about that secret height.

She stood in front of the window, face lifted as if seeking the warming sun. He peered down at her through his field glasses and at once was cold, trembling and afraid. Her eyes seemed to meet his. He pushed the glasses aside in panic.

Did she suspect his presence? Had she known about him all along? Was she toying with him, entering some cruel game in which she made all the rules? He raised the glasses and studied her. Nothing showed on that classic face, nothing but sensual calm.

He laughed at his own fear. Like all the rest, she lived in a dark paradise, unaware of what went on outside her own narrow world. Had she even suspected his presence, she would have been shaken to the roots of her smug existence. She would have recognized him for what he was—the distillation of life. And of death.

Abruptly she withdrew. A wise smile turned his mouth. She would be back to satisfy his silent demand, to exhibit herself as he needed to see her. To please him. To feed the devil that drove him.

Now.

He wanted her now. And she appeared. Wearing nothing. Turning herself so that she confronted him squarely. Her breasts were middle-sized and firm, the nipples brown, tumescent. And the pubic patch was a trimmed triangle, too perfect. A soft groan dribbled across his lips and he felt for himself.

Bitch! Only filth would do this to him. Only filth would show herself so brazenly. Pure bitch, setting her trap, trying to suck him in and drain away his power, his manhood. A cunt who deserved the punishment she got. The cunt and her husband . . . both of them. Both . . .

CHAPTER THREE

I

IN ALL, SEVEN HOUSES STOOD within sight of Simon's Pond. Ranches, Cape Cods, one remodeled barn, and a poured-concrete structure that reminded Loukas of an art museum he had once visited in New York, all angles, curves, and soaring white walls.

Loukas went to each one, spoke to whoever was home. He anticipated no startling revelations. No stunning declaration of guilt. Just a methodical acquisition of diverse bits of information that might eventually form an intelligible picture. A picture that would direct him toward the murderer.

In all but one house, the morning procedure was similar. Husbands had already departed for their jobs; in the remodeled barn, however, the man had remained at home with a low-grade fever and a sore throat.

In all the houses, the wife had gotten her children off to school: nursery school, kindergarten, grade school, and one to high school.

At each stop, Loukas patiently explained what had happened. There were expressions of horror. Then as the realization of how very close violence had come to their own homes, horror changed to dismay, to fear. Loukas offered reassurance: It was unlikely that the person who did this thing would repeat his actions. Undoubtedly he was someone passing through, a vagrant, a drifter, a person without connections to the community. What had taken place was a terrible and unfortunate incident, isolated, not to happen again.

Loukas asked his questions. Had a scream been heard? A stranger seen? An unfamiliar car spotted in the area?

No one had seen or heard anything.

While he was at one house, a truck from Toohey's Gardening Service arrived and two husky young men began the annual fall cleanup. Later, Loukas spotted Mike Jansen making his rounds, collecting the garbage; Loukas had used Jansen for years. And just as Loukas was leaving the remodeled barn, an order from the A-1 Market was delivered. Life in Arcadia went on, simple and ordered, as if nothing unusual had taken place.

It was nearly three o'clock in the afternoon before Loukas completed his questioning and returned to Police Headquarters. He went directly to Captain Henderson's office. Henderson, a large, gloomy man, was in charge of all field operations for the Arcadia Police Department. He had become a policeman in order to become a hero and instead felt himself suffocating under a pile of reports and forms detailing traffic violations and house burglaries.

He greeted Loukas with a nod, indicated the young man standing against the wall. "Tom Petersen, Theo. He'll work on the case with you. Okay?"

"Okay, Captain."

Tom Petersen smiled.

Henderson pointed a bony finger at a second man, seated in the institutional metal chair that fronted his desk. "Mr. Horn," Henderson mumbled, "the victim's husband."

Leon Horn would have been termed handsome and confident under other circumstances. But now his smooth, pleasant face was drawn in anguish and confusion. His eyes were swollen and his mouth was clamped shut. He held himself stiff and erect, as if to ward off attack.

"How?" he said finally, and Loukas knew it was a question he would ask many times in the days ahead. "How could such an awful thing happen to Treysa?"

John Henderson assumed his most authoritative manner. "We're continuing our investigation, Mr. Horn."

"Why?" Horn said.

"We're going to catch whoever did it," Tom Petersen said. "You can depend on us."

Loukas wished he were as confident as Petersen appeared to be, but it was hard to really tell. Petersen could have been one of those sleek, unflappable actors who impersonated cops on television. He always looked smooth, cool, superbright, as if he could drill a man without blinking an eye. Loukas wished he were that way.

Loukas had never fired his weapon at a human being. He doubted his ability to hit a moving target. Even on the pistol range in the basement of the Fort, he barely qualified. The service revolver was a discomforting, heavy appendage on his belt and he'd have been happy not to wear it.

"Why Treysa?" Horn said. His eyes traveled around the room. "What am I going to say to my son?"

A protective coldness settled in Loukas' chest. He wished he were able to wipe away the torment Horn felt, but he had no help to give. Horn was alone with his pain and only time would blunt its sharpness.

Loukas cleared his throat. "Could you answer some questions for us now, Mr. Horn?"

Captain Henderson spoke. "Sergeant Loukas is in charge of the case."

"What questions?" Horn said.

"Was Mrs. Horn expecting anybody this morning? After you left for work? Service people?"

Horn shook his head. "This would never have happened if Livia had been home."

"Who is Livia?"

"Livia works for us. Cooking, cleaning, helps with the house."

"Black, is she?" Henderson said.

Horn rocked in place. "Livia wasn't home this morning. She went into the city yesterday afternoon."

"What is Livia's full name?" Loukas asked.

"Livia Vargas. Olivia."

"Puerto Rican," Henderson said in a knowing voice. Horn's head moved slowly around until he faced the captain. His reactions were hesitant, dulled. "Mexican," he said. "Does it matter?"

"Do you know where she stayed in the city?" Loukas asked. "She must have some friends."

"I don't understand," Horn said. "Why are you asking about Livia?"

Petersen took a single step forward. He held himself straight and tall, his chin aggressively tilted. "Maids sometimes make mistakes. A lot of burglaries happen that way."

"Mistakes?" Horn said, changing his position again.

"They talk to people. Give out information that could be useful to certain people."

"Livia wouldn't do anything like that."

"Duplicate keys can be easily made," Henderson said.

"Livia wouldn't do anything to hurt us," Horn protested.

"Not deliberately," Petersen said.

"Where is she now?" Loukas said quietly.

Horn's confusion seemed to grow more intense. His eyes swiveled and his tongue flicked at his lips. "She said she'd be back in time to prepare dinner tonight. Treysa and I are going to a movie. We wanted to, that is." He covered his face with his hands.

At once he seemed neither confident nor successful to Loukas. Just frightened and miserable, his world ripped apart without warning.

"I would like to talk to Livia," Loukas said.

Horn nodded without raising his head.

"Did you notice anything peculiar this morning, Mr. Horn?"

Horn shuddered, looked up. "What do you mean?"

"Different?" Loukas said. "Anybody strange hanging around? Anything at all?"

Horn struggled to clear his mind. "Only the pond."

"What about the pond?"

"It was drained. I was going to speak to Sensabaugh about it."

"Mike Sensabaugh?" Henderson said. "What's he got to do with it?"

"Somebody opened the sluice gates. It's happened before."

"What about Sensabaugh?" Henderson persisted.

"I was going to telephone him. I promised Treysa I'd call. I forgot."

"I'll talk to Sensabaugh," Loukas said.

"Is there anything else you can tell us?" Petersen said.

"Why don't we have somebody drive Mr. Horn home?" Loukas said to Henderson.

"I must go to my son." Horn was on his feet, wavering slightly. "Daniel must be wondering why his mother hasn't come for him at school yet."

"I'll have a man take you," Henderson said.

When Horn was gone, Loukas lowered himself into a plain oak chair, stretching his legs, crossing his ankles. Lately he'd become aware of his thigh muscles tightening, as if they were tired, as if his body had decided to protest extended use. "A dirty business," he said.

"We're cops," Henderson said toughly. "It's what we do."

"It's going to be hard on Horn," Loukas went on, as if Henderson hadn't spoken. "A man alone with a young kid."

"Don't worry about Horn. He'll find another pair of titties to suck on before the year is up. His kind can't go the distance alone. Okay, Theo, let's have it. What have you got?"

"Not much. The Felton woman, she's the one who found the body, she thinks she might've seen somebody running from the house. No real I.D. No footprints, no tire marks. Hell, it hasn't rained in nearly three weeks. The ground is rock hard."

"The neighbors?"

"Nobody saw anything. Nobody heard anything."

"Citizens," Henderson drawled, making it sound like an obscenity.

"It doesn't make sense," Petersen said. "Mrs. Horn must have had time to scream. At least once."

"Maybe she didn't want to," Henderson said. "Maybe she enjoyed rough stuff, wanted what she was, getting.

Maybe she heard Felton coming and panicked, afraid
she'd be caught in the act. Changed her mind, only her
boy friend wasn't having any. He was too caught up in
the action. How's that grab you, Theo?"

"Could be," Petersen said thoughtfully.

Loukas, massaging his thighs, said nothing.

II

There was a professorial cast to Chief of Police Donald
Wakeman's face. Behind horn-rimmed glasses, his eyes
were watchful, measuring whatever came into sight. He
greeted his visitor with manufactured friendliness, his
words issued from his small pink mouth in thoughtful
progression.

"Victor! It's good to see you."

"Dammit, Chief," Victor Fellows began, voice controlled and resonant, "what the hell is going on?"

Wakeman had never cared for Victor Fellows. The Circuit Prosecutor was too perfectly turned out. Face and
figure, his clothes, everything about him was *right,* coming
up to specifications Wakeman had never learned. Fellows
was ruggedly handsome, with cheeks burnished to a fine
patina, sculpted head riding gracefully on a strong neck.
Men generally thought his too good-looking; women were
drawn to him.

"Please, Victor, sit down," Wakeman said, smoothing
his carefully tended shock of white hair.

Fellows sat, adjusting his trousers before crossing his
legs. His expression was grim.

"I want to know about this killing, Chief. I should
have been informed about it immediately. That was our
agreement."

"Now, Victor, unruffle those tail feathers. Nobody's
out to do you harm. Just happened this morning and before the day was over I'd've gotten to you. Fact is, we're
still pulling things together."

"Who was killed?"

"Lady by the name of Treysa Horn, over near Simon's Pond. Seems like she was sexually assaulted, as they say."

Victor Fellows tried to assimilate what he'd heard.

"Any idea who did it?" he said at last.

"Not yet, Victor. We'll get him, you can be sure of that. We've got a highly professional department here. Our people are trained and competent."

"Has the M.E. made his report?"

"Be patient, Victor. The man hasn't had time to start cutting. You'll get a copy of the report when it comes in, I promise you."

"Donald, I have one thing to say—this is my case. It falls under circuit jurisdiction. The county is not to be involved."

Wakeman showed surprise. "Victor!"

"Nor the state."

"Victor, did you ever know me to go around asking outsiders to do the town's work? Anyway, state or county, neither one can butt in unless they're officially invited. They won't be. I'll guarantee that."

"I'll hold you to that."

"Stop fretting, Victor. The odds are that Captain Henderson and his people will have the guilty party in custody within seventy-two hours. What we've got here is some bum who went a little wild, beat up on a woman and raped her. He got scared and choked her to death, thinking he'd be safe that way. But there's an A.P.B. out for anyone hitching a ride, for anyone suspicious. Seventy-two hours, you'll see."

"Henderson hasn't contacted the State Police, has he?"

Wakeman smiled patiently. "Of course not, Victor. Captain Henderson functions strictly by the departmental guidelines which I've established. We are in constant touch on this affair, constant."

"All right." Fellows appeared reassured. "Henderson's a good enough man, I guess. He'll do things right."

Again that indulgent smile. "Victor, Henderson's my executive officer. He doesn't do field work. Sergeant Loukas is in charge of the case."

Fellows frowned. "Isn't there someone else, more of a take-charge type?"

"Theo's a fine man."

"He doesn't have enough drive."

"Theo's been around, Victor. He's experienced."

"We've got Murder One here. Has Loukas ever worked a murder before?"

Wakeman spread his hands. "This is a peaceful community. There's never been this kind of thing since I've been chief and that's eight years now."

Fellows hesitated. No one on the Arcadia police force had any experience with homicide or rape. Only the county sheriff's office and the State Police had the kind of training and experience that was really needed. But to call them in would defeat Fellows' plans. For the time being he would go along with things as they were.

"You'll keep me informed about developments," he said, standing up.

"Depend on it. Victor."

"If there are any suspects, I'd like to be in on the questioning."

"Now that's up to Captain Henderson. I'll tell John to fill you in as things break."

"All right. But no one makes any statements to the press. My office will handle the media. The rights of the accused must be protected," he added quickly.

"We all want that."

Outside Headquarters a surge of excitement rippled through Victor Fellows. A presentiment of impending triumph. Murder and rape. Here was his chance to establish a statewide reputation. With any kind of luck, he could become another Tom Dewey.

III

"Santa madre de Dios!"

Livia Vargas made the sign of the cross. She sat with downcast eyes, her small face pale, her lips bloodless, hands clasped now in her lap.

Loukas studied the girl. She was young, frightened, intimidated by the police. Leon Horn had phoned as soon as Livia had returned home and Loukas and Petersen had responded immediately. She had been crying but now there was only an occasional sob. Her head came up and she looked around as if seeking aid.

"I am ashamed," she whispered.

"Ashamed of what?" Petersen said. "What did you do?"

Loukas stood back and observed. It occurred to him that Petersen might have been a priest if he hadn't joined the force.

"What have you done?" Petersen pressed the girl.

"Santa madre de Dios."

"Well?" Petersen said.

"What kind of a question is that to ask?" Horn said. "She hasn't done anything wrong."

Horn had snapped back, Loukas remarked to himself. He was stronger than Henderson believed, more resilient, a man who would eventually do whatever was necessary.

"Policemen have to ask certain questions," Loukas said, keeping his eyes on Livia Vargas, "in order to get certain answers that will help us solve a case. How old are you, Livia?"

"Santa madre de Dios."

"Eighteen?" Loukas said.

"Nineteen," Horn answered.

"Let the girl speak for herself," Petersen said, his voice suddenly harsh.

"She's frightened," Horn said.

"Nineteen," Loukas said. He tried to remember what it was like to be nineteen. He couldn't. "Do you have a friend, Livia?" he said. "A boy friend?"

The girl lowered her eyes again.

She was very pretty, Loukas decided. Fragile, almost birdlike, with shining black hair pulled back in a single braid and falling down her back. A little make-up, clothes more in style, and she might be truly beautiful.

"We need your help, Livia," Loukas said.

"Tell them what they want to know," Horn said.

"Sí, señor." She lifted her chin. The pretty face was almost defiant now. "Ask your questions, *señor."*

"A boy friend?" Loukas said.

"I have no special friend."

"You went into the city yesterday," Petersen said. "Why?"

"To shop for clothes."

"On Sunday?"

"No, this morning."

"What did you buy?"

"Nothing was right. I bought nothing."

Petersen leaned forward, his smile encouraging, his eyes cold. "If you weren't shopping all that time, perhaps some of the time you were doing something else. With a man."

"You shame me."

"Tell us his name."

"I was with no one. It is the truth."

Loukas said, "You're a pretty girl, Livia. Many young men must be attracted to you."

"I do not have much to do with boys."

"Why not?" Petersen asked.

She spoke directly to Loukas. "Where I am from, it is a small village, in the mountains north of the capital. The boys are polite and treat a good girl with respect."

"Men are not so different all over the world, I think."

"In my village when a girl does not want a man's attention, her wishes are respected. Here, in this country, what happens to the young men? They do not listen. They do not understand. They have no pride and are unwilling to wait for a girl to wish to say yes to them. So I do not have much to do with them."

"Is there any one boy who has been more persistent than the others?" Loukas said. "One who has come here to see you? More than once, perhaps."

She wet her lips.

"What is his name?" Loukas said.

"I have seen him very seldom."

"Today? In New York?"

"No, no. I saw no one today."

"Could he have been here this morning? Is it possible he thought you were here and came uninvited? Attacked Mrs. Horn?"

"I do not know. *Santa madre de Dios.* He has come without telling me first. He appears without warning. I will not go out with him. I have a responsibility. He comes always without invitation."

"How many times?"

"Three times. No, four."

"His name?" Loukas said.

Her head swung around to Horn, but she found no support in his drawn features. "Jaime Olivera."

Petersen wrote it down. "Address?"

"I do not know."

"You're lying," Petersen said.

She began to weep. "I do not lie. The husband of my brother-in-law's sister would know. It was at his home that I met Jaime."

"What's his name and address?"

"I must look in my little book."

"Then look."

She left the room hurriedly.

"You're pretty rough on the girl," Horn said.

"Not as rough as Olivera was on your wife," Petersen answered quickly.

IV

Originally the house had been the primary living quarters of the Hellstrom farm. Onions had been grown and there was an apple orchard. Fifty years earlier, the farm had been broken down into two- and three-acre lots and sold off for individual homesites. Loukas' father had purchased the land, along with the old farmhouse, and when he died it had been his only legacy to his oldest son, all that remained of a lifetime's accumulations. The old man had begun with a decrepit old truck, carting firewood. Later he began to bag charcoal, selling it door to door. Still later it was home heating fuel. But during the second

World War, business had gone bad and the old man had taken a job slicing meat in an Italian delicatessen.

Soon after the house became his, Loukas began making improvements. He constructed a large living room, complete with vaulted ceiling, floor-to-ceiling windows, and a fireplace of native stone. Next, an enclosed garage, and when Frances announced that she was pregnant, he began to build a playroom.

Loukas was twenty-five years old at the time and he earned his living doing odd jobs around town. But the imminent arrival of a child caused him to reassess his situation. He decided it was necessary to establish a secure future for his growing family. When the examination for police officer was announced, he took it and passed. Six months later he became a probationary patrolman. Three weeks later; Mikis was born.

Mikis was a beautiful child. His cheeks were smooth, olive complected, his eyes nearly black, his hair silky brown. Loukas wished his father had lived long enough to see this boy, this incredible first grandson. The old man would have drunk ouzo and boasted: "A boy like that, a hundred percent Greek, one of the gods."

Loukas agreed, though he never said so aloud. He came to love the boy with a consuming intensity that surprised and frightened him since never before had he felt so deeply for another human being. In his private moments, he made plans for his son's future.

On a Saturday afternoon, when Mikis was twenty months old, he began to run a fever. Loukas hesitated to call a doctor, not wanting to disturb one on the weekend. By Sunday night Mikis was flushed and sweating, crying constantly. A doctor was called and the child was hospitalized. At nine o'clock the following evening, Mikis died.

Doctors blamed the fever on an unknown virus that failed to respond to available medication. They had done all they were able to do.

For nearly a year after Mikis' death, Frances spoke to no one. Then she began to drink. Periodically she em-

barked on wild rages, accusing Loukas of killing their
son, of not protecting her and the child.

Loukas waited for the attacks to pass, for Frances to
become herself again. It never happened. One night, while
Loukas was asleep, Frances climbed out of bed and, still
in her nightgown, walked down to the beach and into
Long Island Sound. An oyster fisherman found her floating face down in the water the next morning.

V

Judith May rolled the Schwinn ten-speed out of the
garage, checked the tires. They seemed okay. She moved
along the driveway with the easy grace of a woman used
to having her body respond quickly and competently to
her command. She was just about to swing into the sad-
dle when her husband came out of the house.

"Must you go?" There was a suggestion of uncertainty
in that strong, even voice.

"I don't know what you mean." Her face was set, the
jawline clean and sharp, her eyes steady and cool, her
tawny hair blowing over her shoulders.

"What's the point of it?" Emmett said, anger twisting
the handsome face. "This time. It isn't like you, Judith.
Who knows what it might lead to."

She raised her brows. The movement was known to all
her fans. It made her seem younger, more vulnerable,
helpless. "The May Look" is what the fan magazines
called it.

"Darling," she offered, "obscurity is not your thing.
Speak out if you have something to say."

"Dammit, Judith, I won't play your game."

"You made the rules a long time ago, my darling. Why
act surprised when I hold you to them?"

He swore under his breath. "You must be careful. We
both agreed. There's so much to lose."

"Trust me, love. Caution is my maiden name. I consider us both in everything I do."

"Yes," he said weakly. Once again he felt as if he'd

been bested in a fight, depressed by defeat. Why didn't
he ever win? "Just be careful," he was obliged to repeat.

He watched her pedal away. She rode well, speed increasing as she went down the driveway. He imagined
her legs under the plaid slacks she wore. Superb legs they
were, tapered, muscular. He'd always appreciated her legs.

He went into the garage, started toward the gleaming
black Porsche, then thought better of it. The Datsun
wagon would attract less attention. He donned dark
glasses and a suede cap before starting the engine.

He drove unhurriedly to the Aspetuck Reservoir,
parked, and sat staring at the still water. Soon the wild
Canadian geese would come down. Emmett thought back
to the time when he brought the children here to see
them. They used to feed the geese bread crumbs and
Emmett would make jokes that always made the children
laugh. But somewhere along the way they stopped laughing at his jokes and lost interest in the geese.

He glanced at his Rolex. Jeanine Stafford was habit-
ually late for each of their meetings. As if by making him
wait she could extract some extra measure of satisfaction.
Only personal perversity could account for her tardiness.
Like Emmett, Jeanine lived in Arcadia, had for years.
Her daughter, Belle, was a student at the high school, as
was one of Emmett's children. Jeanine knew her way
around, knew the roads, the intensity of traffic. And how
much time it took to get from one place to another.

Emmett tapped the steering wheel impatiently and
searched the sky. There was no movement, no geese.

A car drew up alongside. It was Jeanine. He waited,
wishing she would come to him this time. She remained
in place, face averted. She was, he knew from experience,
a woman of immense determination. She knew how to
get exactly what she wanted. He climbed out of the Datsun and went over to her.

"Hello, Jeanine."

"Been waiting long, Emmett?"

Always late and always the same taunting query. He
supposed it was her way of manipulating him, keeping
him in line. It occurred to him that women had always

manipulated him, starting with his mother. Someday he would have to take steps against them, regain control. He withdrew a sealed white envelope from his jacket pocket.

"There you are, Jeanine."

She put the envelope in her purse. "Thank you, Emmett."

He cleared his throat. "You know, Jeanine, this has to stop one day."

Her smile was without warmth or mirth. "It can go on forever, Emmett. And it will."

"It isn't right," he said plaintively.

"Nonsense. Nothing is free in this world. You pay for what you get. For what you got." She examined his face. "A man as handsome as you are, Emmett, you could've had any woman you wanted. I'll bet they fall all over you still."

He made no answer.

She laughed. "Oh, well, different strokes for different folks."

"I've been thinking, Jeanine. How would you like one lump sum, one substantial amount? A lot of money that you could do whatever you wanted with? What would you say to that?"

"How substantial?"

He hesitated. "Twenty-five thousand." He anticipated her reaction.

She laughed, harsh with dismissal. "Don't be a fool, Emmett."

"Fifty thousand."

"Not even close."

"One hundred thousand. You could have an income for life. A safe investment. You could—"

"Emmett, what do you take me for?" The harshness went out of her voice. "Ah, you're teasing, right! Playing games with a helpless lady. I like it the way it is, Emmett. You pay up every other week. Just like always. These meetings of ours, Emmett, they are not without a certain pleasure for me. Not many women get to meet secretly with a handsome movie star."

"I haven't done a movie in years. Jeanine." He felt compelled to keep matters in proper perspective. "Nor a play."

"That's right, isn't it?" Her voice went thin and mean, penetrating. "Just those commercials. Just a voice over all those cartoons, selling soap and breakfast cereals." Her laugh was mocking this time. "But they do make you an awful lot of money, Emmett. Everybody knows that."

"How much do you want?"

"For what, Emmett?"

"To end this . . . relationship."

"Emmett, you are not going to get off the hook. You are my annuity and I am your insurance policy. We need each other. To support and protect each other. In a cold, cold world, Emmett, that is a very rare relationship."

"What a bitch you are."

"Now, Emmett, you be careful the way you talk to me, hear! I know what you are, Emmett. I know and it isn't pretty, Emmett. Not pretty at all. How do you think it would affect your precious career if it became known? Not many sponsors would want a man like you representing them on television. So you just watch out when you talk to me, Emmett." She started her car.

"What if I just broke it off?" he said.

"You mean arbitrarily? Without my consent? Why would you do a self-destructive thing like that? You'd be the one to get hurt."

"Maybe not."

"I don't know what you're thinking, Emmett, but forget it. I am a cautious woman and much smarter than you give me credit for. Anyway, Emmett, the money you pay, it's just a pittance to a man in your position."

He waited until she was out of sight before he went back to the Datsun. On the way home, he began to sing aloud. After all, things could be a lot worse. Despite Jeanine, he was a man who had everything. Every goddamned thing.

VI

Pauline Fellows was small, neatly constructed, with an aristocratic cast to her features. Her eyes were bright and her mouth was a bit larger than she liked, a bit too sensual. She compensated for that with make-up and was careful always to present the correct image, that of a well-bred, properly brought up and educated suburban housewife.

She was reading and drinking coffee from a delicate white china cup when the Mercedes pulled into the driveway. Though no longer able to continue reading, she kept her eyes on the pages of the book when he appeared.

"What are you reading?" he began.

She closed the book. "An art critique."

"Art criticism is a pretentious bore. There have been no worthwhile painters since the Impressionists."

"Is that your opinion, Victor, or something someone else said?"

"It's good to know one's wife holds one in such high esteem. Would you like a martini?"

"Yes, thank you."

He brought her a glass and one for himself, raised it in silent toast. "The ability to make a perfect martini is an indication of the distance man has put himself from the beasts."

"I'd like to think you mean that as a joke, but I know better."

He pointed to the book in her lap. "Why do you waste your time with that kind of thing, Pauline? You'll never go through with it."

"You're wrong, Victor."

"I doubt that I am."

"I've shifted over to your philosophy, Victor. What is it you say—a person can do whatever he chooses to do with his life. Create himself, isn't that your belief?"

"Not all of us are so gifted, Pauline," he said dryly.

She smiled without humor. "You are and I'm not. Nevertheless, I intend to try, Victor, to re-create myself."

"I'm not sure I understand you. Everything a woman could possibly want, you have."

"Then why do I feel as if some essential part of myself is missing? You've never had that problem, Victor. You came complete, every piece in place, every gear and joint functioning perfectly. All you had to do was keep the parts greased and in running order."

"Spare me the sarcasm, Pauline."

"But I mean it, Victor. Being a wife and mother isn't enough. I want more than that."

"Those are still honorable and necessary occupations."

"Yes, and sufficient for some women. But not for me. I want something that belongs exclusively to me."

"Selling second-rate paintings to people who can't tell good from bad. Hardly a lofty ambition, Pauline. I haven't changed my mind, I won't subsidize a New York gallery for you."

"I've given that up for now."

"The first sensible thing you've said in weeks."

She ignored the criticism. "There isn't a really good gallery in Arcadia. Or in the county, for that matter. I intend to rectify that omission. I intend to open my gallery right here."

"A gallery costs money, Pauline, and we are not wealthy."

"There are many people in the world who would dispute that. Anyway, this won't cost a great deal. I've worked out the perfect arrangement."

"Perfect," he said, making it sound like an oath.

She ignored the irony. "Here. This house. The entrance foyer. The living room. The family room. The dining room. All that's required is some spotlights installed on the ceiling."

"You aren't serious."

"I'm very serious."

"You expect to turn our home into a place of business, to invite strangers here? I think not."

"I've already taken the initial steps, Victor. Unless you're willing to rent suitable space elsewhere for me. Remember, Victor, as much as you like to think that you disdain commerce, you do enjoy making money. And this may very well be a profitable enterprise."

"We'll continue this another time."

"No," she said with unexpected force. "This is my decision."

"Pauline, I did not marry a businesswoman."

"You may come to like it."

"I doubt it. Have you considered James? How will this affect the boy?"

"James will probably have a very good time."

"How? By coming in contact with some queer painter?"

"Is that what's bothering you! Fear not, dear husband. Most painters have too many other things on their minds. And those I've met are alarmingly heterosexual. You'd do better to concern yourself about me than James."

"Your sense of humor leaves a great deal to be desired."

She shrugged, eyes bright and watchful.

"Let's end this conversation," he said. "I promised to take James over to the ball field. Makes a bad impression for a player to be late on the first day of practice."

Pauline frowned. "I've been meaning to discuss that with you, Victor. James doesn't want to play football."

"Nonsense," he said, and left the room.

Fellows found James in his room reading a book. He was a willowy boy with yellow hair and watery eyes. His fingers were long, tapering, his features indistinct, his cheeks pale.

"Time to get going, son," Fellows began. "What are you reading?"

"It's a biography."

"Whose biography?"

"Lord Byron."

Fellows frowned. "Are you ready to go?"

James stood up. "Yes, sir." In his football uniform he looked awkward, ill at ease.

They drove to Governor's Field. Everywhere boys were running or doing calisthenics, catching or kicking footballs. Seven large men, in shirt sleeves despite the chill air, wandered about overseeing the activities.

James climbed out of the Mercedes. "I'd better get out here."

"Introduce yourself to Coach Burleigh. I spoke to him myself about you."

"Yes, sir."

"Pay attention to what the coaches have to say. They know the game."

"I will, Father."

"And remember one thing, James."

"Yes, Father?"

"Always hustle."

VII

There was nothing youthful about Belle Stafford. At fifteen, her breastless figure seemed slumped and weary and her face was sullen and distrustful, as if she viewed the world through a scrim of bitter experience.

Belle had learned that deeds counted in this world. Good intentions, promises of future rewards, pleasures scheduled for some indefinite period, were meaningless. *Now* was all that mattered.

In the parking lot behind the high school, she waited. And felt nothing. Not anticipation or fear. What needed doing, she would do. There was, she admitted grudgingly, a kind of kinky lure to it all. It might just be fun.

Jeanine would throw a fit if she knew, but that was Jeanine's problem. Like all mothers, Jeanine worried about what people thought, about her daughter's precious reputation. Worrying was what Jeanine did best. Next to having fits. Jeanine existed on the loud side of hysteria, often reminding Belle of the characters in those awful Gothic novels she was always reading. Set on some misty moor, a girl prim and proper, a house dank and ominous. What bullshit! Jeanine would have thrived in such a setting—a cross between Scarlet O'Hara and Blanche DuBois.

Belle glanced toward the school. Where was Arthur

Slater? In the weight room, she supposed. The teacher was obsessed with his body, puffing it up to grotesque proportions. His torso was round and solid, his shoulders thick with layers of muscle, his arms heavy. Arthur Slater did not have an attractive physique; he would look ill-formed in a bathing suit, peculiar. Nevertheless, Belle wondered what it would be like to be alone with him in a bedroom. Without clothes on. Pounded by that powerful body, helpless in those strong arms. Arthur Slater could hurt a girl without really trying. The idea caused Belle to shiver. She did not suffer pain well.

That was one of the reasons she preferred older men. Men knew how to be gentle and considerate, how to please a girl.

A car pulled into a parking space not far from where she stood. An old Ford badly in need of a wash. Ralph Burleigh, night watchman at the high school, climbed out. He waved and smiled pleasantly before hurrying inside the Administration Building.

What did a watchman do all night in that empty school? The job would have spooked her. Maybe he had a girl friend who came to visit. It pleased her to imagine people making it in a classroom. On a teacher's desk. She looked after Ralph Burleigh with new interest. What would he do if she showed up some night without warning? It might be fun. He was nice-looking in a starched, clean-cut sort of way. And shy. Belle had never known such a shy man.

Arthur Slater came out of the school. He was a stumpy man, thick in the body, his short arms hanging awkwardly away from his sides. He advanced with the splayfooted uncertainty of a wary duck.

At the sight of him, Belle straightened up, tugged her skirt down over her hips. She placed herself in his path.

"Hi, Mr. Slater."

He examined her briefly. "Miss Stafford, isn't it? Why are you here at this late hour?"

"I was in the library studying," she offered coquettishly.

He examined her words. "I doubt it. To study isn't your style."

"Oh, dear," she drawled, touching her hair, "I do mean to try, Mr. Slater."

Nodding, he shuffled toward a green Volvo, keys in hand.

"Is that your car, Mr. Slater? You drive a Volvo? How cool!"

"Don't be impressed, Miss Stafford. It came second-hand and I've driven it for more than five years."

"I've never ridden in a Volvo."

He turned back, gazed skeptically at her. "What are you after, Miss Stafford?"

"After, Mr. Slater?" she said without guile. "Why whatever do you mean? I could use a lift home, if you can manage it."

Slater hesitated. "Very well. You'll have to direct me."

"Oh, I will."

She arranged herself against the door, facing him, skirt as high on her thighs as she dared allow it to go. She crossed her legs and saw his eyes move quickly in that direction, then away. Caution was in order, she reminded herself. Yet not so much that he failed to grasp her intent.

"Is it true, Mr. Slater," she said, "what you said in class this morning?"

He guided the Volvo out of the school grounds, heading east on Frazer Road. "If you expect to get a passing grade," he intoned, "you must produce a higher caliber of work."

"Mom will simply murder me if I fail to pass."

"It's up to you, Miss Stafford."

"Oh, I know. And I am trying, really I am. But there is no use denying it, Mr. Slater, I will never be a really good student."

"Unless you manage a ninety on your finals you are not going to get a passing average, I'm afraid."

"Ninety! Oh, Mr. Slater. That's practically an impossibility for me."

"I'm sorry."

She leaned toward him, voice lower. "You are an extremely demanding person, Mr. Slater."

"Excellence is not too much to expect in a classroom."

She allowed herself a small smile. "You are also a very attractive man, Mr. Slater. All the girls think so."

Slater kept his face set, his eyes on the road ahead. Each year the girls at the school became more brazen, more openly sexual. There were rumors of teachers having affairs with students, a disgusting and immoral condition. After all, a teacher had a certain higher responsibility. As for the students, it was up to their parents to raise them correctly. A teacher could do only so much.

"I feel I am able to reveal my true feelings to you," Belle Stafford was saying. "It is very difficult for a person like myself to hide things. I come from a passionate part of the country, I am a passionate person, I believe in openness and honesty." She shifted closer to him, exposing all of her slender, pale thighs.

"Miss Stafford, you are making a mistake."

She dropped a hand on his arm. It was rock hard, incredibly thick. She squeezed and he shrugged her away.

"Sit back," he commanded with surprising force.

She withdrew, suddenly afraid. But not so afraid that she forgot what she hoped to accomplish. "I could be very good for a man like you, Mr. Slater. Let me tell you what I would do . . ."

"You're a child. You don't know what you're saying. Now sit still and be good or I'll put you out of the car."

She slumped back against the door, sulking. She had expected to be accepted, had wanted to be. She couldn't afford to fail. More, he would have been her first teacher and the idea had excited her. But now! What if he reported her to the headmistress? Or to Jeanine?

"Mr. Slater," she said, "I am sincerely ashamed. The idea of failing upset me. And being so close was overwhelming. You do understand?"

"Let's drop the subject."

At her house, he swung around back, pulled up at the kitchen entrance. She opened the door, looked back at him. "Do forgive me, Mr. Slater."

"We will not discuss it again."

"You are an understanding man. And I will study harder. I promise."

He drove away and she went into the house. Jeanine was waiting at the kitchen window. An older version of her daughter, she had a sullen mouth, a childish pout.

"Who was that man?" she wanted to know. "Whose care was that?"

"Mom, don't fuss at me."

"Who are you running around with? Who was that boy?"

"That was a grown man, Momma. One of my teachers."

"Damn you!" Jeanine screamed without warning. "Can't you learn! You'll ruin everything I've done. Everything."

Belle's face grew sullen. "What about me, Momma? Didn't I have something to do with it? Some little part?"

Jeanine felt a sudden weakness in her limbs. She sat down, staring at her daughter in fear.

"Oh, Momma," Belle said, embracing her mother, "that was just Mr. Slater, my teacher. He gave me a lift, just a ride home."

Jeanine held the girl tightly, trying not to weep. They were so much alike, she kept reminding herself. Mother and daughter.

VIII

He drove with race-driver control and concentration, spine straight, arms extended and elbows locked for optimum steering efficiency. His eyes ranged the road ahead, searching out danger, seeking the unexpected, anticipating sudden death.

Presently his posture grew less rigid and anyone watching would have thought him to be an ordinary man out for an evening's drive. Passing houses new and old, large and small, his mind penetrated the closed doors and drawn blinds.

Who lived here? What manner of person occupied the

house on his left? How did they treat each other? At night, what did husband and wife do to each other?

Faceless figures faded on the screen of his imagination. A man and a woman, bodies graceful in soft light, coming closer in slow, controlled leaps. Muscles rippled as arms stretched. Faces floated together and for a delicious stopped moment of time everything was as it should be.

Then movement. Hands stroking passionately, fingers closing on rounds, curves, thrusts. Crevices and apertures were explored in minute detail, penetrated, anguish and ecstasy declared. He saw it all. Heard it all. He knew both participants as he knew himself.

He adjusted his position. His still finely pressed trousers were swollen under the fly, a hard bulge which his finger traced delicately from tip to root. Mysterious and tentative sensations rippled into his groin.

He stopped the car. The headlights went off, the engine rattled and stopped. In the darkness, there was only stillness.

He stared through a line of cypresses at a lighted picture window. A woman, fully clothed, gazed out into the night. It was a face he had seen many times before, a face he clutched in memory. Closer, the skin was pure cream, the lips so very red, the eyes shining with passion.

He stood alongside the car holding himself and trying to visualize her without clothes as he had done so many times before. Her body would be a gleaming vault of treasure, strong and agile, yet yielding, resilient, rich with promise. It was the kind of body women used against men. Flesh was a weapon, a terrible tool designed to shatter character and decimate the human spirit. Flesh left a man weak and helpless, tortured by searing memories, by heavy guilts. Flesh was the ultimate pit of degradation. A pit in which man suffered as nowhere else.

His trousers were open. His hand reached tentatively into the fly as if exploring a strange and dangerous cavern. Skin touched skin. He shivered and a low animal sound of despair broke out of him. His fingers fitted themselves expertly, drew forward until the great shaft rose up into the cool night.

He pirouetted as if to display himself to an appreciative audience. Wanting someone to be there to see, to envy. He confronted the window and the woman who stood there. Without warning, she withdrew. *Bitch.* Where had she gone? What was she doing? Why did she treat him so badly?

He brought her back into his sight by strength of will. As he desired her to be. Fragile and vulnerable, a floating wisp. His hand moved. Faster, with a rising fury that buffeted the naked shaft, fingers tightening until there was pain, *real pain.* Punishment. Bringing the poison up from the center of his being.

Suddenly, the convulsion. He twisted and bent, clutching at himself in desperation and terror. Drained and chilled, made helpless and ashamed. Left with only his anger.

And hatred.

Part Two

CHAPTER FOUR

I

LOUKAS AND TOM PETERSEN WERE in the Detective Bureau studying the Medical Examiner's report. "Okay," Petersen said. "Posner confirms the rape. Torn tissue, bleeding, some male pubic hairs on her. We already figured it that way."

"Abner can't make it more than it is."

"We're building a nice fat file. Autopsy report, photos, measurements, the interviews. But no suspect. You got a theory, Theo?"

"No theories."

"I go with Captain Henderson. Jaime Olivera, he's the one."

"What makes you think so?"

"It figures. Jaime came around hot for Livia. He finds her gone and Mrs. Horn at home by herself. He's all worked up and tells himself one pussy is as good as another, goes after her. She resists, he insists. She breaks and runs for it. He goes after her, brings her down at the pool. She fights back and he belts her out, puts it to her. Afterwards, terrified that she can put the finger on him, he finishes her off."

"If it had been me," Loukas said thoughtfully, "I'd've taken her watch, some cash, a portable TV, something to make it look like a robbery. Something to throw the law off."

"He was too scared, wasn't thinking straight."

"Maybe."

"It makes sense, Theo. I'm sure of it."

61

Loukas decided that he was sure of nothing. Not personally, not professionally. Once he had been certain of many things, confident, a little smug. But no more. Now each day was a question waiting for an answer.

Traffic patrol had been simpler. A cop took charge on the road, controlling the flow of cars. There was a singular grace to a traffic man's movements, an intricate dance performed with hand and foot, punctuated by head bobbings and changes of expression, eye movements, the blast of a whistle. A great deal could be said for traffic work. Except in bad weather.

"Why?" Petersen said. "Tell me why you don't think it's Jaime."

"Maybe he's the one. I don't know."

The phone rang and Loukas answered. He listened, said "Thank you," and hung up. He brought his feet down to the floor and said to Petersen, "Let's take a trip. Into the city."

"New York! Now?"

"Don't go if you don't want to." He kept his face serious as he headed out the door. "They picked up Jaime Olivera."

II

The basement of the station house smelled of urine and dried vomit. A fat policeman with a jaundiced complexion admitted Loukas and Petersen to the detention cell, hurried back to his desk and a copy of *Playboy*.

Jaime Olivera sat on the floor, legs outstretched, eyes closed, arms folded across his chest. Loukas judged him to be in his early twenties, tight-bodied, with a hint of mustache, his black hair thick and long. A muscle twitched in his jaw, otherwise he made no move.

"I'm Sergeant Loukas and this is Detective Petersen. We're with the Arcadia Police Department, Jaime."

Jaime gave no notice.

Loukas crouched down. The carefully assumed stance

revealed more bravado than insolence. Jaime Olivera, Loukas decided, was scared.

"They tell you why they took you in, Jaime?" Loukas said.

The eyes remained closed. "Nobody tells me nothing."

"Heavy stuff," Petersen said. "Very heavy."

"You guys don't shake me up."

"Does rape shake you up, Jaime?" Loukas said.

The eyes opened. "Rape! Who'd I rape? I enjoy it?"

"How's Murder One grab you, wise guy?" Petersen said.

The glowing black eyes went from one man to the other, fluttered shut. "I'm clean. A model citizen."

"You been in the joint how many times, Jaime?" Loukas said.

"Shit," Jaime said.

Petersen recited the record. "Two collars for breaking and entering, one dismissal, one three-year stretch. Picked up twice for gambling violations, and two drug busts."

"Okay," Jaime said. "I put time in at Elmira. But nothing else. The rest was dropped. I never did nothing. And I'm clean now. Where you guys from?"

"Arcadia."

"Where's that?"

"Not far from here," Loukas said. "In Connecticut."

Jaime shook his head. "Never heard of it."

"You've been there," Loukas said.

"Nah, I don't think so."

"To visit Livia," Loukas went on.

"Who?"

"Livia Vargas."

Petersen smiled coldly. "How is she in the hay, Jaime?"

"I don't know the chick."

"Plowing her steady," Petersen said.

Jaime showed nothing on his face. "This Livia. She the one I'm supposed to have raped?"

"Livia says you knocked her up," Petersen said.

Jaime grinned. "Hey, man, this Livia, she's good-looking? Maybe I give her a break, some of this." He grabbed his crotch.

Loukas straightened up. "Okay, Jaime. We played long enough. Livia made you for us, a positive I.D. You want to talk to us here or in Arcadia? The paper work will take a couple of days. Meanwhile you cool your butt in the can. How do you want it?"

Jaime said something in Spanish. He shrugged, then spoke in English. "Okay, so I was up there a couple of times to see the chick. Nothing going down. You got my word."

"How many times?"

"I don't keep count. Maybe three. Yeah, three. Fucking peasant is what she is. Saving it, y'know. Like it's gonna spoil if she uses it."

"When was the last time you went up to Arcadia?" Loukas asked.

Jaime shrugged. "A week ago, maybe two."

"Yesterday," Petersen insisted.

"Okay. Maybe yesterday. I don't know. What's so special about yesterday? Whenever, the chick wasn't home. Figure it, I go all the way up there and she comes into the city. Dumb dame."

"Mrs. Horn told you that?"

"Who?"

"Mrs. Horn. The lady Livia works for."

"Yeah, I guess that's who it was. She tells me, 'Livia's not here. She went into New York.' So I split."

"What time was that, Jamie?"

"I don't know. Christ, time isn't a big deal with me, can you dig it!" He displayed his wrists. "No watch, see!"

"In the morning?" Loukas said.

"I guess so."

"Early?"

"Yeah, yeah, pretty early."

"About eight o'clock?"

"Could be."

"What train did you take?"

"Train! I don't take no train. I hitch all the way. A trucker, he drops me off on the highway, near the toll booth."

"The Turnpike?"

"I guess."

"Then what did you do?"

"Hang around until it gets light. There's a railroad station. I go over there and drink some coffee in a diner."

"We'll check that, Jaime," Petersen said.

"How did you get over to Arcadia?" Loukas said.

"Walk. None of those bastards'd pick me up. Why you asking all these questions? I told you, I don't do nothing."

"Did you like Mrs. Horn?" Loukas said.

"Like her! I just say a few words to her is all."

"Good-looking woman, wouldn't you say?"

"Hey, what's going on? You guys pimping a little on the side?" He laughed harshly.

"You put your hands on her, didn't you, Jaime?" Petersen said.

"That's weird, man."

"She pushed you away. You went after her and she ran. What did you do then?"

"Hey, look, I don't go near the broad."

"You caught up with her," Petersen said. "You knocked her down, worked her over to keep her quiet. Then you put it to her. How was it, Jamie? Good fucking?"

Jaime's eyes shifted over to Loukas. "Listen, your partner, he's weird, y'know. I don't do what he said. I swear it on my mother's grave."

"You were spotted running away," Loukas said.

The spine went out of Jaime and he sagged in place, his face dissolving. "Holy Jesus! I never do it. I never touch her. You gotta believe me."

"Tell us about it."

"Like I said, I'm looking for Livia. I go around to the back of the house, figuring she's in the kitchen. That's when I spotted the stiff."

"Mrs. Horn?"

"Could be. First time I ever see her. Out by the pool."

"How did she look?"

"She looked dead. Somebody worked her over pretty good. Her dress was up and her legs apart. Listen, you ain't got no dummy here. I knew what was going down

so I split out of there in a big rush. Jesus, you think I
don't know what's gonna happen the cops find a Spic
hanging around!"

"I don't buy it," Petersen said.

Jaime grew agitated. "I swear it!"

Loukas rapped on the bars of the cell. "You want
to let us out of here, officer?" He glanced down at Jaime
Olivera. "You have got a very serious problem, Jaime.
Think about it. Maybe there's something more you'd
like to remember. When you do, the officer here will
know how to get in touch with us. Until then, you stay
right where you are."

III

Bookman, eyes tightly closed, lay on his back. Con-
tentment suffused his body. He felt warm, drowsy, at
peace. He concentrated on the various portions of his
body, isolating each until he could describe to himself
how that part felt. True sexual satisfaction manifested
itself, he was convinced, in the limbs. The knees, particularly. A good come kept a man loose in the joints.

Sex was a necessity to Ned Bookman. Sex with his
wife every night; sex with other women when it could
be sedately arranged. A substantial number of Arcadia's
married women were willing to oblige him, convinced
that psychiatric training lent a special fillip to a man
in bed. As a result, he considered himself an authority
on the quality of the motels within a thirty-mile radius
of Arcadia.

Always before, however, his partners had been ladies
whose acquaintances he had made at parties or while
giving a lecture to some club or college. This was his first
dalliance with a patient. He plumbed his feelings, trying
to understand this strange and already threatening experience. He was, he admitted ruefully, confused.

Enid eyes. He had held her off in session after session,
ignored her efforts to excite him by wearing provocative
clothing, by displaying her cleavage, her fine white thighs.

He offered reasons to himself for refusing her. He reminded himself of how much was at stake and resisted with all his might. But not for long.

Enid Keyes was embarrassed by her failure to seduce the good doctor. At fifty dollars a session, she craved her money's worth. Finally, she substituted action for words.

Bookman let the memory drift lazily across his mind, the memory of the events that had taken place toward the end of her session yesterday when she went to her knees in front of him and pushed her face into his crotch.

He shuddered and struggled to stand. "You are making a mistake, Mrs. Keyes."

She unzipped his fly.

He placed a restraining hand on her head.

She located his swollen member and guided it into the light.

"Ah," she said. She kissed the engorged red head.

"Ah," he said, trying not to fall down. "You must not do that."

She took him into her mouth.

He lowered himself carefully into his chair. "Oh," he said. "Oh, oh."

She rolled her eyes up to his face, mumbled something.

"I beg your pardon?" He didn't want to miss anything.

She removed his penis from her mouth. It quivered damply.

"I see you're human after all," she repeated.

He answered soberly. "This is your time. You may as well get something out of it."

She patted his penis lovingly and tucked it back in its place, zipped him up. "There," she said, resuming her seat.

"What are you doing!" He was dismayed.

"That was just a sample. Tomorrow. I'll get us a room in a motel tomorrow. Is one o'clock all right?"

"I have an appointment at one."

"A patient?"

"I play golf."

"Cancel."

"Well—"

"I'll tell your answering service the name of the motel. I'll use a false name. Won't that be fun?"

"Try the Yankee Drive. It's excellent."

"Why, Doctor, you are a devil!"

When he had arrived on the scene today she was waiting, naked and squirmy. She got his pants down while he took off his jacket and tie and shirt. She dragged at his undershorts and undid his shoes. She heaved herself into the bed to await his coming. He launched himself in her direction in a low dive.

They rolled around, nibbling and licking, rubbing and sucking, until the scent of sex permeated the room. She was surprising strong and adjusted herself on him to her own purposes, until finally he was able to roll her onto her back and finish the job.

Fifteen minutes passed. Fifteen silent, tranquil minutes. He began to fret. And with cause. There were matters about this affair worth worrying about. Namely his reputation, his career. Also his marriage.

Enid Keyes was a threat to everything he had built. A passionate bomb waiting to blow up his world. He shuddered. He should have his head examined, screwing her.

But then the familiar warm glow of self-satisfaction returned. He was a trained psychiatrist, recipient of a successful analysis himself, experienced, intelligent, shrewd. There wasn't a trick he didn't know. He would make her see that this was a temporary and limited arrangement for their mutual pleasure. An arrangement designed to aid her in her search for maturity. When the proper moment arrived, he would release her to go out into the world on her own, make a life for herself. He could handle Enid Keyes. One way or another.

"Well, Doctor," she said, "ready for another go at it?"

"I have to get back to my office." Once a day was his limit.

Her face zeroed in on his shiveled manhood. "How little he is, how cute. I'll make him grow in a hurry."

"I really must go."

Mouth working, she shifted around so that her ample bottom block his sight.

Unwilling to shatter her concentration, he fell back on the pillow. He felt himself grow to the task. She was, he told himself, quite skillful. A fine craftsman, with a true feel for her work.

"There!" she cried suddenly. "Look at him now! Ready for action. Let's put him where he can do us both some good. Come on, Doctor, come on!" She bounced up and down on him with unrestrained delight.

After a moment, Bookman decided that he was in no immediate danger and joined the game. It was fun.

IV

Loukas took the Hutchinson River Parkway and then the Merritt Parkway going back. The drive was slower, but prettier; and you saved forty-five cents in tolls. He felt drained, without energy, and the gnawing had returned to his stomach.

"What do you think?" Petersen said.

"About Jaime? Not much."

"He could be our boy."

"Maybe."

"How long will they keep him on ice down there?"

"The lieutenant in charge will try to pressure the kid, open him up. But he should be out by tomorrow morning."

"We could charge him. He's got a yellow sheet and we know he was up there. A little investigation, I bet he's a sex offender."

"Not on the record."

"Maybe the Felton woman will make a positive I.D."

"She isn't even sure she saw anybody. I got a hunch Jaime's just not our man."

"I don't believe in hunches myself."

"They come in handy sometimes. Give you something to go on. You notice in those mystery movies on the television the cops are always getting hunches, proving them out."

"I don't watch that crap, it's not real."

Loukas smiled. "That's *why* I watch it, because it's not real. But maybe guys who work on a lot of big stuff can develop a special feeling for things."

"A cop is a cop all over."

"I don't think so. Being a cop in a big city is different. They never know what's going to come down on them in the streets. Arcadia, hell, that's just the minor leagues."

"Well, we've got a real one this time. Rape and homicide. Whoever cracks this case is going to make a nice rep for himself."

"You're a pretty ambitious fellow, Tom."

"Something wrong with that?"

"Nothing, I guess. Maybe one day you'll get Wakeman's job."

"Didn't you ever dream of being chief, Theo?"

"Me! No. Just to put in my time, stick an extra six-pack in the fridge. Take it easy."

"I can't stop thinking about Mrs. Horn," Petersen said, after a moment. "Some of the guys around the Fort say that some dames like to be roughed up, that there's no such thing as rape."

"Now you sound like Henderson."

Petersen grinned. "You hear his latest joke? There was this eighty-five-year-old woman who called the cops at midnight, said she'd been raped.

" 'When?' the desk sergeant asks her.

" 'Sixty years ago,' she says.

" 'Well, what do you want me to do about it now?' he says.

" 'Nothing, officer. I just like to talk about it.' " Petersen laughed loudly.

V

Loukas woke the next morning, his reflexes slowed. He examined himself in the mirror. There was a trace of flabbiness above his hips, but otherwise his body was slender and firm. A gift of nature, he supposed. A metabolic rate that burned up calories, kept the fat away. That was important for a man who enjoyed drinking beer.

He dressed without haste, had his morning coffee, listened to the news report on the radio. Temperatures were dropping, soon it would be winter. There was talk of an oil shortage and he wondered how that would affect Arcadia. Not much, he decided. People who had money always managed to fulfill their needs.

At one minute before eight, he arrived at Headquarters. He like the sound of the word, what it suggested. Headquarters. Made it seem as if a small army of policemen was on call to smash down crime wherever it raised its ugly head.

The Fort was the sole police post in town; and there were only nineteen men on the force, excluding Chief Donald Wakeman. Before it had become Police Headquarters, the Fort had served as the local post office. It was a drafty building, too hot in summer, too cold in winter.

The Bureau was on the main floor in what had once been the locker room for the letter carriers. In July and August, it smelled like one.

Loukas helped himself to some coffee from the electric coffee maker and began to study the Horn file. But when he finished, he had learned nothing new.

He went out to the desk and asked for a list of reported crimes during the night. Three burglaries. Two drunk drivers. One fight at the Shore Bar and Grill. One arrest on suspicion of carrying drugs, marijuana.

Loukas took the list back to his desk. He would read the officers' reports, visit the scenes of the burglaries, commiserate with the owners, suggest ways in which they might be able to improve security. But he knew that any time a professional burglar wanted to enter a premises he would do so. By now the TV's, toasters, record players, blenders, and other items stolen during

the night would be in the hands of fences in Norwalk
or Bridgeport or maybe even Manhattan.

Petersen arrived with cinnamon rolls for them both.
They ate and drank coffee and talked about the lousy
season the football Giants were having.

At nine-fifteen, Captain John Henderson entered the
room. The long, lumpy face was sad and drawn. "Jesus
H. Christ. Wakeman's been all over my ass all morning.
Wants action. Doesn't understand these things take time."

Petersen laughed. "People in this town don't like
violence, killing."

"They moved here to get away from that kind of
stuff," Loukas said. "You can't blame them."

Henderson gestured. "Those rolls from the diner?"

Petersen answered, "Yes, Captain."

"What crap. You'd think somebody in this town would
know how to make a decent sweet roll. What about
Olivera?"

"Says he came up to see the maid, spotted the corpse
and took off."

"He did it," Henderson said. "I got a hunch."

"I think so, too," Petersen said.

"I thought you didn't believe in hunches, Tom,"
Loukas said, trying not to grin.

"I believe in this one."

"Let's extradite the sonofabitch," Henderson said.

"If you say so, John," Loukas said. The phone rang
and he picked it up, said his name. "Okay," he said
after a while. "We'll be right over."

"What's all that?" Henderson demanded.

"Unless Olivera got sprung in a hurry, your hunch
about him is wrong," Loukas said.

"Who says so?"

Loukas dropped his hand on the telephone. "We
just got another one."

"Another rape?"

"And another dead woman."

Part Three

CHAPTER FIVE

I

THE HOUSE WAS IMITATION CAPE COD with eight-over-six windows and red shutters. Six bedrooms, a playroom, a family room, a study, and a dry full basement. It sat off Rock Ledge Place within sight of the road, fenced off by a line of tall cypress trees.

Loukas judged it to be about three years old, its worth in the current market nearly 30 percent higher than the original cost. Prices kept going up. Where would it stop? The week before, a real-estate agent had phoned to ask if Loukas wanted to sell his house.

"I can get you seventy-five or eighty for it, less commission, of course."

The house wasn't worth nearly that much, not even with the improvements he'd made. Something was radically wrong, he told himself. Things had to return to normal soon.

Loukas circled the property without haste, ending finally in the horseshoe driveway out front. A blue Chrysler glided into the drive: Abner Posner. The M.E. got out, tugging at his long nose.

"Business seems to be picking up, Theo," he began.

"Who needs it?"

"What's this one look like?"

"You're the doctor, you tell me."

"Have you examined the body?"

"I looked at it, yes."

Posner displayed his large teeth cheerlessly. "I keep

telling you, police work's not for a man of your sensibilities."

"Just look at the body, Abner. Spare me the analysis."

"No extra charge, Theo. Point me to her."

"Inside. On the staircase. What a place to buy it, on the steps."

"A little variety in life keeps things interesting." Posner went inside and a few minutes later Petersen came out.

"There's a kid upstairs, Theo."

"I know."

"No more'n six months old. Slept through the whole damned thing."

Loukas looked up at the sky. It was high, a faded blue. "Make sure the specialists get pictures of everything. Oh, damn, we're not equipped for this kind of messiness. Wakeman ought to call the state cops."

"Ah, Theo, we can do the job, you'll see."

Loukas measured the younger man. "You're enjoying it, aren't you? Lots of excitement. Well, two women are dead. It's all over for them, Tom. When that kid upstairs cries, his mother won't be there to answer."

"I know that, Theo."

"Yes, I guess you do. What about the husband?"

"He has a factory over in Bridgeport. Makes TV circuitry. I called him; he's on his way."

"Good. And the guy who found her?"

"He's in the playroom, like you said, Theo. I put Carl on him. Carl has a mean look. Might shake the guy up a little."

"Always thinking ahead, Tom, that's you."

"Is that bad, Theo?"

"Come on, let's talk to this fellow."

Minute Man was a tall stick of a man, face narrow and knobby, eyes lidded. He sat in a Boston rocker, head sunk between his high, knifelike shoulders.

"I'm Sergeant Loukas."

Minute Man raised his eyes reluctantly. "Terrible," he said. "Just terrible." His voice was honeyed, seductive. Loukas was instantly repelled.

"What time was it when you discovered the body?"

"I can't really say. I was due here at nine and it must have been only minutes after that. Surely no more than five after."

"The call came into the Fort at nine minutes after the hour," Petersen said.

"You see?" Minute Man said. "I don't lie. Don't expect me to solve this case for you. That's not where my abilities lie. I can tell you what I encountered when I got here. There was poor Mrs. Spratt sprawled out on the steps, her legs spread out with everything for all the world to see. It is not a sight I find appetizing."

"You don't like women?" Loukas said.

"It just so happens that I cherish land. No other item is actually real. Land is always *there*. A true value, no matter what direction the economy may take. Whenever I can, I buy land."

"Minute Man," Loukas said. "What's your real name?"

Minute Man screwed up his face. "Blau. August Blau. German, naturally. Call me Augie, please. I hate it when people call me Gus."

"Do you have a family?" Petersen put in.

"You mean, am I married? Indeed. Does it surprise you? Well, I understand why. You'd think that a man with my set of mind would know better. Oh, what a great deal one can discover about females in my line of work."

"Let's talk a little about your line of work, Mr. Blau," Loukas said.

"Augie, please. I clean up after them. All the filthy, slothful women. I make it possible for them to live in neat, ordered houses that their husbands can be proud of. Eat off the floor, if they want to, when I'm finished."

"This cleaning service of yours interests me."

"Let me say, I do not understand how a self-respecting man can tolerate some of these women. Absolutely piggish when it comes to taking care of a home. Your average housewife, she's only too glad to abdicate her responsibility, let other people do her work. Some cleaning services cheat, you know. You can get away with just doing the show spots. But I do an honest job. A superior effort."

"How long were you here alone with Mrs. Spratt?" Loukas said.

"How long?"

"This morning."

"I was not alone with her. Not today, anyway. I told you, she was there, on the stairs. That way. When I arrived. Oh, why am I wasting time talking to you anyway! I have a house to do."

Petersen smothered a laugh. "Don't worry about a thing, Augie. No complaints if you miss today's cleanup."

"Did you spot anybody around the house," Loukas said, "when you got here?"

"Nobody. I'm very observant."

"A car, maybe? Or a car sound?"

"Nothing."

Loukas cleared his throat. "When was the last time you worked the Horn house, Augie?"

"Horn?"

"Yes," Petersen said. "Off Pond Ridge Road."

Minute Man shook his head gloomily. "Not one of my clients. I'd remember if it was."

Abner Posner thrust his long face into the room. "Theo, somebody's getting some very fine nooky. This one's even better-looking than the first."

"Rape?"

"You'll get the coroner's report. But from the look of her, I'd say so. You know something, Theo?"

"What?"

"I think you've got a nut on your hands, a real crazy."

CHAPTER SIX

I

ON HIS DAY off, Loukas went into New York. He had agreed, at her suggestion, to meet Detective Elizabeth Mercer in front of the Museum of Modern Art. She was waiting when he arrived. Slim, dark-haired, surprisingly attractive in her police uniform.

"Why don't we have lunch in the museum?" she suggested. "I'm a member and it's very pleasant." When they were settled at a table, she directed her attention to Loukas. "How can I help you, Sergeant?"

"I told you," he said, "that we've had two rapes in Arcadia."

"Same M.O.?"

"Exactly the same."

"Do the women's descriptions of their assailant tally?"

"That's just it, both victims were killed. Strangled."

Detective Mercer made a face. "That's rough." She lit a cigarette, moved the pack across the table toward Loukas. He shook his head. "No hit and run, that's for sure."

"I figure he's still around."

"I'd say so."

"But I'm coming up empty. No witnesses. No prints. Nothing. I'm afraid he's going to hit again."

"Yes," she said, "unless you get him first. Poor bastard undoubtedly would like to be caught, punished, stopped from doing it."

"It looks to me as if we're going to have to be pretty lucky to collar this guy."

"If he didn't kill— But he does. A live complainant would help. Maybe your man has a yellow sheet. If we could work up a composite from our photo kit, it would give you something to go on."

"It would help if we knew what he looked like."

"Like everybody else," Detective Mercer said. "All shapes, sizes, colors. We get a lot of them in the city."

"This Sex Crimes Analysis Unit you people have set up, what do you know?"

"The idea is to train our people to work with units in the field. Most cops approach a rape victim as if *she* had committed the crime."

"A corpse eliminates that problem." Loukas picked listlessly at his tuna-fish salad. "What can you tell me about rape that might help? About rapists?"

"There are some interesting statistics. For example, forcible rape occurs about once every eleven minutes. That puts the yearly rape figure at approximately fifty thousand per year. Maybe four or five times as many go unreported. Women are often afraid or ashamed to come forward."

"Why should they be?"

Mercer measured Loukas gravely before deciding to answer. "Most cops investigating a rape are men. They see rape as primarily sexual."

"Okay. You're a woman, how else can you see it?"

"Oh, sure it's sexual. That's obvious. But primarily there's the violence. The physical and psychological violence."

Loukas digested that.

"Most cops working a rape try to establish whether or not the victim was fairly active sexually. If she was, they try to encourage her to drop the case. That's a load of you-know-what, Sergeant. Rape is rape, crime is crime."

Loukas felt slow. "What do you mean?"

"It's nothing new, only the degree varies. In ancient Sparta, a man was expected to rape his wife on their wedding night. There's a rape in the Bible, you know.

And there isn't an army that hasn't done it—to the victor belongs the spoils."

"Civilization," Loukas drawled.

"But still I suppose you've heard the theory that all women secretly want to be raped. It works something like this—nice girls don't allow themselves to get raped and bad girls have no one to blame but themselves. Doesn't allow a woman much flexibility."

"Takes the onus off the men. A very convenient theory."

"My, my," she said in exaggerated admiration, "an understanding male cop. I'm impressed."

Loukas grinned sheepishly. "What can you tell me about rapists?"

"Let's see, your average everyday rapist is somewhere between fifteen and twenty-five years old. Usually he's unmarried, but not always. Unskilled labor, you might say, though not necessarily. Often unemployed. Not very well educated, though we've turned up Ph.D.'s from time to time. For the most part, he has a minimum income."

"In other words," Loukas said, "a loser."

"Mainly, except when he isn't."

"You're making it difficult for me."

"Not out of choice. There's a good chance the man you want comes out of a broken home. Or at least an unhappy one. Sex was considered dirty, something secret, done only behind locked doors. Any childhood curiosity displayed was repressed, possibly with violence."

"Sounds like someone I know."

"It's a big club," she said tonelessly. "A lot of cops belonged to it. Here's something you probably didn't know. Most rapes take place indoors."

"I've got one and one," Loukas said.

"Most rapes are planned. In about half of them the rapist is acquainted with his victim. At least he's seen her. Weekends and nights, that's when most of them hit. Let's say after eight in the evening."

"My boy breaks the pattern. He's a morning man."

"No guarantees." She measured him gravely. "That's

it, I'm afraid. Not much help. In most instances the victim is able to identify her attacker. But your man takes care of that possibility very effectively."

"How am I going to get him?" Loukas said, voice tinged with desperation.

"It took a long time to get the Boston Strangler. And Jack the Ripper never was caught. Chances are he's got a scheme, a pattern that he's following. He's choosing his victims. Look into their backgrounds. Maybe they have something in common that will put you on to the right guy. Maybe you can come up with some piece of information that will allow you to anticipate his next move, cut him off at the pass, so to speak. Maybe."

"And if I come up empty?"

"Then he'll make his move and another woman is going to get killed."

CHAPTER SEVEN

I

LOUKAS RANG THE BELL. Russell Spratt opened the door and motioned for him to come inside. From somewhere in the house Loukas heard a baby crying.

"My mother's come to help me with the child," Spratt said. "I think he senses that something's wrong. I was just having coffee. Can I offer you a cup, Sergeant Loukas?"

"Thank you."

They went into the kitchen. "You said to call if I thought of anything," Spratt said. "Milk? Sugar?"

"Black is fine." The mug felt solid and reassuring in his hands, warming the morning stiffness out of his fingers.

"It's funny, maybe nothing," Spratt said, his mouth drawn. "A small thing, but I didn't want to take any chances."

"You never can tell what will help."

"Yes." Spratt's unshaven face seemed to melt and tears filled his eyes. "How could such a thing happen to us? I don't believe it yet. I go to bed at night and expect Charlotte to be there, warming herself against me. She never liked cold weather, never. She was a good woman, so clean and cheerful. What am I going to do now? I can't raise a child by myself."

Loukas drank some coffee. The ulcer pangs came and went.

"Life was getting good for us," Spratt said, snuffling. "The factory, I mean. This house. Charlotte loved this house. the land, her vegetable garden. We used to live in New York, you know. I was a television repairman. When my father-in-law passed away he left us a little money. I was able to go into the manufacturing end. Circuitry. I was doing okay so we decided to move up here. It seemed right, a good place for children. We wanted to get away from the city, you understand. Away from the dirt and the crime, the violence. Isn't that funny? *Why did he have to kill Charlotte?* He could just have— Why did he have to kill her?"

"Why don't you tell me what it is you wanted to talk about?"

Spratt wiped his eyes. He made a gesture. "There, you see. Just the way it was when I came home the other day. Not a single thing's been touched. Nothing. I couldn't even come into the kitchen until this morning."

"You better explain, Mr. Spratt."

"The paper bags, they contained the order."

On the Formica counter top next to the stove, four or five brown paper bags were neatly folded and stacked.

"The order?"

"We were having some people in for dinner that night, the day it happened. Two other couples. Harvey Julian and Lenny Lindner, their wives. Nice people. Charlotte had made up a shopping list, called it in the day before."

"Tell me about the bags."

"Charlotte used them for garbage, you see. Sometimes they would wet clear through with gravy or leftover salad dressing and when I carried them out to the cans in the garage they would break open. It upset me and I yelled at her sometimes when it happened. What the hell did it matter! I didn't have to lose my temper, did I? *Did* I?"

"The bags?"

"That's just it. Charlotte never kept them on the counter that way. My wife is—was extremely systematic. You can see for yourself how clean and organized everything is."

"Yes."

"The bags should be under the sink, in the cabinet

under the sink. They were readily available that way when you needed one. Everybody knew where they were."

Loukas looked at the bags. There was nothing remarkable about them. Plain brown grocery bags. Used in every food store, every market. "Your wife might have unpacked, folded up the bags intending to put them into the cabinet. Something interrupted."

"I don't think so. You see, she had a place for everything." He opened the refrigerator. "There, you see!"

Loukas saw nothing out of the ordinary and said so.

"It's the milk. Charlotte never put milk containers in the door. That was for juice, not milk. There are two containers in the door."

"There isn't any more room in the top compartment."

"Yes, yes," Spratt said, growing excited. "And whenever that happened, Charlotte placed a milk carton on its side on a lower shelf. Always."

"What do you make of this, Mr. Spratt?"

"Somebody besides Charlotte put the food away, somebody else folded up the bags. Whoever did it wanted it to look like Charlotte did it. The man who killed my wife."

"Why would he go to so much trouble?"

"I've been thinking about it and finally worked it all out." A look of triumph came onto the pudgy face. "I know who the murderer is."

"Who, Mr. Spratt?"

"Well, you see, Charlotte shopped at the A-1 Market, generally. She liked their meats. They have quality merchandise."

Loukas waited.

"It was the delivery boy," Spratt said.

Loukas went over it aloud. "The order was called in the day before. The food was delivered the morning Mrs. Spratt was killed—"

"After I had left for work."

"You think that the delivery boy attacked your wife, then murdered her."

"Don't you see, if he'd left the groceries in the bags

we'd have known at once he was here at that time and suspicion would have fallen naturally on him. So he put everything away. He thought he could get away with it."

It was possible, Loukas thought. An order delivered, passion aroused by some innocent remark or imagined invitation. An advance, perhaps a rejection inflaming an already aroused and hostile personality, then the attack. It was a nice theory. Neat. Convenient. Could it come this easily? he wondered.

"Well, thank you for calling, Mr. Spratt. I'll follow through on this."

"I'm right, you'll see. Apply pressure to this fellow and he'll break wide open. You men know how to do that, I'm sure."

"Thanks for your assistance. We'll be in touch."

"I ought to go after him myself. Tear him apart. But I've got to think of my son now. He's got no one else, you understand."

II

A-1 Market was situated in downtown Arcadia. Loukas parked next to a yellow fire hydrant and went inside. He looked around for someone to help him and spied a familiar face.

"Hello, Theo," Ralph Burleigh said, and went on examining a box of Bartlett pears, squeezing each one gently.

"Hello, Ralph, what are you doing here?"

"The best fruit in town," Burleigh said.

"Could be. But out of my salary range."

Burleigh laughed without embarrassment. "Ah, Mr. Miller gives me a break on the price. I used to work here, you see."

"Lucky you," Loukas said. "Is Miller the manager?"

"He owns A-1."

"Where would I find him?"

"In his office, up the stairs at the back of the store."

Miller, a stocky, balding man, was on the telephone when Loukas entered his cramped office. He nodded a greeting, kept talking, measuring the detective. Finally he hung up.

"Can I help you, mister?"

Loukas flashed his shield.

Miller was impressed. "Police. What can I do for you, Sergeant?"

"You deliver, don't you?"

"Deliver. Sure, I deliver. That's part of the service. Best meats in town, daily deliveries, open six nights a week until eight o'clock. How do you think a small operator competes with the big chains? Finast, Grand Union, A & P. Department stores is what they are. Oh, sure, maybe customers can save a few pennies here and there, but if they want A-1 merchandise they got to come to A-1 Market." Pleased with himself, he rubbed his hands together. "Come on, I'll show you what I got. Meat, poultry, fruits. You don't shop my place, do you, Sergeant?"

"Can't afford to. Do you deliver to some people named Spratt?"

"Spratt? I don't know the name but that don't mean anything. I'll look it up. I'm not on the floor so much anymore. Paper work takes up all my time. Once I had a small fruit stand. I bought, I sold, I bought some more. I kept the books and Annie, that's my wife, she worked the cash drawer. Now I got a lawyer, I got an accountant, I got a bookkeeper who comes in twice a week." He opened a ledger, ran down the page with his forefinger. "Here it is. Mrs. Russell Spratt. A customer for two years nearly. Charges and pays on time. Nice lady." He smiled at Loukas. "Why do you ask?"

"What about Horn?"

"Horn."

"Treysa Horn."

Miller returned to his ledger. "Yeah, sure. We deliver to Mrs. Horn."

"How many delivery people do you employ?"

"How many! One is how many. This is no supermarket. I got a little truck. Maybe you seen it, painted a bright yellow with big red letters, A-1 Market—Fresh Produce." He laughed delightedly. "I got a weakness for red and yellow. It's because I got poor color perception. I don't see dark colors so good."

"Who does the deliveries?"

"Virgil."

"A black boy?"

The manager seemed surprised by the question. "As white as you and me. Whiter than you, Sergeant." He laughed. "You got a pretty dark complexion, if you don't mind my saying so."

"What's his full name?"

"Virgil Reiser."

"I'd like to talk to him."

"He's out on orders. Due back in about twenty minutes, I guess."

"I'll wait."

III

Virgil Reiser was tall and slender with long arms and large hands. The manager introduced him to Loukas and left them alone in his office.

Loukas stared at Virgil for a long time. There was an awkwardness to the boy when he stood at ease, as if his knees refused to unlock. "How long have you been in town, Virgil?"

Virgil blinked. "I was practically born here. My folks moved to Arcadia when I was two years old."

"You went to the high school?"

"Yes, sir. Graduated three years ago."

"That makes you about twenty-one."

"Yes, sir. Excuse me, Sergeant, for asking, but what is this all about?"

"Just a few questions I'd like answered, Virgil. Routine investigation."

"Oh, I see." But it was clear that he didn't.

"Maybe you heard about the two women in town

who've been killed. Raped and murdered, Virgil. You
know about that, don't you, Virgil?"

Virgil's expression revealed nothing. "Not really. I
mean, I guess I heard some mention of it, but I don't
read the papers much. Just the sports pages."

"You play sports, Virgil?"

"Ah, not much. I'm not very good at games. Sometimes a pickup game of basketball."

"I know what you mean. I was never much good
myself. I always envied the athletes, the good-looking
guys. They got all the girls. I guess it's still that way
today."

"I guess it is."

"But you do okay with girls, don't you, Virgil?"

Virgil lifted his square shoulders, let them fall. "Sure,
okay. No complaints is what I mean. I'm no movie
star, but I do okay."

"Why, I'd say you're a pretty decent-looking fellow,
Virgil. Got a steady girl?"

"Why are you asking these questions? I don't get it."

"It's like I said, Virgil, just routine. A police investigation takes different twists and turns, goes off at strange
angles sometimes. You didn't say about having a steady
girl, Virgil."

"I see somebody."

"What's her name?"

Virgil answered reluctantly, "Jane."

"Last name?"

"Bonner."

"She lives here in Arcadia?"

"I guess."

"You're not sure where your girl lives?"

"She lives over on Duncan Road," Virgil said with
a mild display of defiance.

Loukas smiled. "There," he said, "no damage done.
Now, you delivered some groceries to Mrs. Russell Spratt
the other morning. Two mornings ago."

"Could be."

"Try to remember, Virgil."

Virgil took a notebook out of his pocket, leafed

through it. "I keep records, you see. Here it is. Yes, Wednesday morning. I was there about nine o'clock."

"How long did it take to unload, collect payment?"

"Mrs. Spratt's a charge; she don't pay."

"How long to unload?"

"A couple of minutes."

"Where'd you go after that?"

Virgil went back to the notebook. "The Henry house, about a quarter mile down the road."

"What time were you there?"

"Five minutes later, I'd guess. I don't run on a time-table, but I don't fool around neither. Mr. Miller, he knows I'm dependable."

"What about the Horns? You delivered to them on Monday. Check your book."

"That'd be Monday morning."

"Time?"

"Eight-forty-five, according to my record. But that's just approximate, you understand."

"What did you think of Mrs. Spratt?"

"She wasn't much of a talker. Some ladies like jawing, not her. All business."

"That bother you, Virgil?"

"Why should it? What are you driving at?"

"Did Mrs. Spratt tip you good?"

"Fifty cents."

"Mrs. Horn?"

"About the same."

"Is that about average, Virgil?"

"About average."

"You live alone, Virgil?"

"With my mother. Why?"

"You're lucky. Before you know it, time passes and your people are all gone. Nobody can take the place of a mother and a father."

"I guess I know that."

"Sure you do. What kind of shape was Mrs. Horn in when you saw her?"

"Shape?"

"Was she okay?"

"What do you mean? Sure, she was okay."

"What about Mrs. Spratt?"

"Say, why are you asking these questions? What's this all about?"

"You saw each of them around nine in the morning, give or take a few minutes?"

"That's right."

"Tell me again about Mrs. Henry. What time you got over to her house."

"A few minutes after nine. It had to be."

Loukas stood up. "You know Mrs. Horn and Mrs. Spratt were both killed, Virgil? Both raped." Virgil wet his lips. He nodded. "Murder," Loukas said, "is a terrible thing. To take a life. A lot of questions have to be asked. You've been very helpful."

"I don't know anything."

"You helped me establish the time of the crimes. If both women were alive when you made your deliveries, then one was assaulted and murdered possibly just before nine and the other shortly after nine. Doesn't that make sense, Virgil?"

"I guess so."

"Well, sure it does. You were probably the last one to see each of them alive. Except for the killer, of course. Kind of spooky, isn't it?"

Virgil didn't answer.

"I've got to go. More questions to ask. Questions and answers, that's what it's all about. See you again, Virgil."

"So long," Virgil said.

Loukas swung back abruptly. "By the way, Virgil, do you usually unpack for your customers?"

Virgil seem startled. "Unpack!"

"You put Mrs. Spratt things away, in the fridge? Folded her bags?"

"Not me. She must've done it. My job ends once I bring the stuff inside. I get my tip and I'm gone."

"Right," Loukas said. "Well, thanks again, Virgil."

IV

Loukas went directly to the Henry house. Gladys Henry was a stout woman in her early forties with a round, pleasant face. Her hair was in curlers when Loukas arrived and she was drinking tea from a glass.

"Come inside, Sergeant," she said cheerfully. "I'll fix you some tea."

"No, thanks, Mrs. Henry. Just one or two questions I'd like answered."

"About poor Mrs. Spratt, I imagine."

"You knew her?"

"Saw her here and there a few times. Met her out walking with her baby only a week ago. Nice young woman, not fancy. Not acting too good for plainer people the way some do. No, I don't want to say I knew her."

"The other morning, you had an order delivered from A-1."

"That's right. Virgil brought it. Nice boy, Virgil."

"How well do you know him?"

"Not at all, actually. He's been delivering for A-1 about a year or so, I imagine. Polite young fellow, well spoken, clean-cut. That's nice to see in somebody working around foodstuffs."

"What time did he get here?"

"That's be on Wednesday?"

"Wednesday morning."

"Well, let's see. Mr. Henry got off to work at his usual time. That's be around ten minutes to nine. He drives to work in a car pool. Meets his buddies out on the road and if he ain't there waiting they'll go on without him. Don't fool around none, those boys."

"What time did Virgil get here?"

"I'd say about nine o'clock. Near as I can tell."

"You can't be sure of the exact time?"

"Never been a clock watcher, Sergeant. I'd make it out to be nine. Yes, nine o'clock."

Loukas felt uneasy, as if there was another question

that should be asked, more information extracted. But he didn't have the question, didn't know precisely what it was he was after.

V

Loukas went around to see Sandy Felton. He rang the bell and waited and felt his nervousness grow. He became annoyed with himself, as if his emotions were betraying him, making him feel what he had no wish to feel. He was about to leave when the door opened and Sandy Felton appeared. In a tennis dress, she was an imposing physical presence, her exposed limbs smooth and brown, the skin pulled taut over clearly defined muscles. Perspiration gleamed on her cheeks and her eyes were bright.

"Sergeant Loukas. Sorry I kept you waiting. I was upstairs. I was half out of this costume and I had to get myself decent when the bell rang."

He retreated a step. "I'll come back some other time."

"No, come in." He trailed her into the den and watched her collapse into a chair, waited for her to invite him to sit.

"Just got back from tennis. You play?"

He shook his head.

"Been at it since I was a kid. Just beat Dana Anderson three straight sets. Do you know Dana? He's the pro at the club. Screaming faggot, but he's got a pretty fair game. Moves okay. But no serve. I can blast him out most of the time."

"Sounds as if you're pretty good at it."

She thought about that. "Used to be. I would have been one of the best if I'd really worked at it. But there was always so much to do off the court. Never concentrated enough. What can I do for you, Sergeant?"

"Just checking a few more things."

"Any suspects yet?"

"We'll come up with something soon."

"I hope so. It's all kind of frightening." In contrast

to her words, she smiled suddenly, the tanned face breaking open. From where Loukas sat, he thought he could detect the sweet sweat smell of her. He struggled not to look at where her thighs came together. "You said you wanted to ask some more questions, Sergeant. Is that really why you're here?"

At once Loukas felt stripped down to some essential portion of himself. He spoke firmly, his manner crisp and authoritative.

"In an investigation it's necessary sometimes to go over the same territory again and again. People forget or omit or are able to come up with something new."

"Have you come up with something new?"

"Do you shop at A-1 Market, Mrs. Felton?"

"I can't afford it, if you want to know the truth. This town is pretty expensive, you know."

"I know."

"But I dig some of the stuff at their gourmet counter. Inside me is a fat girl struggling to break loose. And making a great deal of progress, I'm afraid."

Loukas eyed her extended limbs, her round hips, the fine large breasts. "You have things delivered from there?" He was sorry he'd come, was uncomfortable in her presence.

"Sometimes," she answered. He perceived a deep awareness in her eyes.

"Would you know the delivery boy? Virgil Reiser is his name."

"I guess I might."

"Was he the one you saw running from the Horn residence that morning?"

"I'm sorry, Sergeant, I'm not even sure I saw someone. I told you that."

He stood up. "Just a hunch. You play hunches if you're a cop."

She heaved herself erect, went past him on her way to the door. Walking behind her, he noticed with pleasure that there were no dimples of disintegration on the backs of her round thights. A fine-looking woman.

At the door he stood awkwardly, wanting to say something more to her. "Well," he said finally, "I guess I'd better get back to work."

"Goodbye, Sergeant."

He left with a sense of incompleteness, some part of him not functioning properly; failed, and not knowing why.

VI

Enid Keyes decided to see a movie. By herself. She disliked going to the movies alone but there was no one to go with. That's what came of making it with married men, she reminded herself. The bastards were seldom available when you needed them. Yet for some perverse reason she had not been able to name, she persisted in getting involved with them. As if unmarried men were different. More dangerous, perhaps.

She thought about Ned Bookman, wished she could safely call him, invite him to go with her. Afterward, coffee and pleasant talk, a few laughs, all building up to some good time in bed. He wasn't the best lay she'd ever had, but he wasn't the worst, either. On a scale of one to ten, he was a six. Maybe six and a half. Oh, hell, give him a seven.

She had prepared dinner for her son, Richie, and possessed of no appetite herself, sat silently at the table watching him eat. He was a handsome boy, frequently remote. In that quality he resembled his father, and he looked like Milton. But Milton had loved animals and himself, no one else.

Looking at Richie, and remembering Milton, the loneliness returned to Enid. Six years of living by herself had not made it easier. There was no longing for Milton, no wish for him to return; only a sense of being apart from the rest of humanity, of being one in a world of pairs.

"Richie," she said to her son, "would you mind if I went to a movie tonight? I feel like getting out."

"It's okay." Richie was eleven and enjoyed the feeling of being responsible for himself, enjoyed the lingering fear that rippled under his skin every time the house creaked, imagining all sorts of threatening intruders. "Go ahead," he urged.

VII

An earlier threat of rain had passed and a new moon drifted from behind the clouds, casting a ghostly light on the marina. Boats lifted and fell on the swells, masts swaying in counterpoint to one another. A slight chilling breeze swept in off the Sound.

Tom Petersen smoked a cigarette. Boating had no appeal for him. Boating was a waste of time and never quite comfortable. A man was always too hot or too cold. Stomach close to nausea.

Hunting was the thing. With bow and arrow. Guns were too easy, removed all the sport, left only the killing. Not that Petersen minded killing; he simply enjoyed a contest.

In the parking area behind him, a car pulled up. Footsteps came toward him. Petersen wondered why this place had been chosen for the meeting. Why not some place warm and friendly, where a man could get a good cup of coffee.

"Sorry to keep you waiting, Petersen."

He came around and accepted Victor Fellows' hand. "That's okay, Mr. Fellows. I was just looking over the boats."

"I've got a ketch of my own." Fellows went out on the pier, took a place on a bench. Petersen followed. "Sit down, Petersen. I want to talk about the case. Pressure's building fast."

"I guess so."

"The governor's talking about sending in the State Police, the county's telling us to use the sheriff's office. And the press is up in arms."

"I saw Roy Sullivan's editorial in the *Banner*."

"People want action."

"We're doing our best."

"What about the Mexican?"

"The Mexican?"

"Yes, he seems a likely prospect."

"He was in New York in the slam when the second killing took place. He won't do."

"We need an arrest. People are very unhappy."

Petersen laughed. "I know. We're getting plenty of business."

"Business?"

"Complaints about prowlers, strangers in the neighborhood, that kind of thing."

For a long interval, neither of them spoke. Fellows broke the silence. "I've tried talking to Loukas but I seem to get nowhere. He won't open up."

"Theo is a cautious man."

"I am the Circuit Prosecutor. I'm entitled to know what's going on."

"Theo doesn't always tell me what's on his mind."

"What you're saying is that he doesn't trust either one of us."

Petersen warned himself to choose his words with care. "Sergeant Loukas is in charge of the case."

"What case?" Fellows said tartly. "What have you got? No witnesses. No hard evidence. No suspects. Just two dead women."

Petersen made a sound of assent. "Theo is a careful man. He knows what he's doing."

Fellows shifted around to face the detective. "Do you really believe that? If so, I may be wasting my time talking to you."

Petersen spoke deliberately. "I think I better do most of the listening, Mr. Fellows."

"Loukas is too damned cautious. You and me, Petersen, our futures are in front of us. The best years of our lives still to come. Loukas is ready to retire. He plays it safe."

"He works very hard."

"Okay, he tries. It isn't enough to try. We need results. Loukas is a different generation. The way he thinks, the way he views life. A younger man ought to be in charge of this case. A man with energy and drive. A man like you."

"Captain Henderson makes the assignments."

"Assignments can be changed. If there's cause."

"Theo's a good cop," Petersen said.

"Loyalty is an admirable quality, Tom. But not blind loyalty. Not dumb loyalty. Loyalty to the right cause, the right person. Both of us know that Loukas has never before worked a capital crime."

"No one on the force has."

"But you've been trained differently. You're tuned in to modern crime-fighting methods. You could be chief someday. Don't tell me you don't think about that."

"I think about it once in a while."

"Ingenuity is what's required here. Imagination. Courage to make a decision and stand behind it."

"I don't know what anybody else could do that Theo hasn't done."

"A bright young fellow like yourself might be able to improvise a little, take chances. A little daring is in order, I would say."

Petersen wet his lips. "Like what?"

"Go beyond anything Loukas has done. Follow each lead to the end of the road. A case like this, all we need is someone who seems reasonably guilty. People want an arrest, a conviction. We can give them what they want. Promotion would be a sure thing for the cop who makes this collar, Tom."

Petersen decided to broaden the conversation. "What would it do for the prosecutor who gets the conviction?"

Fellows allowed nothing to show on his face. "One can never tell. A man with the right credentials might go far in politics. Very far. He could take a trusted associate along."

"The state capital?"

"For a starter."

Petersen whistled silently. "You're a very ambitious man, Mr. Fellows."

"Don't allow Loukas to hold you back, Tom."

"I wouldn't want to do anything out of line, anything to hurt Theo."

"Of course not. Just find someone for me to prosecute. I'll do the rest, for us both."

Petersen gazed out at the Sound. Victor Fellows was right, there was no telling how far a man of ambition could go. All it took was hard work, some brains, an ample supply of guts. Petersen figured himself to possess large amounts of all three.

"I'll do what I can," he said.

"Quietly."

"Quietly."

"And when you make the arrest, bring the man to me. Is that clear?"

"Yes, sir."

VIII

The movie was *American Graffiti* and Enid had read a number of glowing notices. She expected to be enthralled, stimulated, thrilled; nothing happened. The story of young people killing time in the early 1960's failed to move her. She remembered 1962 clearly; it had been a bad time with infrequent rewards. She concluded that this was a film made for young people willing to accept the false and fabled world it created.

When the picture ended, she hurried out to where she had parked her car. Richie would be asleep by now, she supposed, and she considered stopping somewhere for an ice cream. But she disliked showing herself in public alone. She drove home without hurrying.

She put the car in the garage and tugged the overhead door. As usual, it was difficult to dislodge and she braced herself for a greater effort. A shuffling sound from within the garage brought her halfway around, just in time to take the full force of his fist on her cheek. She went down.

He came after her, both fists swinging. The pain was dull, not entirely unpleasant. She tried to roll away and that seemed to enrage him. Swearing, he followed, beating her. His fist smashed her nose and a flood of pain spread through her face. She opened her mouth to cry out and he punched it shut, pounding her head against the concrete floor of the garage.

The taste of blood was in her mouth and she found it difficult to breath. A blow landed on her breast and she gasped for air, retched dryly. In a feeble effort to defend herself, her arms rose up. He struck them aside, beat her around the face. She slumped back, still conscious but unable to move.

"This time you're gonna get it," she heard, as if from a distance.

Hands pulled at her panty hose, stripping it away. She stiffened her legs in resistance and he hit her in the belly.

"Bitch! I've been watching you. I know what you are."

He placed himself between her thighs, forcing her knees apart. She moaned.

"You want it," he muttered, coming down on her. "You really want it. Put it in, put it in."

Reflexively, her hand reach out.

He plunged forward and the pain was acute. He banged ferociously at her, body powerful and wild, grinding her into the concrete, ripping her. Giving her what she deserved.

"You love it," he hissed. "You love it. Say you love it."

Sound seeped out of her bloodied lips and as if in response his hands slid up onto her throat, fingers reaching for the warm pulse of her life. He crashed down on her, drove himself deeper, felt her writhe and twist under him, felt her lift up as if to cast him aside.

Infuriated, he went harder and faster until all strength drained into his groin, collected in his shaft. His body grew taut and he cried out in fear and despair.

A succession of eruptions launched him into spasm, flesh jerking uncontrollably, tiny protests muffled behind clenched teeth. His muscles drew up and his hands flexed. The fingers closed, thumbs digging deep. He rose up, weight carried on locked arms, the agony and the joy rocketing beyond all tolerance. His brain swung on an unsteady axis and his vision blurred. He grew dizzy and weak and it became difficult to breathe. He fell forward.

After a while, he thrust himself upright. He adjusted his trousers. In the darkness, her still form was sickeningly pale, ugly. A sound brought his head up, searching the darkness. He felt threatened and exposed. Without looking back, he ran into the night.

CHAPTER EIGHT

I

A SPECIAL FOUR-PAGE EDITION of the Arcadia *Republican* was in the hands of its subscribers by eight o'clock the next morning. It was the first such edition since V-E Day. The only subject treated was the three murders.

Each killing was reconstructed according to the few facts known, and the imagination of the writer. Biographies of each of the dead women were given. There were interviews with Leon Horn and Russell Spratt, as well as friends of the most recent deceased.

A two-column portrait of Victor Fellows dominated the front page, along with a long interview in which he vowed a quick solution to the case, insisting that ". . . the people will have justice."

Chief of Police Donald Wakeman was also quoted: "The full resources of our Department are at work on a round-the-clock basis. There are a number of leads which my people are checking out and I expect to make a dramatic announcement within forty-eight hours."

When asked if that meant the police had a prime suspect, the Chief replied: "I stand on my previous statement."

First Selectman DaCosta said: "Our sympathies go out to the relatives of the victims of these awful crimes and we promise them swift and complete justice in the traditional American manner. The Administration has full confidence in Chief Wakeman and his men to bring their investigation to a swift and successful conclusion."

II

The newsmen came from all over the state. From Norwalk and Danbury. From Hartford and New Haven. From Milford and Westport and Fairfield and Greenwich. They came from New York City and even from Boston.

Reporters went around knocking on doors at random, asking people what they knew about the crimes, how they felt, what they were doing to protect themselves.

Radio interviewers patrolled the country roads with tape recorders, describing the scenes of the killings, dramatizing the fears of the residents.

Television camera crews set up near Police Headquarters and shot film of Chief Wakeman and Victor Fellows. Two crews chased after the First Selectman when he left Town Hall, but he lost them in Morry's General Store, Inc., when he ducked out the rear service entrance. They stopped women on Main Street to record their sentiments about rape, murder, and safety in the home. And CBS filmed Harold McQuillen in his gun shop.

"What would you say the mood is in Arcadia these days, Mr. McQuillen?" the reporter asked.

McQuillen looked fearlessly into the camera. "Uneasy. This is a peaceful place ordinarily."

"But not now?"

"Not anymore. Guess things will never be the same again."

"Because of the murders, you mean?"

"Exactly, sir."

"People are frightened?"

"Scared silly, I'd say."

"What makes you think so?"

McQuillen patter a Remington bolt-action .30-.30 with loving tenderness. "I'm selling a lot more of these beauties to folks lately."

"Then is it fair to say that your business is a good barometer of people's fears?"

"Exactly right. The worse things get, the more guns I

sell. Some folks are buying two, three weapons at a time.
Pistols, carbines, shotguns."

"People are scared?"

"Ask Bill Herkimer, up in Milford. He trains guard
dogs. Bill's got orders enough to last him for two years.
Can't get the right animals. Folks want Dobermans;
they've got the reputation for meanness, you see. And
shepherds are okay, too, I hear."

"Then it's fair to say Arcadia's turning into an armed
camp?"

"People in these parts, they're used to taking care of
themselves. Not depending on outsiders. Reckon we'll
take care of this matter, too."

III

Ralph Burleigh felt uneasy. He was a man who preferred
to do one thing at a time, clearing all else from his mind.
Concentration, thoroughness, these were the qualities he
brought to bear on a problem. He resented being forced
to divide his attention.

Ordinarily he would have been with his football players
on Saturday morning. Making them ready for the game
ahead.

But not this Saturday. As night security chief of Arcadia High School, Ralph felt a special obligation to the
school and to the citizens of the town. He patrolled the
corridors, examined the visitors' toilets, inspected the
aisles of the auditorium. Ralph had learned not to trust
or depend on the cleaning and maintenance staff. During
the school year, when the Adult Education Division con-
ducted classes almost every night, he invariably discovered
uncollected trash or burned-out light bulbs or broken
seats in the auditorium. The successful, cultured people
who attended these classes were entitled to better treat-
ment. He admired their consistently high attendance and
felt a powerful obligation to serve their best interests as
he served the interests of their sons on the football field.

Satisfied that the auditorium was in condition to receive

an audience, Ralph switched on the stage lights, set the podium in place, and arranged two dozen folding chairs, neatly in ranks behind it. Finally he tested the public-address system.

At the main entrance he opened the tall wooden doors and took up his post to one side, ready to welcome his fellow townspeople. But his mind kept drifting to the football team. Kids seemed to lack fighting spirit these days, the will to win. How to motivate them properly, that was his task. What, he asked himself, would Vince Lombardi do?

IV

Ned Bookman sat alone in his office willing himself to remain calm. The effort was unsuccessful. Sweat broke along his sides and he felt chilled. His hands were unsteady.

All his life he had been careful, planning ahead, allotting his time and energies with stringent discipline. His future had been assured. He had accomplished everything he had set out to accomplish, was precisely where he wanted to be. Suddenly it all was in danger, like a house of cards erected on a shaky foundation. What a fool he had been to risk everything for a few moments of pleasure.

He was about to be exposed. A horny shrink without scruples. His practice would be decimated, his position at the Mental Health Clinic and Social Laboratory undermined; he would be fired. His reputation permanently soiled, his future wiped out.

And Moira would be furious, hurt. And rightly so. Betrayed by the husband she had idolized and trusted. Of course she would leave him, taking the children along. The divorce would be ugly.

Now this call. Coming early in the morning, shocking him awake, revealing how close to disaster he existed. He was terribly afraid.

A policeman wanted to see him. To question him. To

link him with Enid Keyes, to reveal to the world his folly. Bookman plucked at his fingers. There had to be some way out. Some way of salvaging all that he'd built. He was, after all, a doctor, a psychiatrist, a person of worth in the society.

By the time Loukas appeared, Bookman had reined in his emotions. His manner was elaborately casual and cheerful, a man totally in charge of himself. He seated Loukas and took his place behind his desk, smiled graciously.

"Now," he said briskly, "what is your problem, Sergeant?"

Loukas measured the other man and was disappointed by what he saw. Bookman gave no indication that he possessed superior qualities that equipped him to deal with the emotional unrest that seemed to grip so many people. Loukas had anticipated a witch doctor. Instead he found a man unremarkable and slightly uncomfortable, the way people often were when confronted by a policeman. Loukas decided to waste no time on preliminaries.

"You knew Enid Keyes?" he began.

Bookman quelled the quick rush of fear and returned the other man's gaze. "A tragic figure, Mrs. Keyes."

"She was a patient of yours?"

"Yes, she'd been seeing me for nearly two months. I can look up the exact time. Three visits per week."

Loukas was disappointed. Every lead proved to have some very logical explanation.

"Your name was on her appointment calendar."

Bookman was relieved. He'd been afraid that Enid might have kept a diary, inscribed details of their meetings. He smiled at Loukas. "Mrs. Keyes did not have a regular appointment. I worked her in whenever possible. Cancellations occur all the time."

Loukas opened his notebook. "Next to the last visit she had written on the calendar the words 'Oh, wow!' Can you explain that, Doctor?"

Bookman produced a puzzled expression. "I have no idea. The session was very emotional. Mrs. Keyes made several helpful revelations that would have been very productive had the therapy continued—" He broke off, shrugged.

Loukas sighed and put the notebook away. Something about Bookman troubled him, some elusive element.

"What can you tell me about Mrs. Keyes?"

"Not much, I'm afraid. I didn't know her that well. It's been a slow process. She was your normally neurotic divorcée"—he smiled wryly—"lost in suburbia and disliking it very much."

"Why was that?"

"A woman alone, longing for a full social life. In Arcadia, she met mostly married men."

Loukas straightened up. "Was she involved with any married men?"

"Not to my knowledge."

"But she might have been?"

"We'd barely scratched the surface." Bookman hesitated. "There is a professional privacy attached to my work, Sergeant."

"This is murder, Doctor. Three rapes, three murders. We need all the help we can get."

"Yes, of course. She used to see a man named Peter. He lives in Bridgeport, I believe."

"Peter Manchester?"

"Oh, you know about him?"

"His name was in her address book. We've checked him out. He's been on a business trip in South America for the last two weeks."

"There were three marriages, you know."

"We've been in touch with both living husbands. They don't know anything. That's the trouble with this case; nobody knows anything. Did Mrs. Keyes ever say anything that might connect her with Treysa Horn or Charlotte Spratt?"

"The other murdered women? Not that I know of. I only know their names through the press reports."

"Did you discuss the killings with her?"

"No, never."

"Did she indicate any fear of rape? Was she threatened by anyone she knew?"

"The subject never came up. But a number of my patients are troubled by these events. One woman I've been seeing is almost hysterical, afraid she'll be raped every time she steps out of the house."

"Are her fears directed toward anyone in particular?"

"Not really. She's just one of your everyday hysterics and this affair has given her something new to think about."

Loukas stood up. "Well, that's it, I guess. If you think of anything that might help, Doctor, please give me a call."

"I'll do that."

Alone in his office, Bookman almost laughed aloud. His fears, his anticipation of disaster, were gone. There was nothing to worry about. Absolutely nothing. Ned Bookman, reprieved man, looked forward light-heartedly to doing the errands Moira had asked him to do this morning.

V

The call was entered in the desk log at 10:42 A.M. The Desk Officer was Lou Pinto, who had been on the force for nineteen years. A large, slow-moving man who had been assigned to rubber-gun jobs for most of his career, he enjoyed taking telephone calls. It gave him a chance to use what he liked to call his official cop's voice, deep, slurred, with just a touch of casual arrogance.

"Police Headquarters," he said automatically, entering the time. "Officer Pinto speaking."

The caller sounded uncertain. People were usually nervous when they had to contact the police, Pinto had long ago noticed. Even when they'd done nothing wrong. Pinto put it down to a fear of authority and he took pleasure in being part of that authority.

The voice said, "May I talk to Sergeant Loukas please?"

"Sergeant's out just now. Won't be back till this afternoon. Anybody else can help you?"

"I read in the *Republican* that Sergeant Loukas is in charge of those killings, those poor women."

Pinto stiffened up. "Who is this?" he said.

"I think I better talk to Sergeant Loukas."

"You have some information about the murders?"

"I'll call again later, maybe."

"Wait a minute!"

The caller hung up.

Pinto was disappointed. But only briefly. Cranks called all the time. One of the burdens of police work. He went back to the paperback book he was reading.

VI

Chief Wakeman had been invited to address the Saturday-morning Parent-Teacher's meeting. He pleaded the press of the current investigation and suggested that John Henderson take his place. Henderson, loath to speak in public, ordered Loukas to go. Loukas considered Tom Petersen as a substitute, but decided otherwise.

He drove without urgency, trying to anticipate what lay ahead. The citizens would be in a foul temper, their ordinarily peaceful lives rocked by a threat they couldn't easily dismiss. Or deal with. To most people, especially those in a wealthy suburb, violent crime was an alien disease to which they were naturally immune. Now the virus had hurdled the social barrier and struck down three of Arcadia's women; the people were confused, frightened, angry. They would demand action, demand that the criminal be caught and brought to justice; they would blame the police for not doing so. They would, Loukas knew, blame him.

Almost all the parking spaces were filled when Loukas got to the school and he was forced to leave his car behind the gym building and walk to the auditorium. Ralph Burleigh greeted him at the door.

"There's a lot of them in there, Theo. And all restless."

"Maybe you'd like to take my place, Ralph."

Burleigh grinned and shook his head. "Not a chance. They're too rough for me."

Loukas nodded. "Team doing okay, Ralph?"

"First game this afternoon, Theo. Come out and give us a look."

"Might do that, if I survive this." He entered the auditorium and moved self-consciously down the side aisle, climbing the steps to the stage. Rita Westphal, the headmistress, greeted him with a smile and took her place at the podium. Gradually the audience quieted.

"Thank you for coming," she began. Her eyes were bright and earnest and her gray hair stood away from her head in uncombed wings. "There was an agenda for this meeting, the question of busing for racial balance . . ."

Hands went up all over the auditorium, fluttering for attention. A bulky, blackbearded man was on his feet, voice booming out in accusation. "To hell with busing. This town has got real problems. I want to tell you, I left the goddamn city to get away from violent crime. I bought a house for ninety thousand dollars. I pay property taxes, car taxes, I pay for water and garbage collection. I travel ninety minutes each way to work every day so that my wife and kids will be safe. Well, dammit, the way things are, I may as well be living in the middle of Manhattan with the addicts and pushers. Let's deal with what's on everybody's mind."

People began shouting for recognition. Rita Westphal pointed to a lanky man in a plaid jacket. Before he could speak, a bird-like woman was on her feet, face distorted with rage.

"Our children are growing up in a gold-plated ghetto! I want them to know what the real world is like."

"Go back to New York!" someone shouted.

"We're being ripped off. Burglars hit our homes. Our women are being raped. Murdered. Nothing's being done."

Rita Westphal held up a hand for silence. Gradually it came. She spoke in a flat voice. "As I started to say, an agenda was drawn up for this meeting but in the light of what has been happening I've set it aside. Instead we have a member of the Police Department with us this morning. Sergeant Theodore Loukas. Sergeant Loukas is conducting the investigation of the terrible crimes of which we are all aware. Sergeant Loukas."

He advanced to the podium, looked down at the audience. These people, so sleek, successful, clever, they made his uneasy. Always when he'd had to deal with them, he'd been made to feel out of place, as if he belonged to some lesser species. He cleared his throat. Before he could say anything, a man rose.

"Isn't it true, Sergeant, that the majority of burglaries are committed by drug addicts and most of them are Negroes? Isn't that a fact?"

Loukas chose his words carefully. "Mostly addicts, yes. Quick hitters. In-and-out guys. A score that can be peddled fast."

"To hell with that crap!" a man cried. "What's being done to stop the killer? That's what we want to know!"

"Our investigation is continuing and—"

"Three women are dead," a woman yelled. "Killed within one week. Three of our neighbors, raped and murdered."

"What the hell's this town coming to?" the man with the black beard bellowed.

"We're doing our best," Loukas said.

"That's not enough! Three killings in a week!"

"How can we be sure there won't be more of them? More rapes? More murders?"

"I can't promise you that," Loukas was forced to say.

The black-bearded man was shouting again. "So we wait until our women are attacked. Is that what you're asking us to do?"

"There are precautions . . ." Loukas began.

A man advanced down the center aisle toward the stage. He moved without haste, tense and gaunt, his eyes dark hollows. It was Leon Horn. He spoke in a low voice that stilled the audience, a voice full of anguish and hate.

"The savages are after us," he said. "Don't depend on the authorities to defend you against them. My wife was murdered and nothing was done. Then Mrs. Spratt. Now

Enid Keyes. Raped and killed. *Why did he have to kill them too!*" His voice rose in a thin wail. He struggled to regain his composure. "The police cannot protect your wives and daughters. They are helpless. All of us are helpless."

"There must be something we can do," a woman said.

The black-bearded man answered. "Get a gun!" he shouted. "Arm yourselves. Learn to shoot, to kill if necessary. Protect your family, your property. We are at war."

"Just a moment," a bespectacled man said from the rear. "That's going a bit too far too fast."

He was shouted down.

"If the local cops can't do the job," came the cry, "let's get the State Police in here."

Another man replied. "As a lawyer, I must tell you that the State Police have no authority to intervene unless invited to do so by town officials. Or unless a state of emergency exists."

"What the hell do you think we've got here!"

"Private patrols," someone else suggested. "Armed men on regular patrol—"

"No vigilantes in Arcadia!"

"We want peace and quiet, safety!"

The man who had objected to the formation of a vigilante patrol turned to Loukas for help. "Surely the police officer can offer some suggestions for protection. We don't want anarchy."

Loukas took a deep breath. "There's no law against owning a firearm in this state. But let me remind you that most accidents with guns occur in the home, to members of the family. And most homicides are committed by people against members of their family, or friends. Few people are equipped to deal with violence—"

"We must do something!"

Loukas nodded. "Leave the police work to us. We're professionals. We're doing our best and outside interference will only complicate matters. But there are precautions you can take. Keep all doors locked. Don't admit anybody you don't know to your home. If someone appears unexpectedly at your door, identify him from an upstairs window. If he looks suspicious, call us. We'll send a car over. Better be embarrassed than sorry."

"What if a person is attacked?" a slight woman wanted to know. "What is she to do?"

"Try to talk him out of it."

"Oh, dear, I'd be too terrified to think of anything to say."

"Make up a story ahead of time. Rehearse it so it comes out naturally."

"What kind of a story?"

"A woman might say she's pregnant. That could stop him. Or claim to have a venereal disease." Loukas waited for the laughter to subside. "Stall if you can. Or run."

"Suppose we do arm ourselves?"

"I don't recommend it. But if you must, if it would make you feel better, a hatpin is easy to carry. Keys scraped across a man's face should discourage him. Or jab your thumbs into his eyes. But no half-hearted attempts. If you fight, fight hard." He hesitated. "There's one thing about fighting back; it may further enrage the assailant. It may incite him to violence beyond his original intentions."

The woman said, "Three of our sisters have been killed. How much more dangerous can it get for a woman?"

Loukas nodded. "You have a point there."

VII

Donnelly peered out from under uncombed brows at Pauline Fellows. He ran one veined hand over his smooth cheek. The sensation was unsettling still; perhaps he would grow another beard. "What," he said without hostility, "are you after, Mrs. Fellows?"

"Work that I like," she answered simply. "Work that I can show and hopefully sell."

"I'm not one of those artistic machines. I don't turn out sculptures on order."

"You've got enough pieces here to satisfy me. I can make a selection."

"I'll make any selection, if one's going to be made."

"Can we make it together?"

His grin was swift, a quicksilver show of teeth, the broad face instantly youthful, enjoying the exposure of his rough effort at a power play. "Once in a while," he said, still grinning, "I begin to think I'm Epstein or Moore."

"You're good, Hugh."

"Not that good, but working hard."

"Let me show your work." Pauline was impressed with Donnelly and his sculptures. He looked like an artist. There was size to him, power, and the ability to laugh at himself. The man and his work would be a great success in her gallery.

"Where?" he said, suddenly gloomy. "The big pieces are too large for any gallery around here. Outside spaces, the sky for a ceiling. That's what I need."

"I can provide it. My lawn is large, the terrain varied. The big things can go there. Inside the house, the smaller works."

"You intend to use your house as a gallery?"

"Yes. Most galleries are nothing more than stores. They might as well sell clothing or health food."

He eyed her suspiciously. "You really like what I do?"

"Very much."

The tension seemed to go out of his powerful body. "I want to tell you what it's like to be a sculptor. People call because you're an artist. Then they chicken out. They can't control you and that frightens them.

"I was asked to make a proposal for a sculpture for the World Trade Center, those twin phalluses in New York. The board of directors interviewed me. Stiff men with pink complexions and bad digestive systems. Told 'em they didn't know their own business. That hooked 'em. Told 'em trade was just an exchange of goods. A piece of green paper with a number on it was nothing but an I.O.U. Worthless unless the givers word is good. Do you comprehend what I'm saying? Told 'em to reconsider the way they lived and functioned as men. Said they should learn their true reason for being."

"What about the sculpture?"

"Oh, I got around to it in time. Told 'em I'd give 'em a quartet of balls to go with those giant concrete pricks. Balls of brightly polished bronze shining in the sunlight. Hah! Those pink faces turned pinker." He laughed raucously at the memory.

"They didn't go for it?"

"Simpering fools. Terrified of anyone who isn't primarily motivated by riches. They don't understand people like me. There aren't many things worth doing in the world. Loving someone, making love, raising kids, doing your work. All the rest is bullshit. Okay, you want to show my stuff, you can do it."

"You may have all the answers, Hugh," she said, meaning it.

His smile was slow and pleasant. "Or none of them. What the hell, that's part of the artistic hustle, isn't it? Some nights I embrace myself in despair and wonder if I have any talent at all. If I know anything. The next day, in the sunlight, I'm brave as hell. All muscle and balls."

"Let's plan the show, Hugh."

"I'm ready."

VIII

Diamond stopped in front of the frozen-food locker at the A-1 Market and studied the shopping list Ruth had prepared. Everything was checked off, the shopping cart loaded. At the magazine rack he picked up copies of *The New Yorker, Newsweek,* and *New York* magazines. He worked his way into the check-out line.

He examined the girl who rang up his purchases. Her face was wide and unlined, the sea-green eyes clear and steady, her lips forced apart by teeth that protruded slightly. She was, Diamond decided, a beauty.

"You do that very well," he said.

She answered without looking up. "It gets to be automatic after a while. They keep changing the prices and that's a drag."

"For us all."

She smiled and Diamond tried to remember if he had ever made love to a girl with buckteeth. What would it be like to slide his tongue against those sharp, white cutting edges?

"You do this part-time?" he said. "After school?"

She glanced over at him. "I'm older than I look. This is how I earn rent money."

"There are other ways."

She looked again, slower, more penetrating. "I've heard stories from the older girls."

"Some guy will come along and drag you off, marry you."

She turned to face him, her manner cool, assured. "Thirty-two fifty-two. For the food."

He gave her two twenties and she made change. Her fingers lingered on his palm. Or was it his imagination? Her expression told him nothing. She began to bag the order.

"I'm in no hurry to get married," she said.

"What are you in a hurry for?"

Her eyes met him. "You're a married man."

There was no point in denying it. He nodded. "What's your name?" he said.

"Jane Bonner."

"I'm Leo Diamond. You live here in Arcadia?"

"Yes." She placed the brown bags in a shopping cart.

He began to tremble. "Do you ever come into the city?"

"New York? Not much."

"I work in Manhattan. Public relations. A lot of show-business accounts."

"Oh," she said. "You want this order delivered?"

"I'll take it," he said. He told himself that he was wasting his time. He was not only married but twice her age. She undoubtedly had a strong, young boy friend who supplied everything she needed.

"I've always had a secret desire to get into show business," she said.

His hopes rose. "We could talk about it."

"Next," she said.

Diamond looked around. Customers were waiting to be checked out. He moved out of the way. Jane Bonner was punching the keys of the register with concentrated skill.

IX

Loukas was on his second coffee when the man called again.

"This is Sergeant Loukas."

"It's about that killing that I'm calling. The last one. You know, the Keyes woman. Her picture was in the paper."

Loukas put the coffee aside. "Who is this?"

"Look, I don't want to be involved. The point is, I think I can be of some assistance."

"Yes?"

"I saw the Keyes woman. At least I saw somebody who was the spitting image of her. I saw her with a man."

"Who was the man?"

"I don't know his name. That is, I didn't know before. But I saw them together."

"Where did you see them?"

"At the Yankee Drive Motel. You know where it is?"

"I know. When was this?"

"Early this week. They checked in about noon and were in a room for a couple of hours. At least she checked in, but I spotted him when he pulled in, parked next to her car and went to the room.

"I see. You don't know who the man was?"

"That's the thing; I didn't. But after I saw her picture in the paper, I recognize her. That set me to thinking. And wouldn't you know it, this morning I was over to Gourmet Kitchen buying some Jarlsberg and English tea biscuits—I got a weakness for cheese and biscuits in the evening—anyway, there he was, big as life."

"But you don't know his name?"

A note of triumph came over the wire. "Didn't know it *then*. But I found out. Went outside and got into my car, waited until he came out, I did, then followed him. Kept my distance, just like one of them TV detectives. Oh, I was real careful."

"And?"

"Followed him home."

"And you learned his name."

"Sure did. Bookman. E. M. Bookman."

Loukas allowed his eyes to close. "You're sure about that?"

"Oh, yes, I don't make mistakes. Details are important in my line of work. Don't miss much, I don't."

"What is your line of work?"

The caller made a remonstrative sound. "No you don't. I'm not that easily found out. Told you all I intend to tell you. Care to have this E. M. Bookman's address?"

"That won't be necessary," Loukas said.

"I see," the caller said testily. "Well, didn't expect no thanks. Just a citizen doing his duty is all. What's that to you people?"

Loukas drove out to the Yankee Drive Motel. It was a low building set down in a huge arc, surrounded by trees. In front, free-form swimming pool and a miniature golf course. Loukas went inside. A thin, middle-aged man with a contrived smile greeted him.

"Good afternoon, sir. May I help you?"

Loukas displayed his shield. "I'm Loukas. You phoned me a few minutes ago."

The thin face paled. "I'm afraid you're mistaken, sir."

"What's your name?"

"Evans. Samuel Evans."

"Okay, Mr. Evans, either we talk here or we talk at Headquarters. Name your pleasure."

Evans lowered his eyes and his voice. "I was only trying to be helpful."

"Keep on helping. She checked in under an assumed name?"

"Miller. She called herself Mrs. Miller. I can show you the register. She phoned beforehand and made a reservation."

"Were they here often?"

"Twice this week. Tuesday and Wednesday. After he left Tuesday, she came to the office and paid for the room for another day."

"You're certain it was Mrs. Keyes?"

"No mistaking it. That picture in the paper looked just like her. And they showed her on the television. Good-looking woman, I must say. Fine figure."

"Mr. Evans, you are going to keep this to yourself."

"Oh, Oh, yes. Won't tell a soul, depend on me."

"I'll hold you to that, Mr. Evans."

"I suppose you'll be wanting me to make a statement," Evans said hopefully. "Be a witness."

"When the time comes, we'll see. Meanwhile, this is private police business."

Evans grinned conspiratorially. "Know exactly what you mean, Sergeant."

Loukas started toward the exit.

"Sergeant," Evans called after him, "how'd you figure out it was me that called? Purely a matter of curiosity."

Loukas almost smiled. "Who else could it have been, Mr. Evans?"

Evans scowled and went back to work.

Ned Bookman struggled to keep his composure. His face was pale and his mouth was stretched thin. His eyes refused to meet Loukas' gaze.

"I'm not sure I understand you," he said.

"Enid Keyes was your patient," Loukas snapped.

"I told you that."

"But you didn't tell me that you were having an affair with her."

Bookman tried to laugh and failed. "That's absurd. I always maintain a discreet distance from a patient, a clinical gap, you might say."

"Don't lie to me, Doctor."

Bookman began to stutter. "You have no right—"

"On at least two occasions you went to the Yankee Drive Motel with Mrs. Keyes. Spent some time in a room with her. Mrs. Keyes made the reservation by phone and checked in as a Mrs. Miller. Do you want me to go on?"

Bookman slumped in place. "Weakness. That's all it was, weakness."

"When did you see her last?"

"What? Oh, two days before her death. Why would anybody—"

"Are you married, Doctor?"

"What? Oh, yes, of course."

"Two children, I believe?"

"Yes, two. Why?"

"Was she trying to get you to leave your wife? Did she threaten to reveal your relationship to your wife?"

"Oh, no. No. My God! You think I killed her? Oh, no, no. I'm not a violent man. Anyway, it wasn't that way. You must believe me."

"You lied once, why not again?"

"I'm telling the truth. All right, I didn't tell you about Mrs. Keyes. But that doesn't mean I killed her. My God, Sergeant, you're a man. You know how it can be with some women. How wild you can get. Making love to such a woman seems monumentally important. Overwhelming. I've always been a sensual man, too much so, perhaps. But I would never take anybody's life." His voice grew intimate. "Man to man, Sergeant, you know how it is. I may be an adulterer, but I'm not a murderer."

Loukas spoke slowly. "You've got one hell of a motive there, Doctor."

Bookman put his hands to his face.

Loukas stood up presently. "Doctor, you had the reason and you had the chance. That makes you a prime suspect in my book."

"She was killed at her house, wasn't she? I never was there. Never."

"We'll see. Just stay in town, Doctor. No unexpected trips. No sudden holidays."

Bookman wet his lips. "You really do suspect me."

"Three women are dead, Doctor. Why not you?"

"You're wrong, you know."

"I don't know yet, but I expect I will."

"Does this have to become public knowledge, about Mrs. Keyes and me? My family, my career . . . you understand."

Loukas went to the door, then turned back. "If you aren't the killer, Doctor, you have nothing to worry about. Not from me."

X

As so often it had, the craving took hold of Emmett May in the middle of the night. It came upon him stealthily, while he slept, nudging him awake. Almost catatonic, he struggled in the lonely blackness to wipe away the tantalizing images. He failed, as he almost always failed. Tension drew down into his groin and he shifted, grew, became swollen with need. He touched himself reflexively, quickly yanked the offending hand away. Shame flooded his brain, and disgust, guilt.

He went into his private gymnasium and rode the stationary bicycle as hard as he could for as long as he could. Next, a series of push-ups and sit-ups. The tension slacked off and he skipped rope for fifteen minutes.

He swallowed a Valium and returned to bed. He slept, but when he woke the craving was back in full force. An incessant gnawing at his central nervous system. Visions danced across his brain, enticing, promising, laughing at him. By midafternoon, he could think of nothing else.

He dressed with attention to detail. Tattered blue jeans, an old sweat shirt, soiled tennis shoes. From his closet came an ancient make-up case. He located a false mustache and applied it carefully to his upper lip. Next, a dark-brown wig went into place on his head. A pair of steel-rimmed spectacles followed. He examined himself in the mirror. A faintly ominous stranger gazed back at him, a man who in no way resembled Emmett May, a man very much in the current mode. Pleased with his efforts, he left the house by the rear stairway.

Popeye's was located up the hill from the Junion High School. Students flocked into Popeye's during their free

periods and at the end of the school day. And especially
on Saturday afternoons. It was a place to gossip, to meet
friends, to be away from discipline and adults. They ate
Popeye's hamburgers, which were flecked with gristle and
fat, and drank his malts, which he made with powdered
milk. It was a world functioning at the top of its lungs,
the air crackling with pubescent energy.

Emmett May took a seat at the counter. From there
he enjoyed an unobstructed field of vision to the booths
against the far wall. He examined the occupants of each
booth carefully, settling finally on one girl.

She was a lovely creature, delicately constructed, with
a small triangular face. Her eyes glowed as she talked, face
animated, hands fluttering. She changed positions swiftly
and often, unaware that the short skirt she wore had
worked its way high up her thighs.

Emmett found it hard to swallow. He approved of her
completely. A flawless complexion. Breasts still only buds.
Arms smooth, tapered.

Emmett allowed his eyes to close and he imagined her
naked. She would be shy, of course, but curious. Pleased
by the attentions of a real man. She would want to please
him and would protest her innocence, but without vehe-
mence, without persistence.

He opened his eyes. The girl and her companion were
leaving. Emmett hurried outside. He sat behind the wheel
of his car and waited.

She appeared alone, turned down the street. Her movements were quick and girlishly awkward, unfulfilled promise. Her round, tight bottom jerked to some primitive
inner beat.

Emmett drove after her, slowing as he came up alongside. She glanced his way without fear or special interest.

"Hi," he said.

She presented an aloof profile.

"Need a ride?"

"Go away."

"It's no trouble."

She walked faster.

"I'm in no hurry at all," he said.

"Go away." Her voice grew insistent.

"I won't hurt you," he said desperately.

She faced him, legs planted solidly apart, hands on her hips, face set. "I am going to call for help if you don't leave me alone."

She was magnificent. All that stormy ferocity in that marvelous little body. He ached to put his hands on her, to smell the pure young sweetness of her.

"You don't understand . . ."

She opened her mouth as if to scream.

He floored the accelerator and sped away. But she remained in his mind for days.

CHAPTER NINE

I

THE BEACH CLUNG to what remained of the day, as if afraid of being cast into the darkness. Across Long Island Sound, night loomed up like a dull gray wall.

In the water, two swimmers splashed a path parallel to the shore. Loukas shuddered. Winter would soon be closing in and the water must be fiercely cold. Those swimmers, what made people punish themselves that way? Surely there could be no real pleasure in such an uncomfortable pastime.

Down the beach, a long figure came in his direction. Joggers were another strange breed.

He walked on. Something about being near the water made him feel good. As if he belonged. His father's father had been a fisherman back in the old country, had sailed the Mediterranean. Maybe heredity drew him to the water.

The jogger was almost upon him. A blurred figure in a crimson sweat suit. Loukas moved to one side, giving the flat sand along the surf to the runner.

"Hello," he said suddenly in pleased recognition.

The runner went past him, pulled up, looked back uncertainly. "Sergeant Loukas?"

"Good evening, Mrs. Felton."

"I didn't recognize you. With what's going on, I'm a little less friendly than I used to be."

"That's probably a good way to be."

"I guess I ought to confine my jogging to daylight hours."

"It's a good idea. Come on, I'll escort you back to your car."

"Okay." They walked a little way without speaking, then she pointed out into the Sound. "Do I see somebody swimming?"

"Two people. They're trying to make it all the way to the Head."

At the distant end of the beach, the land bent into the belly of the Sound in a graceful arc. Where it stopped, rocks loomed up in a rugged, uneven profile.

"Why is it called Eagle's Head?" she said. "Nobody I've asked seems to know."

"Eagles used to settle on the point long ago. Bald eagles. My father saw one when he was a young man. Most of them have been wiped out or gone away to where it's safer for them to live."

"We don't treat wildlife very well."

"Eagles are creatures of habit. They depend on particular nest trees, and if they don't have those trees, they won't breed. Clear-cutting forests for timber drove them out of this area. Pesticides finished the job."

"How do you happen to know so much about eagles, Sergeant?"

He was embarrassed. "I like birds; I like to watch them. We get a pretty good variety around here in the winter. Cardinals, tufted titmice, chickadees."

"You're probably the only cop in the state who watches birds."

"Don't tell anyone."

She laughed softly. "Trust me." She gave him a side-long glance. He was only a little taller than she was and not particularly heavy. She had known so many big men, large men with large, trained muscles, men whose bodies performed on command. Loukas didn't strike her as that sort. Yet he was a cop, carried a gun, was paid to deal with trouble and violence. "It's very reassuring," she said, "to have my own bodyguard."

"I don't think you would have had any trouble."

At her car, she offered him her hand. "Thank you for walking with me."

"My pleasure, Mrs. Felton."

She hesitated, not wanting him to misunderstand. "What do you think would happen if you were to call me by my first name?"

She wasn't able to see the pleased expression on his face. "Nothing very serious. Sandra," he added.

"Sandy," she said.

"People call me Theo."

"Tell me, Theo, how does it make your wife feel, you running around at all hours trying to catch a killer? I don't think I'd like that."

"I'm a widower."

"And I'm a widow," she said simply.

"Any children?" he asked.

"No. Sometimes I wish I did have, a part of Louis to hold on to."

"I know what you mean. It gets lonely all by yourself."

"This is not a good town to be alone in," she answered presently.

"I guess you're right."

"You must be the only unmarried adult male in Arcadia. All the others I've met have wives. I try to avoid the married ones. The single men I meet are bummers often enough. I suppose it's my fault. Maybe I seek out the weirdos."

"You're not very kind to yourself."

"You're a nice man, I think." Settled behind the wheel of her car, she called out, "Next time I go jogging I'll look for you, Mr. Policeman."

II

From behind the wheel of the Valiant, Loukas looked out at the house. Like his own, it was old, without frills, constructed for purely utilitarian purposes. Compact, practical, solid, meant to stand for a long time. The original roof shingles had been replaced with gray asbestos, the siding had been painted an unobtrusive buff, the shutters matched the roof.

Working people had built this house, working people had always lived in it, he was sure. Fishermen or farmers or people who built things with their hands. Not many of that sort still remained in Arcadia. But the houses still stood and were in demand. They had been rebuilt, expanded, designed to the requirements of the strangers who occupied them now.

But not this house. Reiser was the name of the owner. A German name. Loukas recalled a Reiser who had played with the old Brooklyn Dodgers. A very exciting ballplayer, but always crashing into walls while chasing fly balls. Damaged himself so frequently that his immense skills were reduced. Happened that way, life dealing badly with gifted people. Reminded a man that he was a fragile organism entitled to only a brief span of time.

Loukas went up to the door and knocked. A woman answered. She held herself straight so that she seemed taller than she was. Chin lifted, China-blue eyes cold and steady, no sign of uncertainty in her bony face. In the doorway with arms folded, she presented a formidable figure.

"What do you want?" She threw the words out, fearless, challenging.

"Mrs. Reiser?"

"I am Mrs. Reiser."

"I'm Sergeant Loukas. Arcadia police." He flashed his gold shield.

She grasped his wrist and read the inscription on the badge without haste, releasing him when satisfied. "Didn't call the police," she declared. "Don't have any need for the police."

"I'm working on a case—"

"Those murders, I suppose. At least that's what you people ought to be working on. Can't have innocent women being murdered in their own homes. Wasn't that way before, you know. Strangers do it, you know. Too many outsiders in town. Spoils a place."

"I can't say you're wrong," he replied. "My people have been here for a long time."

She measured him coolly.

"My father sold firewood," Loukas said. "Charcoal. Maybe you knew him?"

"Can't say I did. What is it you want with me, Sergeant?"

"In the course of my investigation, I had to speak to your son."

"Virgil told me," she said.

"I see."

"Virgil's not one of those boys who keeps secrets from his mother."

"He tells you everything?"

"Virgil's been brought up in a proper house, a Christian home."

"I'm sure of that. What I want to know—"

"You think Virgil did those things to those women?"

"I'm just checking on everybody who comes into the picture, Mrs. Reiser. Virgil delivered groceries to all of the dead women. Fact is, I'm still trying to make sense out of it."

Her lips thinned out. "Well, Virgil could have done it." She confronted Loukas stolidly.

"What makes you say that?" he said cautiously.

"Virgil's a man and any man is capable of doing rape to a woman. That's men's ways."

"I see. Is there any specific reason you know of that might lead you to believe Virgil would commit rape?"

"Nope."

"You said—"

"I said he's a man and men rape women. Never heard of it the other way around."

Loukas shook his head, smiled sadly.

"Biologically impossible, I'd say."

Loukas found no sign of humor in the grim face. "I'd like to talk to Virgil, Mrs. Reiser."

"When?"

"Right now, if I might."

"You carry a watch, Sergeant?"

"Yes, ma'am."

"What does it say?"

Loukas checked the time. "Seven-twenty."

"There you are," she said with some satisfaction. "Virgil works until eight six nights a week. That's closing time at A-1. I expect you know that already."

"Maybe I heard that somewhere."

"You come to take a look at where Virgil lives. The way he lives. At Virgil's mother. Well, here I am, Sergeant, but there's no reason for you to see any more."

"Why is that, Mrs. Reiser?"

"Your young man's already been snooping around."

"My young man?"

"Petersen was his name. Showed me a badge, too, only he wasn't a sergeant. He's one of you, isn't he?"

Loukas kept his voice steady. "Yes, he is."

"You find out what you need to know from him. Can't have people tracking dirt through the house all the time. As for Virgil, you got any questions for him you put them to him. He's not a boy who lies. His father and I brought him up right."

"Does your husband work in town?"

"Mr. Reiser's been dead for nearly ten years. But I raised Virgil the way Oscar would have wanted. Never deviated one bit. Discipline. Oscar believed in discipline. In doing right. Living right. Whenever Virgil fell off the straight and narrow he heard from me. When talking didn't do it, Oscar's old razor strap is still hanging in my broom closet. I'd take it to the boy right this minute if it was called for."

"I see."

"You tell me that Virgil did those things to those women and I'll bring him down to Police Headquarters by myself. Virgil knows better."

"Yes, I'm sure he does. Thank you, Mrs. Reiser, for your time."

"There was a time a decent woman could walk down Main Street and not be bothered. Now there's those hippies hanging around and dope sold everywhere and all sorts of things going on. You catch the one who's doing these terrible things."

"Yes, ma'am, I'll do my best."

III

Belle Stafford passed the roach over to Willy Morrison. Smoke filled her lungs and she tried to trace the path followed by the good vibes as they spread along her limbs. Her legs tingled below the knees. She giggled.

"Beautiful," she said.

"What is?"

"The sky so black, the stars so white. How clear everything is. Is it like that for you, things so clear? Colors are fantastic for me when I'm stoned."

"You want to know what's best for me when I'm stoned?"

"Bet I can guess."

She wanted Willy Morrison to like her. She'd seen him around, at school, hanging around The Square, at The Coffee House. But until tonight, at the bowling alley, he'd never paid attention to her. For some reason he'd begun talking to her, invited her to go for a drive with him. Then he'd broken out the dope; good stuff, too. They were on their second joint.

"Guess," he said.

"Making it," she answered.

"You win big casino," he said, sliding across the front seat and reaching for her. His hands came to rest on her breasts. "Fantastic," he said.

"Ah, that's good, make circles."

"The damned buttons . . ."

"Let me."

He pulled and her blouse came apart.

"Oh," she said, giggling, "you popped my buttons."

His mouth came down on her breast, teeth working.

She held his head. "That makes me twitch." She located his fly. "Oh," she said, "how nice." She worked the zipper.

He tugged at her panties until they came away in his hands. They shifted and twisted and she arranged herself on his thigh, middle rotating.

"Wild chick." His voice was thick, distant.

"I want to do it to your toy."

"Work for it."

"Conceited bastard."

"You were asking for it."

"Yes."

"Now beg."

"Please."

"You like it?"

"So beautiful."

"Big enough?"

"Biggest in the world."

"Get your head down here."

He smelled of urine and sweat and stale sex; he had been laid already tonight. The knowledge aroused her even more and she made her lips soft, tender, accepting.

His fingers tightened on the back of her neck and suddenly she grew apprehensive. "Don't hurt me. Please."

"Take it."

She struggled to break loose. He pushed harder and for a long moment she was unable to free herself. Bracing her elbows on the seat, she fought back, shoved with all her strength. Abruptly free, she went up against the door, her mouth striking the handle. Seconds later the taste of blood seeped onto her tongue.

"You hurt me, goddamn you!" she shouted.

He clapped his hand over her mouth. "You're okay. It's nothing. I'm sorry. Come on, finish what you started."

She hesitated. "Not that way."

"Why not?"

"Not the first time."

He grinned in the darkness. "By the time I'm finished with you, I'll use every hole you've got."

"Big talk."

"Lay back."

She obeyed, felt him forcing his way into her. "Listen, baby, I'm not using anything."

"Don't knock me up."

"Ah . . ."

"My mother'll kill me if I get pregnant."

"Here!" he cried. "Take it. Take it all. Take it all."

She squirmed, trying to unlock herself, to get him out. With one desperate heave, she succeeded, and a warm flood spurted onto her belly. He pressed himself against her as if afraid of falling off. She held him, waiting until the convulsions ended.

He drove her home, waited for her to get out.

"Don't I get a good-night kiss?" she said.

He complied.

"It'll be better next time," she said. "Next time bring something."

"What about you?"

"I don't have anything. My mother watches me like a hawk. If she found anything like that, she'd murder me."

"Well," he said without intonation, "you're just a kid."

"Jail bait," she reminded him.

"Why do you say that?"

"That's what you said. Call me soon, Willy. Don't make me call you."

"Sure."

"Next time, what you wanted me to do." She slid out of the car, blew him a kiss. He drove away without a backward glance.

Clutching her torn blouse over her bosom, Belle went into the house. The night light in the kitchen revealed four stains on her skirt. Semen. It would dry by morning and she'd get it to the cleaner's before Jeanine could see it. She slipped out of the skirt and for the first time realized that she had left her panties in his car. She giggled and tried to imagine his mother's reaction if she found them. She started up the stairs to her bedroom. Her mother stood on the landing looking down.

"You dirty little tramp," Jeanine cried, coming down the steps.

Belle backed away, shielding her nakedness with the skirt.

Jeanine snatched it away. "Holy Mother of God! Look at you, fifteen years old and look at you. Where are your panties? What have you done to yourself? You're disgusting. Have you no shame at all? How could you do this to me?"

Belle tried to move up the stairs but Jeanine blocked the way.

"Your blouse is torn. Who is it? Who did this to you? He forced you, didn't he?"

Belle confronted her mother. "I wanted to do it. I'll do it again."

Jeanine slapped her face. "Don't you dare talk to me that way. I'm your mother. I won't let you turn yourself into a whore. You know what I'm doing for you? Are you trying to ruin your life? My life? Tell me his name."

"Fuck you," the girl said.

Jeanine hit her again and Belle fell to the floor. At once Jeanine was beside her, cradling the girl, rocking back and forth, crooning assurances. "Don't worry, baby, don't worry. Momma will take care of everything. Momma's going to fix it all. You'll see."

Belle's eyes were fixed straight ahead, her mind made up.

IV

Petersen was on the firing range in the basement of the Fort. Behind him stood Loukas, slightly tense, uneasy. Guns and gunfire always put him on edge.

Petersen was good. Much better than Loukas had ever been. On rapid fire he put six holes in or close to the bull's-eye. He began reloading.

"Tom," Loukas said.

Petersen turned around. "Theo. I didn't know anybody was here."

"I want to talk to you."

"Let me get off another six, Theo."

"Now," Loukas said, before leaving.

He was seated behind his desk when Petersen came into the Bureau.

"What's up?" Petersen seemed puzzled.

"Get me some coffee," Loukas said flatly.

Petersen blinked. "Sure, Theo." He brought it over, offered it to Loukas.

"Black," Loukas said. "I drink it black."

Petersen emptied the cup into the drain and refilled it.

"Put it on the desk," Loukas said.

Petersen did so. "Is something wrong, Theo? What's wrong?"

"You forget who's in charge of this case, Tom?"

Petersen flushed. "You are, Theo. You're in charge."

"That's right. And if I'm not satisfied with the man working with me, off he goes."

"Did I do something wrong, Theo? If I did, I'm sorry."

"You did something wrong, Tom."

"What?"

"Who told you to visit Mrs. Reiser, Tom? Did I tell you to talk to her?"

"It seemed like a good idea." Petersen's cheeks were pale and his mouth worked.

"Did you think you could keep it a secret?"

"I meant to tell you, Theo. I guess I forgot."

"The hell you did."

"Things have been so hectic around here."

"When?"

"What, Theo?"

"When were you going to tell me?"

"I just forgot, it slipped my mind."

"Tom, I know the difference between apple pie and apple sauce when I see it."

"Ah, Theo, there was nothing special. Nothing to get your teeth into."

"You're working for me."

"I know that, Theo."

"Who've you been talking to?"

"Talking to?"

"That's right. My guess is Victor Fellows. You're a cop, Tom, not a politician. What's good for Victor Fellows is not necessarily good for you. Or the Department."

"He wants a collar real bad."

"So do I, dammit. But Fellows is after a spectacular. Lights, cameras, the works. He wants to make a splash. Victor Fellows, gangbuster. He needs something he can ride straight up to Hartford or farther than that. If we let that guy pressure us, we'll blow it."

"I guess you're right."

"Don't guess. The man doesn't care about guilt or innocence, only about a conviction. He tried to use you to get around me, around Henderson. He knows I won't make a collar unless I think it will stick. And Henderson will back me up. What'd he say, he'd take you along on his skyrocket to the top? Jesus, Tom, how dumb can you get?"

"You're right, you're right."

"Okay. It's over. We won't talk about it again. Now fill me in on Mrs. Reiser."

Petersen spoke rapidly, in obvious relief. "That's a pretty cool lady. Like there's an invisible wall between her and the rest of the world. She seemed to enjoy the idea of her son being a suspect."

"Is Virgil a suspect, Tom?"

"Well, he came in contact with every one of the victims, Theo. He saw them all, talked to them all, could have done it."

"We knew that before you went to Mrs. Reiser."

"I wanted to look around Virgil's room."

"Did you get a warrant?"

"Ah, Theo. I thought I'd keep it informal. Mrs. Reiser never asked for a warrant. I didn't conduct a real search, just a look-see. She didn't seem to mind my going up there. She acted sort of proud to show me around."

"And?"

"Nothing. I drew a blank. Cleanest room I ever saw. Virgil does his own housekeeping. His mother told me so. Trained him that way, she said. Everything was in place. Books, magazines, clothes. Tell you the truth, it looked like a room that nobody ever slept in. The whole house was that way."

"What were you looking for?"

"Dirty books, maybe. But now I don't know. From

the look of the room, I'm beginning to think Virgil wouldn't put his immaculate pecker into a dirty old pussy."

Loukas found it difficult not to be amused. "What other salient information did you uncover about our Virgil?"

Petersen seemed more relaxed, his manner easy. "Virgil's been at A-1 for a year now, a little more, actually. Before that he drove a laundry truck for a company over in Norwalk. Punctual, dependable, honest."

"That's the Virgil I know."

"Served in Vietnam. Got himself a Bronze Star."

"His mother tell you that?"

"Showed me the medal. Got it framed under glass and hung on the wall next to a picture of her husband."

"A hero," Loukas said softly.

"War heroes don't usually go around knocking off housewives, Theo."

"Who says they don't? Could be all it takes to be a hero is the right set of circumstances and a pinch of craziness. Have you run a check on Virgil's service record?"

"Good record. He banged up a truck one time and totaled a jeep another time. And he lost a couple of days under the A.W.'s for showing up drunk at reveille one time. Otherwise he was clean."

"That's exactly what I learned when I checked," Loukas said, as if to himself.

Petersen grinned sheepishly and said, "Maybe Virgil got to enjoy killing during the war. Maybe he decided to do a little of it over here."

"Maybe. That's what we have to find out. While you were nosing around, did you turn up anything on Virgil's love life?"

"Not much of a track record. Ran with a Marcy McDermott in Fairfield for a while. From what she says, they never made it. Marcy broke it off finally. Said Virgil was kind've restrained, quiet, didn't drink too much when he was with her."

"But he lost time in the Army for drinking?"

"That's right."

"What about dope?"

"Not even grass, far as I can find out. Virgil is straight arrow."

"That it?"

"All I've got."

"Not much, is it?"

"Ah, Theo, I'm sorry. It won't happen again."

Loukas examined his fingertips. "Did you talk to Virgil?"

"I figured there wasn't much use."

"Did you interview his girl friend?"

Petersen's face stiffened. "Girl friend! What girl friend?"

"A Miss Jane Bonner," Loukas said. He drew out his notebook. "Lives over on Duncan."

"I didn't know about her."

"Virgil could've told you. We ought to have a little talk with Jane Bonner."

Petersen swore. "Ah, Theo, you know what I think? I think Virgil isn't the kind who commits rape."

"What kind does?"

Before Petersen could reply, Captain Henderson came into the Bureau. His mottled face was drawn up in what he meant to be a pleasant expression. "Well, boys, he did it again."

"Another rape!" Petersen said.

"Yeah. Only this time the sonofabitch made a mistake."

"Mistake?"

"The lady is still alive."

V

The classic face was rutted with despair. A glass of Harvey's Bristol Cream stood untouched on the French fruitwood occasional table, but the ashtray was filled with half-smoked and uncounted cigarettes.

Avery Morrison sat stiffly in the brown leather wing

chair that had belonged to his father; and his father, too. Though cracked in places and torn, the leather shone with the soft luster that only time and use can give. Avery cared for the old chair, the way he cared for this house and the land on which it stood.

All that he owned, his things, he held in trust. A legacy from those who had come before him, all would some day belong to those who came later. Avery viewed himself as a link in an ongoing human chain, with responsibilities, obligations, a concern for what was right.

He was a man who struggled to keep his emotions in check, to consider problems as they arose and to act on them for the general good. But in moments of stress his blood ran hot and his muscles tensed and often he ached to give physical release to the wild and frightening yearnings that stirred him.

Now the pressure expanded; he grew sour with resentment and bitterness, anger. Anger at a world that was about to deny him his due; witness to the destruction of all he held important and dear.

He heard the sound of tires on the driveway. Clarice returning from some charitable affair. Ordinarily he would have gone to meet her.

"I'm in the study, Clarice."

His wife appeared in the doorway, smiling pleasantly, politely, glad to have him back, but not given to displays of affection.

"Clarice, where is Willy?"

"He drove in right behind me, dear. He's putting the cars away." Before she had time to inquire about her husband's week in Washington, Willy strode into the study.

"I'd like to talk to you, Willy," Avery said.

"I must go freshen up," Clarice said.

"Stay," Avery said. "Sit down, both of you."

"Is something wrong, dear?"

Avery stared at his son. "The President offered me Argentina," he said. He spoke slowly, voice dull.

"Argentina!" Clarice said. "Buenos Aires is a *beau-*

tiful city. Oh, but aren't they having all sorts of trouble down there?"

"There is unrest," Avery said, watching Willy. "A rising anti-Americanism. The job calls for a good man."

"I'm sure you can deal with it, Avery."

"Yes," Avery said.

"Then you're all set," Willy said, not caring. He had made up his mind; he wasn't going to Argentina or anywhere else.

"The President gave me ten days to consider the offer, to discuss it with my family."

"Avery, whatever you decide to do is perfectly all right with me."

"Willy," Avery said, "we have something to discuss."

"We do?"

The values by which Avery had been brought up, by which he lived, no longer seemed relevant in this strange and rapidly changing world. Yet he knew them to be sound, a strong base on which to erect a life. Looking at his son now, he saw a gap in the family line; Willy was different, soft without being gentle, aggressive without being strong, shrewd without intelligence. The difference between father and son had been made not in this ancient house, with its tradition and sense of duty, but outside. In a world Avery had grown afraid of.

"I went into your apartment, Willy."

Willy's face showed nothing. "You had no right. I don't go into your rooms uninvited."

"Yes. It was not the thing to do. I returned from Washington less than an hour ago. Your mother was out; I thought you might be at home. I was excited and wanted to share my excitement. You weren't there."

"It's Saturday night, dear," Clarice said. "Willy—"

Avery made an impatient gesture, not at all like him. "I had the need of a bathroom."

Willy looked away.

Avery felt the controls of a lifetime sliding into the abyss. He set himself against the slide: "I will not tollerate insolence, young man. I am your father."

"What do you want me to say?"

Clarice was bewildered. Her eyes went to her son, to her husband. "Avery, what is happening? What's wrong?"

The pressure under Avery's skull built up, a pink cloud settled across his eyes. "Those . . . *things!*" he cried.

"If you'd stayed out," Willy said harshly, "you wouldn't have to know about them."

"What things?" Clarice cried. "Won't somebody please tell me what's going on?"

Avery answered. "In Willy's bathroom, television sets, radios, stereo components. Other things. What are they doing there, Willy? Why are they there?"

Willy lifted his wide shoulders. "You want to know? I stole them."

Avery was on his feet, the tall body turned as if in pain, the strong features clenched in distaste. "What are you saying to me!"

"Oh, no!" Clarice managed, as if to herself.

Willy swore. "Okay, here it is. I've been ripping off houses around town. With some guys. And a chick. She takes jobs baby-sitting, cases places for us. So we don't have to waste time. We hit, and boom! We're gone before anybody knows the difference."

"But why?"

A challenging grin lifted Willy's mouth. "You're right, not for the bread. I've got plenty of it. We do it for a charge, for kicks. It's no big deal. Those people, they can afford it. Insurance pays 'em back. Nobody gets hurt."

Avery's mouth opened and closed. "No!" he moaned. "No, no."

"Don't be dramatic, Father."

Avery found it difficult to breathe. "Once before I stood up for you, Willy. I corrupted myself and others for you."

"Oh, come off it, Father. You're just worried about the job in Argentina."

"Willy," Clarice cried, "you will not talk to your father that way."

Avery felt himself struggling to find something solid on which to stand. All the trappings of his existence, the meaning of life, had been ripped away. His honor had been debased, the traditions and teachings of his own father shredded. The crimson cloud thickened and Avery's vision darkened.

Through the mist, a distorted image of his son came into sight, face twisted with mockery and scorn. And his cutting voice—"Don't take it so hard, Father. Nobody has to know."

Not thinking, Avery charged, his big fists pumping. He knocked Willy down and went after the boy, beating at his face. There was the crunch of cartilage being smashed and Willy cried out. Clarice screamed. But Avery, deep in a dark pool of torment and rage, kept trying to destroy the evil he had spawned.

Part Four

CHAPTER TEN

I

ARTHUR SLATER'S EYES SKITTERED from side to side, never resting. He felt alternately chilled and flushed. Confusion gripped him and he made a mighty effort to sort out events. Failing, he began to be afraid. Through the jumble of thoughts and roiling emotions, he knew that he must divert, conceal, give nothing away.

He mustered defiance. "What am I accused of?" He had asked the question before, received no answer.

The interrogation room was a medium-sized chamber with institutional-gray walls and a minimum of furniture. On a small desk in one corner, a lamp splashed a dim yellow light on a straight-backed chair with Arthur seated stiffly on it. Back in the shadows, the other men's faces were indistinct blobs, their voices were heavy, detached, threatening. Arthur was not used to dealing with danger. Crisis situations upset him. In the presence of legal authority, he began to sweat.

"Nobody accused you of anything," came the gravelly voice of Captain John Henderson.

"Then why are you holding me here?"

"Leave any time you want to leave," Victor Fellows said. "You are under no restraint."

"If you think it would be smart," Henderson added.

"I think I want a lawyer," Slater said.

"There's a telephone on the desk. Just pick it up and ask for an outside line. Call a lawyer, if you need one."

Arthur shifted around. "I'm entitled to know why you brought me here."

"Something's happened, Arthur," Loukas said, keeping his voice down. "A crime has been committed. Questions have to be asked, an investigation made."

"I didn't do anything."

"You want to help us find the person who did. Just answer some questions."

Slater hoped he wasn't going to be sick. He felt weak and grew resentful of his body, his carefully trained and developed body, which seemed insufficient to his present needs. He wanted very much to function the way a man was supposed to function.

"Tell us about your evening," Loukas said.

"My evening?"

"What did you do tonight?"

"Nothing. I mean, I was home. Watching TV."

"Who was with you?"

"Nobody. I live alone."

"You were watching television by yourself?"

"Yes."

"That's bad, Arthur."

"Very bad. Are you sure nobody dropped by for a minute?"

"No! What's wrong—"

"Did you phone anybody, Arthur?"

"No. I don't have a phone. That's not a crime."

"Now take it easy, Arthur. Just answer the questions."

"You were watching television. Starting at what time?"

"I'm not sure."

"Think back, Arthur. What programs did you see?"

"The news. Yes, the news."

"What else?"

"I'm trying to remember."

"It shouldn't be difficult to remember. It wasn't that long ago."

"I can remember what I was doing a few hours ago, Arthur. But my conscience is clear."

"What do you mean! I'm not used to being dragged out of my house. Brutalized, carried off like a common criminal to the police station. Badgered interminably."

"Nobody put a hand on you, Arthur."

"Why am I here?"

Victor Fellows spoke. "Tell him."

"Rape," Tom Petersen said.

Attention focused on Slater. The heavy features shifted gradually as the impact of the word filtered through his brain. His eyes fluttered and closed and his head went back. Sound seeped out of him. He was laughing.

Henderson swayed on the balls of his feet. "You think it's a joke, Arthur?"

"Whom did I rape?" Slater said.

"Then you admit it?" Petersen said.

"*Supposed* to have raped," Slater amended.

Loukas retreated to the wall. Something was wrong, something he was unable to name. Slater was frightened, and he should be. But it was not the fear born of guilt. Something else was odd here. But what?

Henderson said, "You've been named by the victim. You took her in your car to a secluded place and forced her to submit."

"Even if you didn't force her," Petersen said, "she was underage, less than sixteen."

Victor Fellows took up a position in front of the teacher, gazed down at him sternly. "Three women have been assaulted, Arthur, and killed. Now you are accused by a minor of committing statutory rape. She has identified you by name. Use your head, man, no jury would fail to convict under the circumstances."

Slater moved around on the straight chair. Sweat rolled down the hollow of his spine. His undershorts were twisted, biting into his crotch. But he dared not touch himself *there*.

"You've been seen with the girl," Henderson said. "Belle Stafford, a student of yours."

"What stopped you this time?" Petersen said.

"Stopped me!"

"You killed the other three. Why not Belle? Why did you decide to let her go?"

Arthur's eyes rolled wildly. "I have never been fond of that girl."

"Is that why you did it, to punish her?"

Victor Fellows leaned forward and Slater drew back. "It might sit well with a jury to be told that you spared Belle Stafford because of her youth."

"What happens to you, Arthur?" Petersen said. "An irresistible urge? You go nuts, is that it?"

"Confession will provide relief to your soul, Arthur," Henderson offered.

Loukas cleared his throat. "Tom, you stay here with Arthur. I'd like a few words with you other gentlemen."

They huddled around the water fountain in the hallway. Loukas bent to drink, remembered that it was broken, had been broken for nearly a year.

"He's the one," Henderson said. "He's got to be the one."

"Why?" Loukas said.

"Because he's the only one we've got," Victor Fellows said promptly. "Because I can make a case against him, get a conviction. As long as the girl sticks to her story, makes a positive I.D."

"I don't like it," Loukas said.

"Theo," Henderson said roughly, "we got to make a move."

"He doesn't fit," Loukas said.

"He fits all right," Victor Fellows replied strenuously. "He fits if the girl *says* he fits. She named him. And the M.E. confirms recent intercourse. He fits if we can get a confession. Or find some other student he had illicit relations with. Who knows how many innocent young girls have been bespoiled by this man!"

Belle Stafford had not impressed Loukas with her innocence. There had been a hardness in her pretty young face, the carved outlines of toughness and experience. The same hostile set that he had seen in Belle's mother, a taste of what was yet to come.

"I still don't like it," Loukas said.

Fellows interrupted smoothly. "We've got a clear-cut situation. A victim on at least one count—age. A positive I.D. Slater could do it all. Look at him, the way he's built. Strong enough to beat a woman into insensibility, strong enough to strangle a horse. And not the kind of man most women would be attracted to in the first place."

"You mean," Henderson said, "he may *have* to go out to get it?"

"Exactly. The thing is to stay at him. He'll break, I know it. Confess to the other killings. I'm convinced he's our man."

"Are you prepared to charge him?" Loukas said.

Fellows felt his confidence mounting. Arthur Slater was precisely what he wanted and he had no intention of letting him get away. He would prosecute with a dramatic flair, calling on all his rhetorical skills. By the time he was finished, women everywhere would understand that he had fought their battle, made them safe. With his fine, even features, his trim figure, women would be quick to flock to his support. And the way the women of the nation went, so did their husbands.

Victor Fellows presented a sober, courtroom countenance as he spoke. "We'll charge him with Rape First Degree and Rape Third Degree. Bring the girl and her mother down here in the morning and get a statement. Also an I.D. in a line-up. Run a check on Arthur. There must be a yellow sheet on him somewhere. He's going to break, I tell you. He'll admit the other killings and that will wrap it all up."

Henderson led them back into the interrogation room. Slater gazed at them blankly when they appeared.

"Sergeant," Victor Fellows said briskly, "inform the prisoner of his rights and the charges against him."

Loukas felt around in his pockets. "Anybody got a Blue Card?"

Petersen found one in his wallet, handed it over.

"You're under arrest, Arthur," Loukas said. "Charged with rape in the first and the third degrees. I will now inform you of your Constitutional rights." He put on his glasses and began to read from the Blue Card. "The Constitution requires that I inform you of your rights:

"You have a right to remain silent. If you talk to any

police officer, anything you say can and will be used against you in court.

"You have the right to consult . . ."

II

Loukas, alone in the Bureau, stared at the half-empty paper cup. He shifted around in his chair. Arthur Slater. No sense to the whole affair. The smell of rot clung to it. He sought to isolate his worry, to give it a name. And failed.

The phone rang. He lifted it, spoke automatically: "Detectives, Sergeant Loukas."

"This is Dr. Rabinowitz, Sergeant. Resident on emergency duty over at Norwalk Hospital. We've got a young fellow here, there's something strange about him. Some guy found him wandering around on a road up your way—"

"In Arcadia?"

"A kid about seventeen. He'd been worked over pretty good, a bad beating, I'd say."

"Has he got a name?"

"Won't say what it is."

Loukas sighed. "I'll come over."

Dr. Rabinowitz, a young man with bright, inquiring eyes, led Loukas into an examining room. A boy was stretched out on the table, eyes closed. Rabinowitz pulled the sheet to one side. The boy's chest was badly bruised.

Loukas examined the boy's face. Cuts and bruises everywhere, a marked swelling of one eye and his cheek. His nose had been broken.

"He'll be okay," Rabinowitz said. "But he'll smart for a while."

Loukas displayed his shield. "Arcadia police, kid. Who did this to you?"

The boy kept his eyes shut.

"Want to tell me your name?" Loukas said. He received no reply. "Where are his clothes?" he said to the doctor.

Rabinowitz pointed to a narrow closet. In a blood-stained shirt, Loukas found a card case.

"That's mine!" the boy cried. "You have no right."

"You trying to protect somebody, kid?" Loukas said, thumbing through the cards in the case. An I.D. from Arcadia High School, a driver's license, a Social Security card. "William Morrison," Loukas said. "Why would anyone beat you up, William?"

The boy remained silent.

"William Morrison," Loukas repeated. "You related to Senator Morrison?" Again, no reply. "I'll have to call him."

"Does he have to know?" Willy Morrison said.

"Tell me what happened."

"I was out walking—"

"Alone?"

"Alone. I like to walk alone."

"Okay. You were taking a walk."

"Some guys stopped and offered me a ride."

"Just like that?"

"Sure."

"How many guys?"

"Two."

"Driving what?"

"What?"

"What make car?"

"I don't know. I didn't notice."

"Most kids would notice. Go on."

"I got in."

"And?"

"We drove for a while."

"And then?"

"They worked me over."

"Just knocked you around, for no reason?"

"They robbed me."

"Ah. They get much?"

"Not much. Twenty bucks, maybe."

"Why'd they beat you up?"

"To keep me quiet, so I wouldn't call you guys. They tried to scare me and they succeeded."

"I see. That's why you didn't say anything. You were afraid."

"Yes."

"Tell me about the two guys. What did they look like?"

"I don't know. I don't remember."

"You're still scared?"

"It isn't that."

"What is it then?"

"It was dark, nighttime. They pulled under a tree. It was hard to see."

"How old were they?"

"In their twenties, I'd say."

"Black men?"

"Well . . . yes. Yes, they were. They must've figured I'd be easy."

"Apparently you were," Loukas said dryly. He hung the shirt back in the closet, went through the pockets of a pair of blue jeans.

"Hey!" Willy protested. "Don't do that! You have no right!"

Loukas brought a handful of bills out of one pocket. "There's more than a hundred dollars here, Willy."

"They missed it," Willy said sullenly.

"Couple of amateurs, I guess."

"Maybe."

"Willy, Willy," Loukas said, shaking his head. "There must be something more you'd like to tell me."

Willy lay back down on the table, eyes closed once more.

Loukas clucked sadly. "A few years back, Willy, it comes to me that you had some trouble. Remember that?"

"You must mean somebody else."

"I mean you, Willy. You and Hugh Clinton and Ted MacIntosh. You jumped that woman, Willy, the three of you. Gang-banged her. Wasn't my case, but I remember it. Word got around it's Avery Morrison's boy, so don't push it. And nobody pushed. Okay, Willy, let's say your daddy went out on a limb for you that time. Does it follow he'll do it for you one more time?"

"My father had nothing to do with this."

"Guess you do figure he'll fight your battle again. We'll just have to see, won't we? I'm going to talk with him."

"Leave him out of this!"

"Ah, Willy, you're a smart boy. You know I can't do that."

Although it was after midnight, the butler was on hand to usher Loukas into the study. "The Senator will join you in a moment, Sergeant."

"Thank you."

"Would you care for something? Some coffee, perhaps?"

"Nothing, thanks."

The butler withdrew.

Loukas looked around, and was impressed. Paneled walls, old leather chairs, a massive desk, first editions.

Loukas grew uneasy, wondered if he should have come. He had never before dealt with a man of Avery Morrison's stature, but he'd taken the call, visited Willy Morrison at the hospital. The job was his, it was the way the Department functioned.

"Sergeant Loukas," Avery Morrison, in a navy-blue velvet smoking jacket, advanced into the room. He gestured Loukas into a chair, settled opposite him. "How may I help you?"

Even seated, Loukas felt intimidated by the other man, made smaller by his fine good looks, his authoritative manner. Loukas cleared his throat. "It's about your son, Senator."

"What about my son, Sergeant?" No hint of concern, no suggestion of fear, came onto that handsome face.

"He's in the hospital. In Norwalk."

Morrison blinked once. "I see." Morrison rose. "I'd better go to him."

Loukas remained seated, his nervousness vanished. Something *was* wrong. The boy's story, obviously untrue. And now the father's reaction: too controlled, too unconcerned.

"Aren't you going to ask me what happened to Willy?" Loukas said deliberately.

"Yes, of course. What did happen?"

"He was beaten up by a pair of muggers. Two men gave him a ride, beat and robbed him. That's the story he told."

"I see. Is he badly hurt?"

"A broken nose, bruises. He'll ache for a while, but nothing serious."

Avery exhaled and smiled. "That's good to hear. I'd better get down there. His mother will have to be told—"

"Senator," Loukas said, "the boy wasn't telling the truth."

"I beg your pardon."

"He said he'd been robbed. But he had a large amount of cash on him still."

Avery chuckled. "Not very efficient, were they, the robbers?"

Now Loukas stood up, and Avery Morrison no longer seemed so large and intimidating a presence. "I don't believe Willy's story, Senator."

"My son is not a liar, Sergeant. If he told you—" Avery broke off, voice unsteady. Willy was shielding *him*, protecting him from pubic scandal, willing to accept the responsibility of his father's loss of control. The Senator blinked rapidly. "We have nothing further to discuss, Sergeant. I must go to my son."

"Senator," Loukas said flatly, "a few years ago Willy and two of his friends raped a woman here in town. Rumors went around about pressure coming down from the state house and all the way from Washington. There was talk about money changing hands. The detectives on the case, both of them, retired within the year, long before they'd put in their time. One of them bought a ranch in Nevada; the other went into the charter-boat business on Long Island. Up till then they barely got by from one payday to the next. And Hillary Carter, the Circuit Prosecutor in those days, ended up as an assistant attorney general in Washington. Hillary was always complaining about not having the right connections. Funny how those things happen, isn't it, Senator?"

Avery Morrison spoke in a low, cold voice. "As you said, Sergeant, rumors."

"It's as if the rape never took place. The woman left town. The official record never showed a thing. You can wipe records clean but you can't do that to a man's memory."

"This kind of talk can do no one any good, Sergeant."

"Is that a threat, Senator?"

"I never make threats. But I am suggesting—Sergeant, Willy was mugged, that's all. If you can locate the men who did it, I'm sure my son will be happy to cooperate in their prosecution."

"This is a lousy business, Senator. You can't keep buying the boy out of trouble. One day he'll go too far, and there'll be no way to get him off the hook. Even you won't be able to pay the price."

"I think it's time for you to leave, Sergeant."

"I guess it is."

When he was alone, Avery picked up the telephone and dialed his attorney. "Charlie, it's about Willy. He's in the hospital in Norwalk. No, not serious, but have Dr. Wilson look in on him tonight. You, too, Charlie. And Charlie, a Sergeant Loukas of the Arcadia force has taken an interest in the matter and I'd like it to end at once. A couple of phone calls should do it." He hung up and sat down, suddenly weak, drained and frightened. He wanted to cry but no tears came. Nothing seemed to matter anymore.

III

Loukas switched off the headlights and lifted his foot off the accelerator. The Valiant rolled silently into Homestead Lane. He parked the car on the side of the road, under the trees, and turned off the ignition.

In the darkness, he checked the number—22. Samuel Lubin, president of a marketing research company, owned the massive colonial mansion, had lived in it with his family for nearly eight years and leased the guest-house to various tenants. At the moment, it was rented to Arthur Slater.

Loukas, carrying a flashlight, advanced without haste around the big house. The guest quarters consisted of a single-story cottage with a narrow porch. The door lock was a simple spring affair that gave way easily to a flexible steel pick Loukas always had with him. Inside, he drew the shades, closed the draperies, and used the flashlight to look around.

He was in the living room. An old couch stood opposite the corner fireplace and a braided Early American rug covered the floor. In the other corner opposite the couch, a portable TV stood on a small table. Magazines and newspapers were strewn about and books were everywhere. Shelves were crowded with them and they were stacked on the floor and piled carelessly in chairs. There were more books than Loukas had ever seen in any one place before, except a library. He read some of the titles and marveled at the wide range of Arthur Slater's interests.

He worked the light beam around the room. On the far wall, hung on wooden pegs, in neat formation, guns of every size and shape. Some fairly new, most old. Rifles, shotguns, pistols. A Springfield 1903, its metal parts chromed and shining; a Japanese Army rifle, caliber .22; an ancient muzzleloader; a derringer no bigger than a man's palm; a .357 magnum which Loukas had heard called "The Beast." All the weapons were clean, oiled, operating parts in working order. Arthur Slater was a gun freak. Loukas put it down as an extension of those big muscles.

He directed the light into the tiny kitchen where it showed dirty dishes piled in the sink, a frying pan that hadn't been washed in days, and an open can of peaches. Arthur Slater was a rotten housekeeper.

Loukas followed the light into the bedroom. He found a single bed, unmade, a chest of drawers containing underclothes, socks, handkerchiefs, some shirts, a closet that revealed two suits, a thick woolen coat sweater, a raincoat, and some ties. A pair of worn hiking boots and a pair of sneakers stood next to a cheap suitcase.

In the corner of the room were a set of barbells and weights, a rowing machine, a stationary bicycle.

Loukas went back into the living room. On the desk he found some letters from various parts of the world. They were chatty, discursive, concerned with nothing of interest to him. A half-filled stamp album lay open and next to it a cigar box filled with old coins, including two twenty-dollar gold pieces. Arthur Slater collected all sorts of things.

A magnetized chess set, arranged as if a game were in progress, drew Loukas' attention. Did Slater play against himself? Or by mail with a friend? Or possibly by telephone? He slashed the light from corner to corner; no phone, just as Arthur had said. Apparently he had no need of contemporary communications.

Loukas went through the desk drawers, found nothing. He sat down and tried to give a name to whatever it was he had come here to find. Some suggestion of the kind of man Arthur Slater was, the key to the parts that made him tick.

Loukas got down on the floor. The magazines, with the exception of a few physical-culture books, told him nothing: *Time, Playboy, Rolling Stone, Atlantic, The Saturday Review*. On his knees, Loukas moved over to the books along the wall, scanning titles. Arthur Slater had a powerful concern with the lives of great men, biographies of Jefferson, Bismarck, Napoleon, and more. There were histories, particularly histories of war. There was a one-volume encyclopedia of weaponry from the Stone Age through Vietnam. It was, for Loukas, all of a piece, consistent with what Slater appeared to be.

Then the policeman's attention was drawn to a row of looseleaf binders. Each one a different color, seven in all. He supposed they contained academic work Slater had done, perhaps while in college, and decided to keep. Out of curiosity, Loukas pulled one of the binders from its place, opened it at random and began to read. Excitement soon gripped him and he read on. Arthur Slater

had kept a detailed diary of his life, an autobiography in
outline.

Loukas removed the binders from the shelf and arranged them in order, according to the dates inscribed
on the first page of each. Then he settled onto the old
couch and began to read.

Daylight had leaked beneath the draperies before
Loukas found what he was after. Three pages of single-
spaced writing. Painfully inscribed, the anguish of the
author evident in every phrase. Loukas read the three
pages over again. When he left, Loukas took the binders
along.

IV

It was almost noon when Loukas reached the Fort.
Earlier he'd had a long talk with Rita Westphal at her
home, apologizing for intruding on her Sunday morning. After a number of other interviews, he'd gone home,
had shaved and showered, changed clothes and drunk
some coffee. He had also phoned Captain Henderson.

"Where the hell have you been, Theo?"

"I'm coming in now. Get the Circuit Prosecutor over."

"What are you up to, Theo? I'm warning you, you're
making a lot of people unhappy."

"I'll be right down."

At the Fort, Loukas asked the Desk Officer to tell
Captain Henderson he was in, ordered Arthur Slater
brought up from the holding cell, then ducked into the
Bureau. He filled a paper cup with coffee and chewed
on a soggy doughnut.

Henderson showed up first. The long face was drawn
and blotched, chin pulled down to his chest. "Goddammit to hell, Theo, what's going on! How'd you like me
to dock you a day's pay for not showing up this morning? You're responsible to me, remember that." He
propelled himself into a chair, feet swinging up to the
metal desk. "Don't fuck up, Theo, is all I can tell you.
Don't fuck up."

An officer appeared with Arthur Slater. The teacher was unshaven, the whites of his eyes streaked and dull.

"Sit down, Arthur," Loukas said. He waved the officer away.

"You're looking at an unhappy man, Theo," Henderson said. "Very unhappy."

"Arthur didn't do it," Loukas said.

"I'm getting unhappier by the minute, Theo."

"I can prove it," Loukas said. "Arthur can prove it."

The teacher stared at him without comprehension.

Henderson spoke as if in pain. "Jesus, Theo. This town is ready for an arrest."

Loukas let his hand fall on the stack of loose-leaf binders on his desk. He watched Arthur Slater.

The teacher rocked silently on his chair, making no sound.

"What are those?" Henderson wanted to know. "What's going on?"

Victor Fellows strode into the Bureau. He wore a dark-blue suit with hairline stripes, a blue shirt, and a blue tie with small crimson anchors on it. His smile was possessed, his manner assured. "Gentlemen, what have we here? Have you decided to confess, Arthur? Make it easier on all of us that way."

"Arthur's innocent," Loukas said.

"Goddammit, Theo," Henderson said.

Victor Fellows faced Loukas, eyes glittering aggressively. "We've got a sound case. The victim will press her charges. Mrs. Stafford and her daughter will be in Judge Portabello's chambers tomorrow at one."

"It won't wash," Loukas said. "And don't count on the Staffords."

Fellows spoke in a voice surprisingly peevish. "You're making a bad mistake, Sergeant Loukas."

"I'm doing my job," Loukas said.

"He's guilty," Fellows insisted.

The gnawing pain came alive in Loukas' middle. He kept himself from rubbing it. "If he was it'd be convenient. But Arthur never did it, not any of it. He couldn't."

"Use your head, Theo," Henderson said angrily. "Look at this mother, he's strong as a bull."

Loukas took one of the loose-leaf binders in hand. "It's all in here."

Henderson eyed the binder as if expecting it to explode. "What the hell is that!"

"That's mine!" Arthur Slater cried desperately. "You have no right to read it."

"I'm trying to help you, Arthur," Loukas said.

"It's private!" the teacher protested. "My private work."

"Let me see that," Victor Fellows said. He held out his hand.

Loukas ignored it. "For crying out loud, Arthur, tell the truth."

"You had no right to go to my place," Slater moaned. "I never said you could."

"Evidence illegally acquired . . ." Fellows broke off, smiling thinly.

"Wait a minute," Henderson said. "Have we got an illegal entry here, Theo? Maybe you better not say anything."

"Tell them, Arthur," Loukas said. "Tell them or I will."

Slater began to tremble.

Henderson reached for the binder. "What kind of a nut house is this! I'm running a circus, not a police force. What's in that fucking book anyway?"

Loukas held on to the binder. "Arthur, would you be better off spending the next twenty years in prison? You won't like it, Arthur. You won't like it at all."

"I never did anything wrong," Slater said feebly.

"Tell them."

Slater looked around as if seeking support. "Why should I be punished when I'm innocent?"

"Tell them," Loukas said.

Slater's shoulders slumped and he turned his eyes to the floor. "I never did anything to that girl. To Belle. I'm not that kind of a man. Nor those other women.

It's not in my nature to hurt anybody. I would never do anything to a woman."

"Damn this business," Henderson growled.

"Prove it," Victor Fellows said, struggling to keep his demeanor cool.

"Tell them about the diary," Loukas said.

"It's in the notebook," Slater said.

"It's a diary of Arthur's life," Loukas explained. "A kind of autobiography."

A sputter of energy brought Slater's head up. "I wanted to write. Someday I was going to write a novel about a man who existed truly only within his own head, his own heart. A man who never lived the way most people do."

"I don't get it," Henderson said. "So he wanted to write a book!"

"A self-serving document," Victor Fellows said. "Not the strongest piece of evidence."

"Arthur doesn't have sex with women," Loukas said. "He never does. Not ever."

"A queer," Henderson said automatically.

"Not exactly," Loukas said, the words obscured under the force of a verbal outburst by Arthur Slater.

"I'm not!" he screamed, fists raised up, arms locked and trembling. "Don't call me that! I'm not what you said! I'm not!"

Fellows considered the legal aspects of the situation. "A homosexual might very well commit rape and murder. A homosexual might have a deep and abiding loathing of women, all women. A homosexual might act out his hostility in the extreme. I'm afraid, Sergeant Loukas, nothing said up to now has altered the situation."

Loukas turned to Slater. "Either you tell them, Arthur, or I will."

Slater had turned in on himself, body sagging, eyes almost closed, his breathing shallow.

"Okay," Loukas said. He wanted to get it all out, to be rid of the responsibility. "When Arthur was nine years old, his father and mother got drunk. They drank a lot, you understand, partied a lot. He was used to the noise and the partying, used to the fighting that went on."

"Get to it, Theo," Henderson said.

"This time it was different. Sometime during the night, Arthur's mother came into his bedroom—"

"Mothers do check on their children," Fellows said.

"—she climbed into his bed—"

"Jesus!" Henderson said.

Fellows raised his voice. "Do you expect me to believe—"

Loukas said, "Name it and she did it to the kid. Everything."

Henderson made the sign of the cross.

"I don't believe it," Fellows said.

Loukas went on. "Arthur's father walked in. He dragged the mother out of there, then came back. He blamed Arthur for what had happened, said he was evil and beat him. Said it was all Arthur's doing. He told the kid that the only way to make up for what he'd done was to live a perfect life. Arthur's been working at it ever since."

"The entry in the book may not be true," Fellows said. "People let their imaginations go."

Loukas stared steadily at the Circuit Prosecutor. "You can't wait to get your hands on this poor sucker. It won't work, Mr. Fellows. It just won't work."

Fellows turned to Arthur Slater. "You said you were writing fiction, a novel. That's what it all is, the product of your imagination. Isn't that the case, Arthur?"

"It's fact, not fiction," Loukas said. "Arthur *can't* make it with a woman. He can't do it with any woman."

"Why not?" Henderson said. Understanding broke. "Jesus, you mean he can't get it up?"

"He can't."

Arthur began to weep.

"He's tried," Loukas said. "With girls he knew, with hookers, with older women. Nothing worked for him. It's been more than ten years since he even went near a woman. It's all in here."

"That doesn't change anything," Fellows said. "Belle

Stafford named Slater and she is a minor. We can get him on that alone, her word."

"Not with this book in evidence," Loukas said. "Anyway," he said, watching Fellow's face, "she's going to withdraw the charges."

Fellows' eyes hardened and his mouth thinned out. "The hell she will!"

Loukas struggled to keep his satisfaction from showing. "I showed the book to Belle and her mother. Maybe I even frightened them a little, you never know. Anyway, between the book and me, they were convinced and did some talking. Seems like Belle likes men a lot. This time she came home looking as if she'd been worked over pretty good and Mrs. Stafford blew her top. They went round and round. The girl wouldn't say who did it to her. Seems she makes this dude out to be somebody special, a prize package. She wants to protect him, keep him for later use, I guess. That's when Arthur's name came into it."

"I don't believe it," Victor Fellows said. "I'll talk to them."

"It was the mother who came up with Slater. Seems that Arthur had given the girl a ride home one day and Mrs. Stafford spotted them. She put it together and made Arthur her kid's lover."

"There!" Victor Fellows said. "You're establishing my case."

"Not really. I spoke to Rita Westphal, the headmistress at the high school. Belle is not your most outstanding student. She's failing Slater's class. She admitted to me that she tried to get a passing grade out of him, tried to seduce Arthur. He turned her down."

"That's Arthur's story," Henderson said hopefully.

"That's Belle's story," Loukas said. "But when her mother came up with Slater's name, Belle figured she could protect her boy friend and dump on Arthur at the same time. Sweet girl."

"The Staffords told you this?" Henderson said.

"Let's have his name," Fellows said. "The man who did sleep with her. He could be our guy."

"The girl won't name him."

"Very nice," Henderson said.

"You believe this fantastic story?" Fellows said.

"I talked to some other people this morning, too. Some of Arthur's pupils and some other teachers," Loukas said. "Whatever the pupils think about Arthur, nobody even suggested that he ever did anything improper sexually with a student. The other teachers say he's got his faults, a loner, stiff-necked, but a good teacher, a decent guy.

"As for Belle Stafford, she's done her seduction number with at least three other teachers. One of them was a woman, the way I understand it. You wouldn't want to depend on Belle Stafford as a witness, Mr. Prosecutor. She'll never stand up for you."

"Why?" Henderson said. "Why would she do a thing like this?"

Loukas shrugged. "It's nothing new. In Genesis, the Old Testament. Potiphar's wife attempted to seduce Joseph, and when he refused, she accused him of raping her. A woman scorned, I suppose . . ."

"Well," Victor Fellows said, after a moment, arranging a generous smile on his full mouth. "There seems to be no case against you, Arthur. And that's what it's all about under our system of justice. You're free to go, Arthur. You have nothing to worry about anymore."

"Not a thing," Henderson said.

Loukas drove Arthur Slater home. In front of the guest cottage, the teacher got out.

"Arthur," Loukas said, "these things happen."

"I know."

"People can be so damned mean sometimes, Arthur."

"I know."

"You wouldn't have told them, about the business in the diary."

"Probably not."

"I don't understand."

"Part of me wanted it to be true, I guess. I wanted to be *able* to have done those things. I almost felt like a real man." A suggestion of a smile turned the corners of his mouth.

Loukas understood and was startled that he accepted the idea so readily. "It shouldn't have to be that way," he heard himself saying.

"It's not a should-be world, is it, Sergeant? It's real and very often rotten."

"All that time in the joint. Believe me, it would not have been worth it."

"You're probably right."

"It's over. Now you're free."

Slater's face closed in again. "It's not over yet. And I've never been free."

Part Five

CHAPTER ELEVEN

I

A SURGE OF EMOTION brought him upright in the narrow bed. For an extended interval he sat without moving, eyes fastened on shifting images inside his head. A shudder racked his body and he stood up, placed himself in front of the long mirror.

The white nylon briefs he wore cupped and outlined his genitals. A delicate curve, a gentle ridge, a long, slack line. He lifted his eyes. The body reflected in the glass was strong, well proportioned, muscles clearly defined, skin smooth and hairless.

He tensed his legs and the thigh muscles swelled and bulged. He came up on his toes, admired the strong, round thrust of his calves.

He flexed his right arm. The bicep formed a hard, round ball. Sinews and veins streaked along the length of his arms, disappearing into the wide, powerful shoulders. He considered his posture—almost military in bearing. His chest was broad, his belly flat and ridged. A perfect body, without a flaw or blemish.

One swift, practiced movement and the white briefs came off. He examined his limp member in the mirror. He went into the bathroom and removed a pair of scissors from its place in the medicine cabinet. He spread a clean bath towel on the floor and stood over it, his legs spread. Carefully, his hand steady and sure, he trimmed the pubic hairs.

The job done, he showered. First he wet down his body, then soaped himself to a thick lather. He cleaned around his crotch with a particularly soft sponge. He rinsed thoroughly, repeated the process. He dried himself with tender care, patting his skin dry. Baby powder went under his arms, on his feet, around his genitals. After-shave lotion stung his cheeks.

Back in the bedroom he put on clean white briefs, starched khaki trousers, and a newly laundered sweat shirt, soft white socks, a pair of slippers. He moved without urgency to where the worktable stood, confronted the great formless ball of clay. It shone wetly in the soft light, needing his magic touch to transform it into something meaningful and beautiful. He waited for some massive blast from on high to stimulate his genius; nothing happened.

He retreated a stride or two, allowed his eyes to close. He released his mind. And it flowed backward in time to the last one.

How long had he watched her?

How long yearned to place himself next to her?

What a bitch she was! All of them were the same. Disgusting creatures willing to perform the most degrading of acts. Using their bodies to reduce a man to a whimpering blob of meat. Diminishing a man's strength, making him soiled and used up.

None of them were any good. Spreading their legs in beguiling invitation. Reaching, grabbing, stuffing a man into themselves, into that diseased and corrupt sump hole, draining away all manhood.

They deserved to be struck down. Wiped out. His hands slid along his sides, came to rest on his engorged penis. His fingers bent and closed. He mustered all his strength and squeezed.

His eyes opened. His hands swung up and out, smashing down around the damp, soft ball of clay, shaping, giving it form, pressing it between his cupped palms. Like lava forced out of the earth, it rose upward and out. At once he slashed at it, one finger molding and prodding, until pursed lips were manifest in the gray stuff. Lips parted and inviting.

"Dirty cunt!"

A bone-handled hunting knife rested on the table. His hand closed on it and his arm swung up, drove with explosive force, sinking the blade into the lips of his creation.

Moaning as if in pain, he sank to his knees, fumbling with his trousers, desperately seeking himself. Rolling on the floor until the torment was eased.

CHAPTER TWELVE

I

ARTHUR SLATER TRUNDLED ALONG the north corridor of
Arcadia High School. Eyes to the front, broad jaw set,
the massive body pulled together in preparation for attack. Murmurs and giggles followed him, becoming louder,
more distinct. Searing voices that sliced through all de-
fenses.

"Get it up, Arthur."

"Rape me, man, rape me."

"Old Softy."

Arthur Slater heaved himself around, wheezing, a
blocky, awesome figure full of terror and rage. Faces
turned away, voices fell.

He sought a place of safety. In a deserted classroom,
he stood behind the oak door, body trembling, weak,
frightened. His muscles were useless now, weights that
wore away his courage and his strength.

When he was able, he made his way to the office of
the headmistress. "I would like very much to see Mrs.
Westphal," he told the secretary. She was a plump woman whom Slater had never learned to appreciate. There
was no emotion in the round face, no feeling for other
people. Her voice was strident and querulous.

"Mrs. Westphal is extremely busy this morning."

He ached to strike her, to punish her for treating him
without understanding or compassion. But then he'd always known it was this way; none of *them* were sensitive
human beings. Selfish and mean creatures, without affection or kindness.

"I insist, Mrs. Delaney. It is imperative that I speak with Mrs. Westphal. Immediately."

The tension he communicated frightened her and she went into the headmistress's office. She returned shortly. "You may go right in, Mr. Slater."

The headmistress looked up from her work. Her expression was one of meticulous preoccupation, a woman busy but not uncaring. Slater saw only judgment in her face, rejection. Mrs. Westphal's tone was brisk, her words businesslike.

"What is it, Arthur? This is not a good day." She had decided to treat him as if nothing had happened. No charges had been levied. He was free, innocent; wronged.

He interpreted her attitude as condemnatory. "There has been some trouble," he said tentatively.

Mrs. Westphal removed her glasses. "A mistake was made, Arthur. It's over." She was dissembling and she knew it. By tonight, half the homes in Arcadia would carry some grotesquely distorted version of Arthur Slater's situation. His personality, his character, his history, all would be dramatized to make the story more interesting, the gossip more insidious. Phone calls would come to her office from concerned parents questioning his right to teach their offspring. Committees would be formed for the "protection of our children." The Teachers' Union would be denounced and the School Board would be attacked. Arthur Slater, the headmistress knew, had been transformed into a threat to children and to their education.

Slater spoke in a thick, dull voice. "I am resigning."

"You don't have to do that, Arthur." The headmistress warned herself not to try too hard to keep him. Resignation would make it easier on them all. He could go away, find another job elsewhere, and life in Arcadia High School could continue much as before. Mrs. Westphal decided that she didn't like herself very much. "Stay on, Arthur," she said. "We'll fight this through together."

"Everybody knows about me."

"The charges were dropped."

"They're all talking about me, what I am. But I'm not any of those things."

"You're a good teacher. That's all that matters to me."

"You'll have my resignation in writing."

She nodded. He was a beaten man, worn, drawn, his skin pallid. Defeat was etched in the line of his body.

"Oh, Arthur," she said, "I'm so sorry." And she was. "Nothing's the way it used to be. Or should be. Teaching used to be an honorable profession. Now we're little more than watchdogs over the growing beasts until they're legal.

"The girls here get pregnant and their mothers take them to New York on Friday afternoon and have them aborted. A couple of hundred dollars and they're back in class on Monday morning, good as new. And I'm not supposed to know about it.

"They buy pot in the gym building, and share it with their parents. And I'm not supposed to know about that either.

"Ninety-odd percent of our students will go on to college. Sixty-five percent will get degrees. Many of them will go on to masters and doctorates. But they're moral slobs who demand instant gratification and denounce such refinements as right and wrong as fascistic."

"Arthur, I'm sorry."

"They've always laughed at me. But I was a good teacher."

"Stay and fight, Arthur."

"It's an inconvenience for you, having to replace me in mid-semester this way. But you'll find somebody."

The tension drained out of her spine. "Where will you go?"

"Go? I have no idea."

"Think about it overnight. Change your mind. You can still change your mind."

At the door he spoke without looking at her. "Thank you for not laughing at me."

Arthur Slater wrote out his resignation that night. He reread it, changed some words, typed it on his portable machine, and signed it. He found a stamp and walked out to the mailbox at roadside, deposited the letter. The postman would collect it in the morning and the head-mistress would receive it the next day.

Back in his rooms, he located a plastic garbage bag and took it into the living room, spread it neatly on the coffee table. From its place on the wall he took down the Smith and Wesson .357 magnum revolver that he had had for so many years. He enjoyed the feel of it in his hand, solid, heavy, powerful. A man's weapon. From the desk drawer he took a single bullet, dropped it into the cylinder. He spun the cylinder.

He took his place on the battered old sofa and placed The Beast in his lap. Very carefully, he drew the plastic garbage bag over his head, concerned lest he make a mess, then put the muzzle of The Beast into his mouth. The taste of the cold metal was slightly offensive, but not excessively so.

He brought The Beast back to full cock, listened to the sear fall into the hammer notches. He closed his eyes, exhaled, and squeezed down on the trigger with his thumb.

Click.

A jolt of terror wrenched his body. He cocked The Beast again.

Click.

Once more. If a third attempt failed, he would take it as a sign that he was meant to survive. One more time, and he grew confident that he would not die at this time in this place. He squeezed the trigger.

The slug ripped into the roof of his mouth and pain radiated upward into his brain. His eyes stung, his nose grew stuffed, his teeth ached. Fear was everywhere in him and he felt control of his bodily functions loosen and fall away. And in that fractured moment of time, he understood for the first time the dimensions of the mis-take he'd made—Belle Stafford was the one he should have killed. And her mother.

Not himself.

II

Duncan Road angled off Main, ending in a turnaround. The houses were undistinguished for the most part and small. It was a quiet street without much traffic. Loukas couldn't recall ever visiting it before. He stopped the Valiant in front of a gray clapboard house.

"Converted," Tom Petersen said. "Four, maybe five apartments. Bet the landlord's illegal. Bet the Zoning Board never approved the conversion."

"When you've got nothing better to do," Loukas said dryly, "go through the records. Right now let's try and stay with business."

They went inside, climbed an unsteady staircase to the second floor. At the rear they found Jane Bonner's apartment. A pretty girl with red hair and green eyes answered their knock.

"Excuse me, miss," Loukas said. "I'm looking for Miss Jane Bonner."

"She isn't home."

"Are you her roommate?" Loukas said.

The girl eyed the two men warily. "Who are you?"

Loukas flashed his shield. "Sergeant Loukas, Arcadia police."

Relief washed the tension out of the girl's face. "I've been a little jittery lately with what's going on. What do you want with Jane?"

"Would you mind telling us your name, miss?"

"Holly Mason."

"I'd like to ask you one or two questions, Miss Mason," Loukas said. "If that's all right with you?"

"Sure." She opened the door wider and stood aside. "You want to come in?"

The apartment was cramped, the spaces small and crowded with furniture. Loukas took it all in at a glance, smiled encouragingly at the girl. "Where is Jane tonight?"

"On a date."

"With her boy friend?" Petersen said.

Holly looked up at him. "Boy friend? Jane doesn't have a boy friend. Nobody regular."

"What about Virgil?" Petersen said.

"Who?"

"Virgil Reiser," Loukas said in a still voice.

Holly said the name aloud. "Oh, I know, the delivery boy at the market."

"That's right."

"She never dated him. But he digs her, always giving her the eye."

"You mean they never went out, not even once?" Petersen said.

"Never. Jane likes a good time too much. No delivery boy can afford Jane. Not that she's only interested in money," she amended quickly.

"How about that!" Petersen said to Loukas.

Loukas said to Holly, "You said Virgil was always watching Jane. Does he hang around, watch this house?"

"I don't think so." She hugged herself. "That would be creepy. I hope he doesn't do that. No, I meant down at the market."

"You and Jane shop there?" oukas said.

"Jane *works* at A-1," Holly said. "Check-out girl."

Petersen looked over at Loukas but received no response.

"Has this got something to do with the killings?" Holly wanted to know.

"Just a routine investigation," Loukas answered. "You don't have to tell anyone we were here, except Jane."

"I hope you catch that guy soon," she said. "You will, won't you?"

"We'll catch him," Loukas said, with more assurance than he felt.

"Nice-looking chick," Petersen said when they were back in the car. "Maybe I'll give her a call."

"There's a nut going around wasting women. People are on edge. Just keep your pants on until this one is wrapped up. A weird case, you can't tell what's liable to happen. Look at poor Slater."

"No guts, knocking himself off. A man ought to face things."

"Maybe he didn't see a way out. Maybe killing yourself takes more guts than we know. Now let's get back to the job. I want to double back on everything, everybody. Run another check on all the people who had access to any of the homes involved. I made up a plastic overlay. Marked off the three houses where the deceased lived. Place it over a map of the town and you discover that all three crimes took place within a one-mile radius of each other, in the general vicinity of Simon's Pond—the northwest corner of town. Find out what services work that area. Get a list of names of anybody who had a reason to show up there. Check out everybody. I want to know who might have seen those women at any time."

"What about Virgil? He keeps cropping up."

"Especially Virgil."

Part Six

CHAPTER THIRTEEN

I

LOUKAS PARKED ON LEMMINGTON DRIVE between a char-
treuse Sedan De Ville and a lemon Impala. At the private
road leading up the hill to Victor Fellows' house Sam
Barker directed traffic. He tossed a casual salute toward
Loukas.

"Didn't know you were an art lover, Sarge." He laughed
without sound.

"Culture brings advancement in police work, Sam."

"I didn't know that."

"Stay on your toes, man."

Walking the long driveway Loukas identified a Mercedes, a Jaguar, a Porsche, a Rolls-Royce, a Peugeot,
two Fiats, three Datsuns, three Toyotas and six Volks-
wagens. American cars, it seemed, were unpopular in
Arcadia.

Inside the house, an oscillating babble assaulted him.
There were people everywhere, in chattering bunches, in
intimate pairs, at rest or on the move.

These were the citizens Loukas was paid to protect. Sleek
and beautiful in pants and shirts and skirts by Galanos
and Saint Laurent and Pucci and Bill Blass and Halston.
They spoke in French or German or Italian or Spanish
and traveled the world on jumbo jets, belongings tucked
neatly into cases by Vuitton. The men were meticulously
barbered, slickly turned out. The women had bright eyes
and shining teeth; and not a brassiere in the place.
Loukas judged it a mistake to have come.

A woman advanced in his direction and he made ready to flee. Her mouth was open, her hands outstretched.

"Sergeant Loukas!"

Eyes swung toward him and he felt sweat break out on his back. He tried to remember her name. He drew a blank.

"How good to see you," she cooed. "A madhouse, isn't it? All these people. Where did they come from! Do have a drink."

Victor Fellows' wife. He searched for her first name; it eluded him. "It's a very nice party, Mrs. Fellows."

"Pauline, everybody calls me Pauline. The bar's that way. The show is everywhere. Victor's somewhere being a host. Do enjoy yourself. We'll find a moment later and talk, I'm sure."

She faded into the crowd.

Loukas went in the opposite direction, toward the bar. He asked for a beer.

"Miller's, if you've got it," he said to the barman.

The man gazed at him as if he were some rare and despised laboratory specimen. "No beer," he drawled.

"Rye and ginger ale, please."

Glass in hand, Loukas retreated. He tasted the drink: bourbon. It was too much trouble to return to the bar. He went into the entrance hall and found a place for himself in front of a large painting of a sliced apple, a paring knife, and a chunk of Swiss cheese.

"What do you think?" a man said, taking up a position alongside.

"I don't know much about painting," Loukas answered.

"Which means you think it's bullshit."

"Is that what I said?"

"This is the third time I've looked at that abortion," the man said. "Each time I hate it more."

"Why do you keep looking?"

"Because my wife loves it. I get a great deal of satisfaction from knowing that my wife doesn't know her ass from a hole in the ground."

Loukas said nothing.

"I've shocked you," the man said.

"I'm not shocked."

"But you don't approve of a man talking that way about his wife?"

"Does my opinion matter to you?"

"Not much. In my old neighborhood, my wife was what was called a dumb broad. You're asking yourself why did he marry her? I'll tell you why. Her old man had money and he bought me a practice when I got out of school. I'm an orthodontist. You know what an orthodontist is? He's a man who charges higher fees than a dentist. You don't approve of me, do you?"

"I'm a listener by profession."

"What's your profession?"

"I'm a cop."

"A cop! An honest-to-God cop?"

"That's right."

The man walked away, shaking his head. Loukas found space in front of another painting. Parallel blue lines angling across a yellow field. Shellacked to a high gloss. Another man approached him, a vague smile on his face. It was Ralph Burleigh, night security over at the high school.

"Hey, Ralph. You an art lover?"

"Ah, I just like to look at the pictures and all. Sometimes on my days off I go into the city, visit the galleries. You can go into any one you want, you know. All free. It must be great to live in New York and be able to do that whenever you want to."

"I guess so."

"I admired your speech to the Parent-Teacher's, Theo. People ought to pay attention to a man like you."

Loukas never felt comfortable in the presence of a compliment. "Thanks."

"Well, I better get along. I'm on duty tonight. I got to change clothes and get over to the school. See you again."

Punch was available in one corner of the living room. White wine, ginger ale, and strawberries, served up in champagne glasses. Ruth Diamond accepted a glass, sipped nervously at it.

She wished Leo had come and at the same time was glad to be alone. Leo's presence was often a burden. Nothing she did or said ever pleased him and in public she feared she would commit some awful faux pas that would draw a scathing criticism. Still, had he been there, she would not have felt so lonely, so frightened.

She shuffled along the wall, devoting no less than three minutes to each painting. Creative people were an enigma to her, as was their work. This nude, for example, breasts stacked up like a pair of washed-out globes, the nipples a glaring cherry color. What did it mean?

"Figured it out yet?" a voice asked in her ear.

She dared not face the speaker. The question was repeated, the voice more suggestive. Coming had been a mistake.

"Symbolic," the voice said. "But what does it symbolize?"

He stepped in front of her, blocking her view of the painting. Only slightly taller than she was, he was immaculately groomed, dramatically handsome, the kind of man who always seemed terribly sure of himself.

"Ask the painter," she said at last.

"Too simple an approach. I prefer solving puzzles for myself. Does the white represent the purity of women?"

She said nothing, convinced he was mocking her. She wanted to walk away, but could not.

"No vagina," he pointed out. "What shall we make of that? A blow for women's freedom, do you think? Find pleasure and purpose in one another. Close out mankind."

"You're very good with words."

"I'm glib," he acknowledged. "And shallow. A very small talent. Did you pose for this painting?"

Ruth didn't know whether to be pleased or insulted. She assumed her remote manner. "Have you noticed a resemblance?"

"I'm just trying to provoke you," he said.

"I see," she said, but she didn't.

"Have you ever been a model? You're very attractive."

"I was a cheerleader in high school," she felt compelled to explain. "But it isn't the same, I guess," she ended lamely.

"It's better. Did you twirl the baton?"

"Oh, I was never very good at that."

"I'll bet you were a hell of a cheerleader, though."

"You're making fun of me."

"No. Just enjoying you. You're a very attractive, very pleasing woman."

She drew back and that caused him to laugh. Her cheeks grew pink.

"Do you have a name?" he said.

She told him.

"I'm Alan McCambridge." His eyes searched around. "Which one is yours?"

"Which one?"

"Your husband?"

"He had something else to do, in the city."

"Oh, I see."

"And where is your wife?" She was surprised to discover that she hoped he was unencumbered by a wife. She reminded herself that she was respectable, conservative, happily married. At once, conflicting emotions surged up in her, giving rise to fragmented ideas, thoughts, desires. Tears were close to the surface and she set herself to hold them back. She tried to smile at Alan McCambridge.

"My wife?" he said. "Looking to score, I imagine."

"Score!"

"Dear Ruth Diamond, Lily and I have an arrangement. It keeps our marriage intact, the bills paid, the house in order, and the connubial bed content. She goes her way and I go mine."

Ruth decided that she didn't want to hear any more. She took a step away. He reached for her arm.

"I am what is vulgarly known as a swinger. Lily and I express our sexual proclivities in a number of different ways. Nothing too bizarre of painful, of course. I'd like very much to express some of them with you."

She disengaged her arm. "I have to go."

"You're frightened."

"I'm not what you think."

"You don't know what I think you are. For that matter, you haven't quite decided that question for yourself. You're an explorer on the verge of adventure. Who knows what you may find out? I chart a very sound route and you're ready for the journey."

"You're wrong," she blurted out.

"I doubt it," he said.

The words trailed after her and she wondered if he could be right. She wasn't certain about anything anymore.

"It's good, isn't it?" Donnelly said without conceit.

The sculpture consisted of two bronze rectangles of different sizes, the centers hollowed out, and entwined like a Chinese puzzle. Loukas had been studying it for nearly five minutes.

"Are you the sculptor?" he asked.

Donnelly, solidly planted on the other side of his creation, jerked his broad, bony head once. "I am. What do you think of it?"

Loukas hesitated. "I keep thinking I should be able to take it apart, then put it together again."

"That's good. Nobody's said that before."

"Is that what you had in mind?"

"When I did it? Not consciously. Listen, you don't have to *understand* it, you know. All you have to do is respond. Like it or loathe it, your prerogative."

"Does it have a name?"

"*Unity Two.*"

"What was *Unity One?*"

"Circles."

Loukas grinned and Donnelly grinned back at him. "Don't ask me why I called them Unity. Otherwise I'll make a heavy speech about the oneness of mankind and the rest of that crap. Let's keep it simple. Can you afford to buy it? It would please me to think you owned it."

"How much is it?"

"Two thousand."

Loukas whistled softly.

"Ah, well," Donnelly said in regret. "Writers don't determine who reads their stuff, either. I thought everybody around here was loaded."

"Meet the exception."

Donnelly snapped his fingers. "Bad luck. See you around."

Victor Fellows took Loukas into his study, saw him settled in a blood-red leather club chair. "This sort of thing"—he gestured toward the door—"all those people, not at all my style."

"The opening seems to be a great success," Loukas said.

"My wife has this fantasy about becoming an art dealer. I find modern art puerile, empty, contrived."

Puerile. Loukas made a mental note to look up the meaning of the word.

"What's your impression of Donnelly?" Fellows said. He laughed at the puzzled expression on Loukas' face. "The sculptor. Brawny sort of chap in a flannel shirt."

Loukas had known Victor Fellows for nearly five years, had worked with him on other cases. But they had never been close, never discussed anything personal, never had a brew together. The idea of Victor Fellows drinking beer at Jerry's Pool Hall was an amusing one.

"We just talked," Loukas said.

The prosecutor lit a cigarette, making the brief act almost ritualistic. "Donnelly's not a man I can admire. his work is practically pornographic." He dragged on the cigarette in a delicate, almost effete, manner, didn't inhale. "Those people out there, has it occurred to you that one of them is likely to be the man we're looking for?"

Loukas agreed. "It's on my mind all the time. I keep looking into people's faces—can this be the one? I don't think about much else now."

"Too bad Slater didn't measure up. I'd've torn him apart in a courtroom."

Loukas lowered his eyes. "Three people were at the

funeral. A kid from one of his classes. He said Slater was a good teacher. And a distant relative. An old man."

"You said three."

"I was there."

"Right." Fellows placed the cigarette between his teeth, letting it hang there while he spoke. "We've got to break this case, Theo."

Loukas tried to recall whether the Circuit Prosecutor had ever before used his first name.

"And soon," Fellows added.

"I'm for it."

"Pressure's building, from the state house down."

"The state cops have got the manpower, the experience. Maybe—"

"No," Fellows snapped. "If you feel you aren't up to the job, say so. I'm sure Chief Wakeman will find someone to take your place. Without prejudice, of course."

Loukas turned a steady glance toward the other man. "I want this guy a lot. I guess I'll just keep pecking away."

Fellows was disappointed. He ground out the cigarette. "It seems to me we're operating in the dark."

"Not totally."

"You have information I don't?"

"More like a candle flickering far off. Nothing solid."

"I want reports on anything you get."

"Absolutely, Counselor."

"A thing like this is contagious. First thing you know, some other pervert will start attacking our women. We don't want that to happen, do we, Sergeant?"

"No, sir. Sure don't."

CHAPTER FOURTEEN

I

RUTH DIAMOND EASED THE STATION WAGON into the garage, being particularly careful not to scrape Leo's Cord, and went into the house. The baby-sitter was asleep on the couch. She woke the girl, paid her, and watched her car draw away before checking on the children. Both of them were sound asleep.

In her bedroom, she undressed and lay down in bed. Without Leo next to her, she felt surrounded by vast, threatening spaces. You got used to sleeping with someone, you wanted him to be there. Where was he? Since their wedding day, whenever she needed him most, Leo was absent.

Loneliness was a more constant companion than her husband. Children, a big house, expensive furnishings. Nothing assuaged the emptiness, the sense of being the only one in the world.

Tears came into her eyes. All those people tonight, so cheerful and friendly. She had been an outsider.

What had happened!

There was a time when she had been active, popular, in control of her own fate. She had believed it would go on forever. Captain of the pep squad in high school, valedictorian; a cheerleader in college, prom queen in her senior year. She had dreamed about a stage career, had come to New York and appeared in two off-Broadway plays, one Equity Library Production.

Then it all seemed to grind to a halt. A career became

too much trouble to pursue. The necessary drive was
absent.

Then Leo Diamond materialized. At first all so right.
Her dreams of love and marriage being acted out. Gradually life began to change. After the initial excitement,
pregnancy was a bore, a burden. Nor was raising a child
all that she had been led to believe.

She had tried hard, harder than she supposed she could.
Or at least so she told herself. She vowed to become the
best mother in Manhattan. And later, the best mother in
Arcadia, Connecticut. She cooked, she cleaned, she
shopped.

Slowly, behind the beginning tears, back where the dull
ache always lodged, some remnant of the person she had
been and might have been stirred. Please, God . . .

Slowly, reluctantly, she recognized what was taking
place. Her hand, always the same hand, had drifted between her separated thighs, the fingers stroking absently,
dispatching tiny ripples of sensation into her belly.

Ahhh . . .

She commanded herself to stop. But the need seemed
to grow, her body tingling with desire, tension locking her
joints into place. She rolled onto her stomach, filled with
self-hate, and knowing that nothing else would allow her
to rest.

The fantasy was always the same. She was at a party.
A very crowded, very noisy party. People were drunk and
getting drunker, stoned on grass, floating on unnamed ex-
cesses. She was wearing a long, gossamer-thin skirt made
of green and pink panels, a sheer pink blouse. Men flocked
around hungrily. Their eyes told her what they wanted.

One was bolder than the others. He took her hand,
led her off to a darkened room. Once there he backed
her against a wall, pressed his body against her. She accepted his tongue and then his hands were grasping her
naked breasts and she moaned so that he would know her
desperate need and fulfill it.

She needed to be *touched*.

The stranger's hand plunged under her skirt. How good,

how very good. Her body thrashed about in response, lifted and heaved, caught in spasmodic release.

At last she fell back on the bed, alone, vaguely dissatisfied, sleep a dark, enticing shroud. The garage door brought her instantly awake. She had forgotten to close it, to lock it. Leo's precious collection of old cars would be exposed to the night; he'd be furious. She sat up, silently protesting the effort. She searched for her robe; it was not in its accustomed place across the foot of the bed. She was unable to summon up the energy required to look for it. Naked, she went downstairs.

It was dark in the garage. A bright moon lit the back lawn in ghostly silver. The night air was cold on her skin and she shivered, embraced herself, felt daring, wanton, thought about dancing across the grassy slope in the moonlight. She gave up the idea as silly, childish.

She would close the garage, return to bed, and in the morning make breakfast for the children as she always did. Then there were chores to be done. A list of items Leo wanted purchased. She took a last glance at the moon and turned back to the garage.

A shadow detached itself from between the Alfa Romeo and the Bentley. A shadow hunched and threatening, advancing ominously. For a long moment she refused to believe her eyes. She blinked, certain it was a trick of the night. Then the shadow was within arm's length and there was no longer any doubt. She opened her mouth to scream but before she could a fist crashed into her middle with paralyzing force and all sound died in her throat. Another blow sent her tumbling to the concrete.

He came at her, pushing her down, turning her body into a more compliant position, swearing when she failed to respond immediately. Pain stabbed into her breast as he punched out in frustrated fury.

He placed himself between her legs, and when she resisted, he struck her thigh with a hard fist. She cried out weakly and the muscles went slack. She spread her legs.

"Dirty cunt!"

The faceless voice was honed with the cutting edge of retribution. Here, astride her, the fears of a lifetime, the terrible fantasies and night terrors, all set down between her thighs. As if to protest this terrible intrusion, her mouth opened. He slapped it shut with heavy blows.

"Put it in."

The words were Diamond's. Used by every man she'd ever known. In cars on back roads, on the darkened porches of fraternity houses during beer busts, on the unyielding bench of the football stadium, in the stairwell of the apartment house she had lived in when she first came to New York. *Put it in!*

She obeyed. He felt immense. A throbbing weapon designed to rip and sear and violate. Once again her body was an object of pleasure for somebody else. Never for herself.

"Put it in."

He pounded between the spreading lips, against the tightness, sent chilling pain up into her belly. His fists beat at her shoulders and he called her names she had never before heard. The swollen ferocity ripping at her made her weak and afraid.

He was slamming at her with growing power, grunting, rasping, almost oblivious to her presence, beating her body into submission. His fingers were at her throat, tightening gradually. The closing pressure caused her to gasp and she began to choke.

His body trembled, jerked, and twisted, and she was aware of the full force of his semen spurting into her. Mustering all her strength, she rolled hard, still locked in his killing embrace.

She was on top!

Not thinking, she struck out and made contact. His hands loosened and she broke away, came onto her knees. Hot semen splashed her thighs and she heard him protest at the interruption. He was moving toward her, reaching to complete his attack. She was halfway to her feet and from that position she brought one knee up with all the force she was able to muster. He groaned and fell back.

She fled into the house, slammed the door, threw the bolt. She plunged into the family room, tripped and fell.

Flat on the floor, she dared not move, certain he was coming after her. Certain he meant to kill her.

The children!

She got up, looking wildly around for some weapon. There was nothing. She cursed Leo Diamond as a weakling and a fool, a man who would leave his family defenseless.

Outside there was the sound of running feet. She went to the window and saw him. A graceful figure in the moonlight, moving swiftly. He disappeared onto the access road that bordered the property. Seconds later she heard the sound of a car engine, wheels spinning, and through the trees a flash of movement. He was gone. Shaking uncontrollably, she sank to the floor and this time remained there for a long while.

II

He stood frozen in the darkness of his bedroom, fighting for breath. Each awful beat of his heart rocked his body, threatening to destroy him. Fear scurried along his limbs and he set his sphincter against the rising terror.

"Cunt!" he cried in a muffled voice.

How had it happened? After all his planning. The careful working out of every detail. Every move plotted first. Just like the others. There was no reason for it to go wrong.

She did it. It was her fault, all of it. They were all the same, corrupt and stained, enticing a man until he became so agitated he could find comfort and release only in their despoiled flesh.

A sense of dirtiness took hold and his skin seemed to slither along his bones, prickly, heavy with filth, with the lingering smell of her. God! What if she'd been menstruating, if she'd bled all over him!

He went into the bathroom, tearing off his clothes, desperate to examine himself. No sign of red anywhere. Just the heavy female stink, the rottenness of her insides. He turned on the shower and steam rose up in the tiny room.

He cupped his genitals, fingers exploring the fall of the scrotum, the wrinkled skin, searching for some blemish, some evidence of impending disease. He milked himself; no leakage. He brought his fingers to his face, inhaled. The cavities of his skull filled with the ripe stench of his own sexuality. An anguished cry broke from him and he stepped into the shower.

He slipped on the wet tile, almost fell. He set his feet firmly and allowed the scalding water to burn his skin, turning slowly so that no place remained untouched.

He soaped himself and scrubbed, using the special sponge for that special place. He rinsed and repeated the process. He tried not to think about what had transpired, but was unable to close her out of his mind.

She had spoiled it for him. Destroyed that delicate and feverish instant. Deprived him of that marvelous sense of growing larger than he was, of being consummately powerful and godlike.

She deserved punishment. Suffering. Pain. His groin throbbed where her knee had landed and he cursed her name.

He stepped out of the shower and using an aerosol can covered his pubic area with white foam. Very carefully he shaved, cleaning away all traces of her.

He returned to the shower. Had she recognized him? Even in the dark, it was possible. What if she informed the police? He concentrated fiercely, launching his thought through the space that separated them to her brain. Silently he conveyed to her the inevitable retribution that must descend upon an informer. Eternal damnation. Death.

He reassured himself. Nothing could touch him for he existed within a magical protective cocoon that kept away all danger. He was unlike other men. Smarter. More creative. Stronger. He functioned outside the normal guidelines of human behavior. Above the petty restrictions that most men surrendered to.

He patted himself dry. Sprinkled powder and sprayed cologne. He studied himself in the long glass. The hairless look of his groin was strange but immensely pleasant to behold. Made him feel young again, innocent.

He dressed in his usual manner and studied himself again in the mirror. The face and figure that he saw were those of a normal person. Ordinariness was what he chose to display. No hint of the special person he was. Pleased with himself, he left to do what he was expected to do. To fulfill his obligations.

III

Loukas drove Sandy Felton home. He parked, left the motor running, his hands tight on the wheel.

She studied him. The high-bridged profile, the smooth olive cheeks, the clean line of his jaw. She liked what she saw. Rugged, but without the swaggering look of a jock. Not pretty, he was the sort who looked better as time went on.

"We keep bumping into each other," she offered.

"It's okay with me." He avoided looking at her.

She tried to recall when last she had known a man who was shy with women. No one came to mind. "It's okay with me, too, Theo."

"I almost didn't go," he said.

"Why not?"

"Oh. It's not my league, those people. I'm a ham-sandwich-and-beer guy myself. Tonight was a whole other ball game."

"You did pretty well for yourself, I'm sure." She smiled at him and he looked away quickly. "You're not one of these blue-collar snobs, are you, Theo?"

"I don't understand."

"Not everybody is lucky enough to be born poor or brought up working class, you know."

"You're kidding me."

"Only a little. I watch TV sometimes, I eat sandwiches, and I love a nice glass of cold beer."

"Yeah?" he said dubiously.

"Yeah." She grinned. "So what're you going to do about it?"

"Well," he said without haste, "there's a place over at the beach—Jerry's Pool Hall. Mostly it's for drinking but Jerry makes pretty good chili."

"I like chili."

"You do! Well, some nights there's a piano player and guys stand around and sing a little bit."

"Are you one of them, Theo?"

"I'm not much of a singer."

"I bet you're great."

"No, no." He laughed sheepishly. "I'm really not." He grew sober. "Maybe you'd like to pay a visit to Jerry's some night?"

"Are you inviting me?"

"Well, yes. Sure."

"I would be honored to visit Jerry's with you and eat some chili and drink beer and maybe sing a little. Do they let women sing at Jerry's?"

"Come to think of it, I never heard of a lady singing. But I guess nobody'd mind."

"We'll have to see about the singing."

"When do you want to go?" he said anxiously.

She touched his hand lightly. "Why don't you call me?"

"You're sure?"

"Oh, yes, I'm sure."

"I'll give you a ring soon," he answered quietly.

He waited until she was inside the house before driving away. Back home, he phoned the Fort. Clay Simmons, a new man, was on the desk.

"What's going on?" Loukas said.

"Break-ins, Sarge. The usual drunks, a couple of car crashes. Oh, and one good citizen decided to be a hero."

"What was that all about?"

"Seems like Toohey Smith was sleeping off one of his drunks and this citizen spotted him. Toohey gets scared and takes off with the citizen on his tail. Toohey got knocked around a little bit and the citizen called in and said he'd caught the rapist."

"Is Toohey okay?"

"Sleeping like a baby in the cage. You should've seen the citizen, Sarge. Came in like a puffed-up bantam rooster. Went out like a pricked balloon."

"Give Toohey some coffee in the morning. He takes it black."

"Right, Sarge. Good night."

Loukas took a cold can of Miller to bed and lay in the dark sipping it, going over his talk with Victor Fellows, the people he'd met, the paintings he'd looked at. But mostly he thought about Sandy Felton.

Part Seven

CHAPTER FIFTEEN

I

LOUKAS INSPECTED RUTH DIAMOND OPENLY. He didn't want to miss a thing.

There was the same incredulousness, the inability to accept the evidence of his own senses. If he'd seen her at Pauline Fellows' the previous evening, he could not recall. In any case, she would have looked dramatically different.

Now her face was swollen and discolored, her upper lip cut and bloated out of shape, blood-crusted. One eye was partially closed and her hair was uncombed. In a flannel robe and pink slippers, toes pointed inward, knees pressed together, she represented human defeat.

At the far end of the long living room, Leo Diamond stationed himself behind an oversized easy chair. He was paler than usual, and his red hair flared wildly out from his narrow head. The washed-blue eyes were never still, as if seeking a familiar landmark in a strange and threatening terrain.

Loukas, his features arranged in an officially unyielding mask, leaned toward Ruth Diamond. He felt a rising desire to find the man responsible for these crimes, a compulsion to catch and personally punish him. Disturbed by the dissolution of his professional objectivity, Loukas made himself remain calm. Objective.

"Mrs. Diamond," he said, "it's necessary to ask some questions."

If she heard, she gave no sign.

"I know what you've been through," Loukas said, and instantly recognized his error. Ruth Diamond drove it home. Her words were chosen to damage, spoken stridently.

"To have my body *penetrated*. No man knows! I am consumed by . . . hatred."

A vein in her forehead, a vertical blue line from brow to hairline, pulsed fiercely. A thick, wordless lament ripped past the swollen lips and she bent her head again, concealing her grief.

Loukas persisted. "You're our only lead, Mrs. Diamond. There's every reason to believe the man who did this to you also killed three other women. Help me find him before he does it again."

The silence that followed was broken only by her rasping efforts not to cry, to be strong in front of her husband. Finally she lifted her head and said, "Ask your questions, please."

"You saw the man?"

"He was all over me."

"I mean, were you able to make out his face?"

"It was too dark."

"There was a moon."

"It happened in the garage."

"Where did he come from?"

She made a face. "I don't know."

"From outside?"

"I . . . don't think so."

"He was already in the garage when you got there?"

"Yes. I think so. He must have been."

"But you were in the garage earlier, when you arrived home from Mrs. Fellows'?"

"Yes."

"You heard nothing then? Saw no one?"

"Nothing. No one."

"He could have come in after Ruth went upstairs," Diamond said. "He must have been lurking around outside, waiting."

"That's probably how it happened," Loukas answered, not looking at Diamond. "So he was inside. Okay. Where did he conceal himself?"

"I don't know. Behind the cars, it seems logical."

"I collect antique cars," Diamond explained. "And we have two more for everyday use."

"Do you usually leave the garage open at night, Mrs. Diamond?

She felt the anger rise again. More than anger, resentment and rage directed toward Loukas. Toward Leo for failing to protect her, for making her feel guilty about the garage door.

"We always close the doors," Diamond said. "Dogs come in otherwise and knock over the garbage cans. There have been raccoons—"

"I went right to bed," Ruth said tonelessly. "I was tired. I forgot about the doors. I was almost asleep when I remembered."

"How could he have known my wife would come back down?" Diamond said.

Loukas lifted his eyes. "If he'd been watching the house, studying your habits . . . He knew the door would be closed, that it was your custom. Or else he was prepared to wait until morning."

Tom Petersen, from his place near the entrance, spoke. "Oh, he's good, really good. He knows his job."

"Maybe he's not so good," Loukas said. He swung back to Ruth Diamond. "You were naked, you said?"

Guilt returned and a full measure of shame. Perhaps she had been to blame, the way she had manipulated her own body earlier. Somehow the lurking stranger must have sensed her need, been aroused by it, come to her as punishment and reward.

"My wife was in bed," Diamond put in peevishly. "It was late. She had no reason to believe—"

Loukas cut him off with a short gesture. "Of course. Now, Mrs. Diamond, what did he look like?"

"It happened so quickly."

"He came at you from behind a car?"

"I . . . think . . . so"

"And then?"

"I seem to recall hearing a sound. I turned and he hit me. In my stomach. It hurt and I couldn't breathe. It still hurts."

"I'm sorry," Loukas said. "What did he do next?"

"He hit me again. I fell down."

"Can you tell me something about his build? Was he a big man? Tall?"

"It's difficult to say."

"As big as Detective Petersen? Or built like your husband? Was he my height?" Loukas stood up.

She glanced at each of the men. "I don't know."

"Approximately?"

She shook her head.

Loukas sat down. Bad feelings swirled around inside him. He was going to come up empty again. His prize witness was a dud. She had never had a chance to see anything. Struck down without warning, she had been hurt, frightened, stunned. The man had gone before she was able to function normally again.

"All right," he said. "He knocked you down. What happened then?"

"He raped me," she rasped.

Loukas gave her no additional time. "Did he have a weapon?"

"A weapon! No, I don't think so. I didn't see anything."

"How many times did he hit you?"

"I don't know."

"During the sexual assault itself, did he strike you?"

"What? What do you mean?"

"Did he hit you while he was having intercourse with you?"

She screamed at him, half out of her chair, "We did not have intercourse! I was raped! Raped, raped." She fell back, sobbing.

Diamond took a step in her direction. Loukas stopped him with a raised hand.

"You were afraid," Loukas said. "Rightly afraid. The man had killed and intended to kill you."

She looked up. "I want to die."

"Did he say anything to you?"

"What?"

"Did he speak at all?"

She nodded once.

"What was his voice like?"

"What?"

"Was it a baritone? A tenor? Did he speak with any kind of accent? A drawl? A lisp? Anything at all?"

"I don't think so. No accent. Shrill, I'd say. But whispery, too. Oh, I can't be certain."

'What were his exact words?"

"What good is all this going to do?" she said. "He did it to me. It's over. You'll never find him."

"With your help, we may. We have to try. Otherwise—"

She sat straighter "I'll try, too. What was your question?" She seemed more secure, as if she had assumed new and stronger controls over herself.

"His exact words?"

"You can't expect my wife to remember," Diamond said aggressively.

"Shut up, Leo," she said without turning. "Just keep your mouth shut." Then, to Loukas, "He said I was . . . a . . . dirty *cunt.*"

"I see."

"That was all I was to him, a cunt. The rest of me didn't exist. No other part of my body. Not my brains or my feelings. Nothing but that one thing."

"Anything else?"

She looked at him without comprehension.

"Did he say anything else?"

"Oh. Yes. He said, 'Put it in.' "

"Jesus!" Diamond said.

"And?" Loukas said, barely loud enough for her to hear.

She seemed surprised. "Why, I put it in, of course. What else could I do?"

"Oh, Jesus," Diamond said, making it a lingering groan.

"I was very afraid," Ruth said.

"Did he say anything else?"

"He cursed me. As if it was my fault . . . as if I had forced him to do it. It was not my doing!" Her voice rose.

"No," Loukas said. "Of course not." Loukas gathered his resolve, spoke in a clear, commanding voice. "There are details I have to know, Mrs. Diamond."

"Let my wife alone," Diamond said. "You can see the condition she's in."

Loukas spoke only to Ruth Diamond. "All right. He knocked you down, forced your legs apart, ordered you . . . He made a complete entry?"

"Why do you have to ask that?" Diamond cried.

"He was inside me," Ruth replied deliberately. "All the way inside. He was doing it to me."

"He assumed the dominant position?"

"What?"

"He was on top?"

"Yes. On top."

"He was inside you, lying between your legs."

"Yes."

"Mrs. Diamond, where were his hands?"

"His hands?"

"Was he holding you? Embracing you? Were his hands on your arms? At your waist? Holding your . . . backside?" Loukas fought back a spreading disgust.

"You have no right!" Diamond screamed, his face livid. "No right at all! I want you to leave."

Ruth allowed her mind to reach back. "No, it wasn't like that. No embrace. No holding. He was beating at me, my shoulders, my chest. Damage was what he wanted to do to me. His hands went to my throat."

"He took your throat in his hands?"

"He began to choke me. I remembered those other women. I was so afraid."

"Go on."

"I moved. I think I got onto my side somehow. I kept moving and suddenly I was on top."

"He released you?"

"Not right away. No, not right away. I think I hit him."

"In the face?"

"I can't be sure. I just struck out."

"Then what did you do?"

"I kicked him with my knee. I would have done anything to get away."

"And then?"

"I ran into the house."

"He came after you?"

"No. No. I don't think he even tried."

"You locked the door behind you?" Petersen said.

"I locked it."

"What did you do then, Mrs. Diamond?"

"Do? Why, I cried. I lay on the floor and cried."

"Okay," Loukas said. "He didn't try to get in the house."

"He went away."

"How could you be sure?" Petersen said.

"I heard him running. On the gravel driveway. I went to the window and I was able to see him."

"You saw him in the moonlight?" Loukas said hopefully.

"He looked evil and ghostly in that light. His face was a round white blob."

"You're sure?" Petersen said. "He wasn't black?"

"I'm sure."

"We have to explore every possible avenue," Loukas said. "There's an identification process called a photo kit. If you could recall what you remember about this man's face—his mouth, his nose, his eyebrows—from parts the police artist will show you, then all the parts can be worked together until a composite is formed. Can you do that for us. Mrs. Diamond?"

"I'll try."

"He was running," Petersen said. "Which direction?"

"Toward Old Country Road."

"Were you able to see a car?"

"You can't see the road from the house," Diamond said.

"I heard it," Ruth said.

"Describe what you heard," Loukas said.

"A loud sound . . . I remember, I thought that he'd wake up the neighborhood."

"Like a racing car?" Petersen said. "As if the muffler had been removed?"

She considered that. "No. Not like that. Just loud, full of thumps and cracks."

"Backfiring," Loukas said.

"Timing needs adjustment," Diamond said knowledgeably. "An old car, most likely."

"Is there anything else?" Loukas said.

Ruth Diamond shook her head.

"We'll have to get a statement," Loukas said. "If you could come down to Headquarters later today—"

"You mean I have to go through it all again?"

"Give us a call first and I'll have the artist on hand. Save you a trip that way."

II

When they were alone, Diamond stationed himself opposite his wife. He inspected her as if seeing her for the first time.

"You're staring," she said presently.

"I'm looking at you."

"Nothing's changed," she said defensively. "I'm the same."

"Don't be ridiculous."

She hung her head.

"Can I do anything for you? Get you something?"

"Nothing. I just want to forget it."

"How do you feel?"

She glared in his direction, at a point past his left ear. "Rotten."

"The doctor said you weren't hurt badly. Nothing's broken."

"He reached inside of me. How could such a thing happen to me?"

Diamond conjured up an image of Ruth lying under another man. He strained to see the expression on her face, to hear her voice. A shudder wrenched his lean frame. "The doctor said . . . he said you'd be all right down there."

"I'll never be all right."

"He said that should you contract a venereal disease, not to worry. It can be treated."

"The doctor . . ." She shivered. Why the guilt? she asked herself. Why the shame? The sense of personal wrongdoing. She had not invited that man to enter her. Had not sought him out. Had never desired him.

I've done nothing wrong!

Her husband was asking for attention, saying her name, speaking. She turned back into the present. "It would be too much to hope you were wearing your diaphragm."

She stared at him uncomprehendingly. "I wasn't expecting to be *fucked!*" she yelled.

"I know *that.*"

"You weren't here. And I didn't invite him in."

"I only meant—"

"I know what you meant. You should have been here, Leo! You should have been at home with me. With *me.* It wouldn't have happened."

"I see. It's my fault."

"A husband should be with his wife."

"Next time you'll remember to lock the garage door."

"It's human to forget."

"Maybe if you didn't run around bare-assed none of this would have happened. Did you see the expression on that cop's face when you told him? Coming downstairs with nothing on, a woman your age."

"You bastard!"

"There's a word for women who show their bodies off."

She stood up, glaring. "He was going to kill me."

"But he didn't. Four times he's raped and you are the only one he let off. Why, Ruth? Were you such a good lay? Did you give him something the other women didn't?"

"I hate you, Leo! I've hated you for a long time."

"Did you invite him back for seconds?"

"I fought him off."

"Sure, *after* he screwed you. Maybe you should have fought harder before you put him in."

"I was raped!" Her voice was shrill. "I didn't do anything wrong."

"Not the way I heard it."

A low wail broke out of her and she fled the room.

III

The First Selectman's secretary brought them coffee in paper cups and a selection of breakfast pastries. They helped themselves.

Loukas stared at his coffee. He hated coffee in paper cups. He tried to imagine how many gallons of bad coffee he had drunk out of paper cups in the last year. Hundreds of gallons, he told himself.

"Had another call from the governor this morning," the First Selectman said. "He's bucking for the White House, all right, and coming down pretty heavy on me. Says either we wind things up in a hurry or he'll declare a state of emergency. Move the state cops in."

Wakeman swore. "He can't do that, can he, Victor?"

Victor Fellows fingered the knot of his paisley tie. "He can do it, but he won't. Home rule is too big an issue in New England. He's too politically shrewd to alienate half the voters in the party. No, he won't do that. The point is, he'll find some other way to deal himself in unless we make an arrest soon."

"We're giving it our best effort," Wakeman said. "Aren't we giving it our best effort, Captain Henderson?"

"Positively our best effort," Henderson growled.

"We could put extra men on the job," the First Selectman said hopefully.

Henderson kept his long face still. "Where do they come from? The entire force is doing double shifts now. Calls are up by nearly forty percent. Every time the wind blows, some citizen calls in. We send a car. You want to let everything else slide by?"

"Not at all," the First Selectman said heartily. "We must maintain the appearance of normalcy. Town's getting a bad name. Jokes are being made—Johnny Carson called us the Rape Capital of New England last night."

"We need an arrest," Victor Fellows said.

The First Selectman puffed himself up. "People come to Arcadia for peace and quiet. I mean, they leave the city to get away from violence and crime. They don't want to be afraid. Isn't that so, gentlemen?"

Victor Fellows spoke firmly. "It is our responsibility to put an end to this outbreak."

"Very well put, Victor," the First Selectman said, wishing he had said it. "The point is, every citizen has to help, do his share."

"My own feeling is it's an outsider," Wakeman said. "Okay, not a transient. But someone from one of the surrounding towns."

"Norwalk most likely," the First Selectman said. "We all know the kind of people they've got over there."

"You're wrong," said Loukas. "He's one of us; he lives here. He moves around freely. He probably went to school here, works here."

"If you're so sure of that," the First Selectman said aggressively, "why can't you catch him?"

"Because he's practically indistinguishable from the rest of us, for one thing. He thinks the way we do, he acts the way we do, he looks like us. White and polite. No visible scars."

"That doesn't get us closer to the man who did it," Victor Fellows said.

"There must be somebody we can pin it on," the First Selectman said.

"Pin it?" Loukas said.

"A figure of speech," Wakeman said. "The First Selectman means we better find the guilty man and soon. I feel exactly the same way."

Victor Fellows crossed his legs, smoothed his sharply creased gray worsted trousers. "My doubts about the delivery boy have never been completely satisfied."

"Reiser," Henderson said.

"What do you think, Theo?" Wakeman said.

"Certain things point to Virgil," Loukas conceded. "Opportunity, certainly. Access to all the women involved. He seems to fit the psychological profile. But—"

"But?" the First Selectman pressed.

"No concrete evidence. I have a hunch Virgil didn't do it."

Fellows said, "My hunch is Virgil is our best bet. Under pressure, he'll crack wide open."

Wakeman agreed. "Why not do a hard job on him? Move him around to the crime scenes, confront Mrs. Diamond. Scare the pants off him."

"Am I being ordered to arrest Virgil?" Loukas said without expression.

"If he's guilty . . ." the First Selectman said.

"Let's give him a little tossing around," Wakeman said.

"If he's innocent?" Loukas said.

Victor Fellows leaned forward, his rugged face open and sincere. "Then he'll be cleared. I have no desire to prosecute an innocent man."

Loukas looked over at Henderson and he turned away. Loukas stood up. "I won't do it."

"We have to do something," the First Selectman cried.

"Bring Reiser in," Wakeman commanded.

Loukas placed his detective's gold shield on the massive desk and slid it toward the Chief.

"You do it."

"Dammit, Theo," said Henderson, "put the tin back in your pocket. This is your case. Theo runs it his way or you can take my shield too."

"My goodness," Wakeman said, rocking his head in disbelief. "Everybody's getting awful touchy. No need for temperament. We all want the same result, don't we?"

Minutes later, the meeting was terminated. And an hour after that a call came into the Bureau. Tom Petersen answered. He listened, dropped the phone back into its cradle.

"Theo," he said in an almost musical voice, "this time we really got a winner."

Loukas waited for him to go on.

"It's Judith May."

"The actress?"

"She's dead. Sounds like another rape."

"Sweet Jesus." Loukas took his pistol out of the desk drawer, snapped it onto his belt. "That'll put us on the network news for sure tonight."

IV

Even in distress, Emmett May presented an almost boyish figure. His face, evenly tanned, remained unlined and handsome.

A maid served coffee in a small sunlit room. Loukas sat in a Mexican leather-and-wood chair that squeaked whenever he moved and waited for the actor to speak.

"Judith and I were very close." There was a suggestion of grief in the resonant voice, grief held back for the sake of appearances. "She was my third wife, you know."

"I didn't know that," Loukas said.

"Oh, yes. I was married twice before I was twenty-two and divorced as many times. I never expected to get married again. But Judith came along, gave me real happiness. I loved her dearly. She loved me."

"You found her body?"

"I was on my way into New York. I intended to stay for a couple of days. A number of voice-overs. I had to cancel them all."

"You were driving away when you saw her?"

"Mark was doing the driving."

"Mark?"

"My oldest son, by my first marriage. He lives with us. And there she was. Off to the side, behind the hedges. Mark spotted her bike, you see."

"In understand Mrs. May did a great deal of bicycling."

"Judith loved exercise. Both of us do. Actors must stay in condition. Judith rode, took dance classes, played tennis. I can't believe she's gone."

"Mark saw the bike. He stopped the car. What next?"

"We got out and looked around. I saw Judith first. I thought she might have fallen, injured herself. I was going to carry her back to the house. I told Mark to phone for a doctor. There's a phone in the car. Then I realized that Judith was dead."

"What made you realize that, Mr. May?"

"No vital signs. No breath. No pulse."

"Then what?"

"I placed her back down on the grass."

"Did you know that she'd been assaulted?"

"Not at first. The reality of her death was difficult enough to digest. The other, what difference does it make?"

"But you did come to realize it?"

"Yes, of course. She was naked under her skirt. Judith was a very proper lady. Careful to present a suitable image."

"Do you have any idea who might have done this to your wife?"

"The same madman who has killed those other poor women."

Abner Posner appeared in the doorway. Loukas excused himself, walked into the adjoining room with the doctor. "What have you got for me, Abner?"

"Probably rape."

"Probably?"

"Well, I'm sure of one thing, Theo. She's dead."

"No jokes today, Abner."

"As near as I can tell it was a one-punch job. A single blow to the jaw. Snapped back her head, broke her neck."

"Very nice."

"The autopsy will confirm it all, I'm sure." Posner tugged at his long nose. "She wasn't beaten like the others, Theo."

"Strangled?"

"No indications."

"No finger marks?"

"Nary a one."

"Abner, you're complicating my life."

"Don't tell me your troubles, Theo. You should never have become a cop; you don't have the emotional set for it."

"It's a little late to change my job classification. Get that lab report over to me as soon as you can."

Loukas went back to Emmett May. The actor smiled sadly. "Some more coffee, Sergeant?"

Loukas kept his eyes on May's face. "With all due respect, Mr. May, did you wife have a friend?"

"A friend? My wife had hundreds of friends. She liked people, people liked her."

"A lover, Mr. May?"

A cold expression crossed May's handsome features. "Judith and I were very much in love, I told you that. There was no one else for either of us. Judith was killed just like those other women."

"I understand." Loukas felt uneasy. At first glance everything seemed as it should be, but faintly sour notes were sounding. "We still have to find this murderer." The actor didn't reply and Loukas stood up. "Thank you for talking to me, Mr. May."

"You'll keep me informed?"

"You'll be hearing from us."

Loukas found Petersen waiting at the car. "What did you find out?" he said when they were on the road.

"Nothing," Petersen said. "The servants, everybody, walk on eggs around here."

Loukas swore under his breath. "It's contagious."

"What, Theo?"

"Our guy had nothing to do with this one."

"Are you sure?"

"Somebody was sore as hell at Judith May, killed her with one good belt. This was an explosion, somebody with a grudge."

"The question is who?"

Loukas answered matter-of-factly. "Somebody who knew her. Somebody who knew her pretty damned well."

CHAPTER SIXTEEN

I

TED KEARNEY HUNCHED over the piano, head following his fingers on the keyboard with feverish intensity. Around him, five men were singing "Sweet Rosie O'Grady," oblivious to the click of pool balls up front and to the sounds of talk and laughter from the rear. By the time Loukas and Sandy Felton were settled in the last booth on the right, Kearney had begun a medley of George M. Cohan songs.

"I've lived in Arcadia for so long," Sandy said, "and never heard about this place. It's nice."

"A joint for working stiffs."

"Don't be a snob, Loukas."

A waitress came over and Loukas ordered two Millers and a bowl of chick-peas to nibble on. "It's a place to watch a football game on Sunday afternoon, to talk."

"What about the blue laws?" she said.

"Ah, who'd make a complaint against Jerry!"

She grinned mockingly. "So Sergeant Loukas decides which laws to enforce, does he?"

He answered solemnly, "Judgment is a very important factor in effective police work."

Her head went back as she laughed, the soft sweater she was wearing stretching tight across her breasts. It was clear to Loukas that she wore no brassiere and he didn't know whether to be pleased or disappointed. She was unlike any woman he had ever known. Her background was foreign, and he wasn't convinced there was

any constructive reason for them to be together. Still,
being with her made him feel good.

"It's strange," she said. "I've never known a cop
before."

"We're no different from anybody else."

"Other people aren't walking around with guns on their
belts."

"I never used it. Not much call for that kind of action
in Arcadia."

"Until now."

"We're going to catch him."

"When?" He looked away and she touched his hand,
bringing his eyes back to her face. "Ah, Theo, don't let
me be hard on you. You're doing your best, I know that.
But it's scary. We're all scared. The house creaks at night
the way it always creaked and I jump. When that happens
now, there's no sleeping for the rest of the night."

"This won't last forever. Arcadia's still a good place
to live."

She detected the hurt in his voice and tried to change
the subject. "It's the times we live in. Craziness everywhere. Tell me what it's like to be a cop. Police work
seems very exotic to us ordinary citizens. Do you go
around collecting clues? Picking up dust in glassine en-
velopes and making casts of tire tracks?"

"The specialists do that. Anyway, I'm just a displaced
traffic cop. I hate this crummy business we got going
now."

"What are you looking for?"

"Nothing in particular. Just trying to see what there
is to see. You go someplace, you leave a piece of yourself behind. Everybody does. The trick is to recognize
that piece, put it together with the perpetrator."

"Perpetrator," she echoed. "You sound like one of
those cops being interviewed on the six o'clock news."

"It's the job." He sighed. "The jargon. Most cops are
afraid of sounding like they're illiterates, which they
almost are. You keep hanging around lawyers, court-
rooms, getting flyers from the F.B.I. You try too hard.

The way most cops talk, you couldn't have them saying
those words on the television."

"I know all the words."

"Everybody does, I guess. But nobody wants to admit
it in public."

"You like being a cop, don't you?"

"I guess I must. I've been one for a long time. But now
I don't know. I hate this case, what it's doing to the
town. I've been thinking about early retirement."

"But what would you do?"

"Move down to North Carolina, maybe. My brother
lives there. Maybe play some golf, just sit around. Lately
I've been thinking about one of the Florida Keys, where
there's not so many people. When I'm too far away from
the water, I get a little nervous."

"That's because you're a Greek."

"You think so?"

"Greeks have always been seafaring people."

"I'm not exactly a great sailor. But I like to throw
a line in once in a while."

"It sounds nice to me."

"Come along," he said casually.

"Is that an invitation?"

"It's something to think about," he said seriously.

"Theo, Theo, you don't know me at all."

"Well, you might like living on the Keys, lots of sun-
shine, easy living."

"I'm not an easy person to get along with."

"Nobody is."

"You wouldn't be a problem for a woman."

"I've got my share of bad habits."

She produced a loud, clear laugh, face shining in the
semi-darkness. "I'll tell you my bad habits if you tell
me yours."

"All right," he said, meaning it.

She studied him, shook her head. "No way, Loukas.
That's a deal bound to lose ground for me. I think I'll
let you find out about me for yourself."

"I think you're a special lady," he said.

"Ah," she said, reaching across the table, touching his cheek lightly. "That's nice, Theo. It really is."

II

It was barely past midnight when Carl Johnson, a tightly knit black man of medium height, walked into Police Headquarters. He brushed snow off his mackinaw and slapped a red watch cap against his leg. He had warm eyes and seemed ready to smile, a pleasant-looking man with a narrow head and regular features. The night manager of the Hamburg Delight on Main Street, he sometimes made deliveries to the Fort himself. Ten years before, Johnson had been a pretty good high-school halfback in Norwalk. He was a friendly man, easy to talk to, and well known to everyone around the Fort.

Andy Raines, the Desk Officer, was taking a report from a prowl car when Johnson appeared. He waved a hand in greeting, completed the call.

"Hey, Carl, how about this snow!" He picked up the telephone, dialed. "Simmons ran his car into a snowbank. He's stuck. Got to get him a tow. Be with you in a minute, Carl."

"Take your time."

The call completed, Andy swung around to face Johnson. "Business slow? Bet it is on a night like this. People stay close to home."

"I closed up the place."

"Wish I could here. Hardly anything going on all night."

"Who is handling the May case, Andy?"

"That's Loukas, Carl. He's become the resident authority on rape. That Mrs. May was one good-looking woman, I'd say. Saw her one time over at McAnally's Hardware."

Carl Johnson spoke in a subdued voice. "Might be a good idea to get in touch with Loukas, Andy."

"Why should I do that, Carl? It's practically the middle of the night."

"He'll want to know."

"Know what?"

"That you've got Judith May's murderer down here."

The officer's eyes widened. "You mean what I think you mean, Carl?"

"I killed her, Andy."

Raines jumped up, his finger pointing. "Carl, you just stand there. You hear me!" He started to reach for his pistol, changed his mind. "No trouble, Carl. Just don't make an unnecessary move."

Johnson smiled. "Take your time, Andy. I'm not about to go anywhere."

CHAPTER SEVENTEEN

I

BY SIX IN THE MORNING the snow had stopped falling. The main roads were cleared by ten, but an abrupt temperature drop caused an icy veneer and driving was hazardous and slow. Commuter trains ran late and five of them were canceled. At eleven-forty, a power line heavy with accumulated ice tore loose, cutting off electricity from more than two hundred homes in Arcadia. The offices of Southern New England Power & Light were inundated with complaints.

Power remained off in some homes for nearly seventy-two hours. In seventeen of those houses water froze in the pipes; when the thaw set in the pipes would burst. Four hot-water systems were ruined and had to be completely replaced and nearly 30 percent of the basements were flooded.

Loukas was personally concerned with none of that. His house stood on a low hill and the drainage had always been excellent. The power remained on and the heating system never faltered.

He spent most of the night at the Fort talking to Carl Johnson, getting his confession on paper and signed. At intervals, he made Johnson repeat his story, but was able to find no discrepancies in it, no contradictions. Johnson revealed details of a relationship with Judith May that could not have been fabricated and much of his story would be easy to confirm. Satisfied there was nothing more to do, Loukas went home and was back in bed by five-fifteen and asleep minutes later.

SECRETS

At eight o'clock the telephone jarred him awake. He shaved and showered before returning to the Fort, arriving a little after nine at Captain Henderson's office. Victor Fellows and Emmett May were present.

Both men seemed well rested, though the actor's eyes were concealed behind large dark glasses. It occurred to Loukas that Victor Fellows was even better-looking than the actor. He was younger, of course, slightly taller, and his cheeks glowed with good health. Loukas shook hands with each of them and sat down.

Henderson was just hanging up the phone. "That was Wakeman," he said. "The Chief is accepting congratulations."

"Because of Johnson?" Loukas said, and at once his ulcer began to act up. He swore at the doctor. It *was* an ulcer, growing larger every day, devouring his stomach. He was going to need an operation. His knees grew weak at the thought of being cut open.

"We got a collar," Henderson grumped. "The Chief's scheduled a press conference for eleven o'clock. You're invited, Mr. Fellows."

Fellows drew down his smooth brow. "My understanding was that I'd handle the press."

"Take it up with the Chief."

"I will."

"Wasn't much of a collar," Loukas said, barely audible. "The man came in and gave himself up. Hardly got the chance to play Sherlock Holmes."

"The Chief," Henderson said sourly, "holds that the Department has solved our recent crime wave."

"He thinks Johnson did them all?"

"That's what the man said."

Loukas grunted, the muted sound of disbelief.

"I'll tell you gentlemen one thing," Emmett May said, voice hoarse with anguish but sincere and forceful, "Carl Johnson is playing his own game. Perhaps he killed those other women, but he very clearly did not murder my wife."

"How do you know that, Mr. May?" asked Loukas without looking at the actor.

Said May, "My wife and I were very much in love. She was not unfaithful to me. Not ever in all the years we were married. Nor I to her. Surely you don't believe that a woman like Judith May would be consorting with a black short-order cook."

"I've read the confession," Henderson said. "Lots of details."

Loukas pressed the heel of his hand against his stomach. "Carl's a pretty nice-looking fellow," he said. "Young, vigorous."

May displayed compassion. "I don't think you men fully realize how Judith and I lived. In our world, in the theater and television and films, physical beauty is not uncommon. Some people might say that I am not without a certain masculine appeal."

"Women," Loukas said, swallowing bile. "They don't always do what a man expects them to do."

"You're willing to accept that man's story, Sergeant?"

"I am."

"Well, I am not." May's face grew hard, rosettes of pink and white alternately appeared at his jawline as he clenched his teeth. "It's clear that I'm dealing with a collection of fools."

Resentment collected in Loukas; he set himself against it.

"The man confessed," Victor Fellows said. "We have no reason to doubt the confession."

"My wife," Emmett May replied tersely, "was not unfaithful."

Henderson shifted around in his chair. "Carl claims it was going on for a long time. Couple of years."

"Nonsense."

Loukas raised his eyes. "Under Mrs. May's right breast, did she have any kind of a mark?"

May laughed, but it was contrived and late in coming. "Possibly Johnson saw Judith in a bathing costume. She looked marvelous in a bikini."

"Where would he have seen her?" Loukas said.

"How would I know?"

"Was he a guest at your pool? Was he welcomed as

a friend in the houses of your friends? Did Mrs. May ever patronize the public beach?"

"I cannot be expected to account for every detail—"

Loukas yearned to return to bed, to sleep. "Mrs. May had a scar," he said.

"I do not have to listen to this," May said.

"On the right buttock," Loukas continued. "The result of a boil when she was a young girl. Is that right?"

"I am not going to allow this man to destroy my wife's name."

"The M.E. confirms," Loukas said. "A liver mark about the size of a quarter under her breast. Johnson described the shape and color perfectly. And the boil scar."

"This is all some horrible kind of mistake."

"Carl Johnson and your wife were sleeping together for two years," Loukas said harshly. "They met at his apartment in Norwalk in the afternoons. Four days ago they had a fight. She wanted to end it, he didn't. She walked out, said she'd met another man."

"No," May said.

"Another man," Loukas said again. "He's over in Redding. A construction worker. Twenty-two years old. White, which might make you feel better. I talked to him last night. He confirms Johnson's story."

"Pure fantasy."

"Carl wanted to patch it up with Mrs. May. Yesterday he went up to your house to try to talk her into resuming their relationship. She was out bike riding. He waited in the bushes for her return. He grabbed her. She laughed at him, insulted his sexual abilities. That's something that gets all of us, I guess."

May produced a clumsy laugh. "What we have here is the sexual fantasy of a poor, misguided black man. Spent his entire life dreaming about making love to someone like Judith May. Here was his chance to make all his friends think that he had a movie star. Can't you see how it all fits?"

"Sorry," Loukas said. "Carl lost his temper. He dragged Mrs. May into the brush. She fought back. He hit her. Just once. Carl is a pretty tough guy, good with his fists. Fought professionally for seven years or so. He didn't realize that she was dead and he had sex with her. Only when he couldn't bring her around did he realize what he'd done. He panicked and ran. Last night it got to be too much for him to handle and he turned himself in."

May was on his feet, backing toward the door. "I will not allow my wife's name to be sullied. I will hire the best private detective agency in the country, the best lawyers. They will get at the truth. Let's get it all into the open, why you people are determined to damage my wife's memory."

After he was gone, Henderson spoke first. "You were pretty rough on the guy, Theo."

"Crap. All May cares about is his own precious image."

Victor Fellows said, "Could he be right? Did Carl make it all up?"

"No."

"Has he confessed the other killings?"

"He isn't going to," Loukas said. "He had nothing to do with them."

"I'd like to talk to him. Maybe I can get him to open up."

"You really mean to make a score," Loukas said.

"Take it easy," Henderson said.

Victor Fellows smiled thinly. "Some of us handle pressure better than others."

Loukas pushed himself erect.

"Where do you think you're going?" Henderson said, but not abrasively.

"Home. To get some sleep."

II

The telephone rang and Emmett May shivered, as if under attack. He stared at the instrument warily before lifting it to his ear.

"Yes . . ."

"I waited until it was almost dark; you didn't come."
There was a petulant complaint in Jeanine's voice. "What
is going on, Emmett? I don't like being stood up."

"Don't you know?" he said. "About Judith, I mean?"

"I read about it. I'm sorry for her. But it doesn't
change a thing."

"What a cold bitch you are."

"Look here, Emmett, you'd better put a check on that
tongue of yours, I'm warning you."

Suddenly he wanted to be rid of her, to end this conversation. "I'll meet you tomorrow. Same time, same
place."

"That's better. There's just one thing."

An anticipatory fear seeped into his middle and he
felt chilled and lonely. "What do you mean?"

"You know how things are," she was saying. "It gets
more and more difficult to maintain a decent level of
existence. There is going to have to be an upward adjustment in our financial arrangement."

"That's crazy. A thousand a month is—"

"Is not enough, Emmett. There is no reason to argue
the point. I am going to have to have more. Another
five hundred will do. A total of fifteen hundred a month.
That really isn't so much money, when you think
about it."

"Don't you have any respect?" he cried. "This is a
house of mourning."

"Emmett," she cooed, "you do have my deepest sympathies. But life must go on, mustn't it? Every one of us
has to fulfill his or her responsibilities. I have mine."

"You and that brat of yours are not my responsibility."

"Nonsense, Emmett. You know better than that. Fifteen hundred, Emmett. Tomorrow. Same time, same
place." She hung up.

He sat trembling. Gradually he calmed himself, began
to think. A single mistake should not condemn a man to
a life of degradation and deceit, or economic servitude.
It must end, once and for all.

The idea surfaced in his brain and he examined it

with clinical interest. He tested it in every way possible. Put it aside, then considered it again. He could find no flaw. He wrote it down on a yellow legal pad, step by simple step. He studied what he had written. Perfect. He burned his notes in the fireplace and sat back to contemplate his shrewdness, his courage. Not many men would do what he was going to do. Most lacked his creative imagination. He reached for the phone and called Jeanine.

"I won't be able to make it tomorrow," he began, voice cradled in apology.

She became shrill. "You're trying to pull a fast one. Well, let me tell you, it won't work. I—"

"Nothing like that, Jeanine. I have to work all day tomorrow, in the city, one commercial after another. You do want me to remain solvent?"

She laughed with satisfaction. "I knew you were a reasonable man, Emmett. And so am I. The day after will do."

"Why not now?"

"It's late," she said.

"That doesn't matter. Suppose we meet in forty minutes. That should give you enough time."

"I guess it's all right. Belle's out and I'm all alone. But you be there on time. It's bad enough being out by that reservoir during the day, but when its dark—ugh."

He dressed swiftly. Jeans, sweat shirt, soiled tennis shoes. He studied himself in a mirror and approved of what he saw. A desperate man, ready for anything. He set his jaw and left the house.

He decided to take the Porsche. It lent the correct image of power that the evening called for. It was right for a man of action.

He drove without haste toward Putnam Circle, parking on Hillary Drive, less than one hundred yards from Jeanine's house. He cut across a stone fence onto her property, went around to the back. He was in luck, the garage door was open. Her five-year old Mustang sat there. Using a key, he let the air out of the left front tire.

When the tire was flat, he retreated into the storage room at the back of the garage to wait.

Minutes later, the light went on in the garage and Jeanine came out of the house. The tilt of the car caught her eye and she saw the flat.

"Oh, damn," she muttered aloud. "Some other arrangement will have to be made."

She started back toward the house. Emmett grew panicky. He'd intended to make his move in the dark, but time was running out. A few more strides and Jeanine would be back inside, his opportunity lost. He charged forward.

At the last moment, she heard him and pivoted around. No fear showed on her pretty face, only surprise, a hint of confusion. "What—What are you doing *here?*"

He reached for her throat, fingers closing. She tried to twist away, lost her footing and began to fall. He went down with her.

"You bitch," he said amiably. "You think I'd permit you to blackmail me for the rest of my life! You're going to die, Jeanine, and when you're dead I'm going to screw you. The cops will blame the rapist. No one will ever suspect Emmett May. No one."

Her body arched and he bore down, adjusting the angle of pressure. He was proud of his control, of his ability to act under stress.

She rolled and lashed out, the edge of her hand catching him in the throat. Free, she scrambled to her feet and screamed. He went after her, brought her down, working to smother her cries. She bit his hand. He swore and struck out, too late. She was up and running again.

Lights went on in the nearby houses. A man's voice cried out, "What the hell's going on?"

Jeanine yelled: "Rape! Rape!"

A shotgun was fired into the air, the blast reverberating. Heavy footsteps came nearer. Emmett moaned desparingly and ran for the trees. Twice he fell and once a branch whipped across his face. At last he reached the Porsche and sped away, lights off, heart pounding. His

eyes were watering and his hands were shaking. Everything was ruined. He would be exposed. Finished. His
life was over.

III

On Saturday morning, at eleven-twenty-two, under a
lowering gray sky, with high banks of snow framing the
playing field, James Fellows fractured his clavicle. The
pain was acute and the boy writhed on the frozen ground,
struggling not to cry.

Ordinarily James would not have been in the game
with Weston so early. But when Ralph Burleigh saw that
Victor Fellows was standing along the sideline, he put
James in the starting line-up. Ralph was not a man to
by-pass opportunity.

In addition to being Circuit Prosecutor, Fellows was a
member of the Planning and Zoning Board and chairman
of the School Board. A word from Victor Fellows and
Ralph would find himself transferred to the high-school
athletic staff, where he would be one step closer to his
consuming ambition—to become head coach of the high-
school football team.

James, then, was the key to Ralph's future. And the
greatest roadblock. The boy was a physical klutz. He
lacked running speed, strength, and the kind of determination all true studs possessed. James was unable to
block or tackle with authority and he almost never could
catch a pass.

But Ralph viewed the boy's athletic deficiencies as
small obstacles. With Fellows on the scene, the boy
started the game.

It happened on the second play from scrimmage. Ralph
blamed the quarterback, calling James's number. James
went downfield for seven strides, cut to the right, taking
the pass on the third step.

Nothing went right. James and the ball arrived at
approximately the same time. The pass was good enough,
just a tiny bit high. James went through the motions of

jumping, his hands stiff, the fingers closing even before
the ball arrived.

The corner back came up fast. A little kid with a lot
of guts. A kid who knew how to hit. He laid a good
rolling block on James.

The ball went flying. James flipped over, landing
heavily on his right shoulder. Ralph, on the sidelines ten
yards away, heard the bone snap.

By the time he reached the stricken boy he was sure
Victor Fellows would blame him for his son's injury.
But Victor Fellows, crouching over James, trying to keep
the boy from doing further damage to his collarbone,
seemed almost proud.

"Grit you teeth, son," Fellows said. "Pain and football go together. Pain and life."

Ralph's hopes soared. As soon as the game was ended,
he'd visit James at the hospital. And that evening he'd
pay a call on the Circuit Prosecutor at home. This situation might yet turn out to be to his advantage.

IV

On his way to the restaurant, Leo Diamond kept
remembering how it had been in the hotel room with
Jane Bonner. That incredibly proportioned body without
blemish, legs long and full at the thighs, breasts round
and heavy, the nipples soft and brown.

She had treated him as if he were a high-school boy.
Tantalizing and taunting him, controlling him every step
of the way. They had rolled on the bed, kissing and
embracing for nearly an hour before she allowed him to
put his hands under her blouse. That first contact with her
breast had made him dizzy and he begged her to get
undressed.

She had refused.

She had laughed at him.

And would do nothing to alleviate the ache in his
groin.

Hurrying along the street now, he despised her, despised himself even more for wanting her. For needing her. Next time he would plan his moves more carefully.

Ruth had selected the restaurant. Leo, as usual, disapproved of her choice. It was small and dingy, without style or class. It smelled of Parmesan cheese, which Diamond likened to the thick, offensive odor of vomit. He located Ruth at a tiny table set back in the farthest corner of the place.

He started out complaining. "I can't stand being next to the kitchen. The noise, the smells."

"Sit down," she said.

There was a disturbing note in her manner. A sullen, hostile edge, a new authority. Who was she ordering around! He sat down. A waiter came and Diamond ordered a drink.

"What's so important?" he said. "The way you sounded over the phone, I though something had happened to the kids."

"I have something to tell you."

The drink came. Not nearly enough bourbon. He fingered the rim of the glass.

"This is important," Ruth said.

"Couldn't you tell me over the phone? Who's with the kids? I hope you got a reliable sitter. Some of these girls—I didn't trust that one we had last time."

"The children are at my parents'."

He drank some of his drink. "Let them stay there for a couple of days. Keeps the inside of the house quiet." He chuckled at his own joke.

"You'll have plenty of quiet from now on."

"Okay," he said, cocking his head. "I'm supposed to ask what that means. I'm asking."

"I am leaving you."

He examined her face as if there to find the true meaning of her words. She seemed strangely at ease, the usual tension no longer visible around her mouth or in her eyes. "That isn't very funny," he said.

"It's over, Leo. Our marriage. We are finished. Separating. I have moved out of the house. Goodbye birds and bees. Goodbye crab grass. Goodbye house and color TV, and goodbye you, Leo. The marriage is terminated."

He touched the bald spot at the back of his head. "You're my wife," he reminded her.

"Slave is what you mean. Chief cook and tender of your children. Not a person."

"Say it straight out, Ruth. Something's bothering you."

She stared at him in disbelief. "Everything is wrong. The way we lived. The fact that I've allowed you to intimidate and make less of me for so long. The way the children are growing up, self-indulgent, selfish, with no sense of anything but their immediate gratification."

"There's nothing wrong with the way we live."

Her brows went up. "There's everything wrong with it."

"It's all my fault, is that it?"

"Mine, too. But I want out. I want a chance to begin again."

"The rape, that's what's got you so upset."

"The rape made me understand a great deal. The way we make love, for instance. Whenever the planets are in proper conjunction, you launch yourself at me. Bang, bang, bang. A spurt or two and off to sleep you go. It's better than a sleeping pill and makes you feel like a man.

"But what about me, Leo? I toss around half the night trying to find out what happened to love and caring and to my self-esteem. There was a period in my life where I actually liked myself."

"I don't want you to put yourself down."

"It's over between us, Leo."

He eyed her speculatively. "You've found another man?"

She wanted to laugh, but couldn't. "That's not why I'm leaving."

"Then why? Do you suspect me of being unfaithful to you?"

"You have a certain charm, Leo. Even now. Somehow you manage to relate everything to yourself. Leo, I *know* you've been unfaithful. It's your style to be

unfaithful. How many women since our wedding day?
Fifty? One hundred? Not that it matters. Your women,
your business, your garage full of old machines. Your
four-channel stereo. Me. The children. All items on Leo
Diamond's check list. Reminders that you're alive and
doing well. You're a collector, Leo, but you don't really
care about anyone."

"Ruth, this is not at all like you."

"You don't have the staying power for the long haul.
Promiscuity is a necessary ingredient to your mental
health."

"This is hardly the time to discuss such matters."

"When would you suggest?"

"At home. When you've calmed down."

She shook her head. "The decision is made. I've left
you."

"A trial separation might be a good thing. Give us
both a chance to examine the priorities. Then, when we
get back together again, it will be with a renewed appre-
ciation of the value of the other person."

"My God! You sound like an essay on the Op-Ed
page of the Sunday *Times*."

"I mean it, Ruth."

"Leo, try to understand. I've rented an apartment."

"An apartment!"

"On West Sixty-ninth Street."

"I won't have it."

"You have nothing to say about it. Two bedrooms,
living room, a kitchen. All we'll need."

"We?"

"The children and I."

"You're taking the children!"

"Of course. We may even get to know one another
after a while."

"The West Side," Diamond said scornfully. "Do you
realize the kind of neighborhood that is?"

"It will do nicely."

"Dope addicts, muggers."

She smiled grimly. "Are you afraid I'll be raped?"

"You know what I mean."

"Arcadia had its chance at me. Let's give Manhattan a crack!"

"If you insist on this ridiculous course, Ruth, at least do it properly. I know a real-estate agent who specializes in co-ops. I'll find a suitable apartment for you and the kids. That makes a great deal of sense. That way we can have the best of both worlds. The house in the country for weekends, the apartment for during the week. I never did enjoy commuting."

"If you want an apartment, Leo, find you own. I've got mine."

"That's not a very generous attitude."

"And while you're at it, find a lawyer."

"A lawyer!"

"We should each have one, I'm told."

"What for?"

"To handle the divorce."

"Divorce!"

"I am filing for a divorce, Leo."

He still refused to believe her. "Ruth, I will not let this happen. This is a phase you're going through. You'll outgrow it. We are married until death do us part. I believed in those words, I believe in them now. I intend to woo you, Ruth, and win you back."

She rose, looked down at him. "Leo," she said conversationally, "you are an asshole."

V

Clarice Morrison watched her husband while he talked on the telephone. His normally serene and handsome face was strained, puffy, pale. He appeared to have aged ten years in the last ten days. His voice was low and hoarse.

"Yes, Mr. President," he was saying, his manner deferential but firm, "my decision is definite. No, not the station, on the contrary. That's right, a personal matter.

I appreciate your generosity and patience, sir. Yes, perhaps another time. Goodbye, Mr. President."

He sat in place staring at the telephone.

"You could change your mind," Clarice said, wishing she hadn't spoken.

"It's over," he muttered. "None of this would have happened if I'd been at home more, spent more time with Willy, been a better father."

"Oh, Avery." She fought back the tears. "You're an extraordinary father, an extraordinary man. It isn't you, it's Willy."

"I won't believe that the boy is inherently bad."

"Have you decided what we're going to do?"

"I've made some inquiries. Several schools are set up to accept boys who are . . . difficult. Horton Military Academy seems like the best of the lot. It's in Colorado."

"So far away!"

"Yes. That's rugged country. The discipline is strict and the administration is firm. There are few opportunities for a boy to get into trouble. It will do Willy some good, I'm convinced."

"What if he won't stay there? What if he runs away, gets into trouble again?"

Avery came around the wide desk, took hold of his wife's hands. "Willy has to change," he said intently. "Become responsible for his actions."

They embraced, stood holding each other. A sob racked Avery's large frame.

"My God. I've become the kind of man I've always despised. Corrupt, corrupting, weak . . ."

"Not you, my dear, not you."

"This is Willy's last chance. I will not help him again. I can't keep concealing the truth, using my position, my money, to buy him out of trouble. He must do it himself this time, he *will*. . . ."

"Yes," she murmured against his cheek. "He will, my dear."

VI

She was imbedded in his memory. Passing before him, flaunting herself in that brazen, careless way girls did. The way they held themselves, breasts and bottoms bulging. Laughing in that way that girls laughed. Often at him.

He tried to lose himself in the magazine in his lap. In the photographs and drawings. In the articles that described the things people did to each other. To themselves. But she kept forcing her way back into his head.

Daring him.

Those mocking eyes.

She had been with him for months. As much a part of him as the magazine or his clothes or his work. No longer could he recall the exact moment when he'd first seen her. Not that it mattered. She was with him frequently now, as the others had been. Crowding other images out of his mind, giving birth to the hot yearnings that he'd come to know so well. Thinking about her now, he felt his flesh respond and he resented the response. She had no right to take advantage of his weakness.

It was the way women were.

Devious, evil creatures.

He looked at his watch. He knew where she lived. Knew her habits, the patterns into which her life fell. He had been attentive to each of them, and to her. Quietly attentive. Never showing himself. Never revealing his need.

First, the search. Not really a search, for he had never *chosen* this course. It had been thrust upon him by *them*. The way they were, the way they acted, the way they made him *feel*.

Then came the surveillance. Lengthy, slow, thorough. No detail was too small to be overlooked. And it had paid off in every instance, things going exactly according to plan. Except the last time. His throat locked at the memory and he wondered if it would be possible to go back, to complete matters, to make everything clean and orderly. It was better not to think about it. Not yet.

Last was the kill. To plunge his flesh into a woman. To rip and tear and bang away. To cause pain and sense fear. And at the same time to receive so much pleasure and reward.

He put the magazine aside and allowed her to drift back into view. That lovely, seemingly innocent face, the open laugh. She was lithe and youthful. He imagined her struggling under his own body and his excitement mounted.

He took off his clothes and showered. More quickly than he liked, but time was of some concern. He had obligations to fulfill. He applied baby powder, cologne, combed his hair.

In front of the mirror, he inspected himself. Nowhere a blemish. Cleanliness was a most admirable quality in a person, *the* most admirable. Cleansing the body inside and out. Rites of purification. The image in the glass smiled back at him. Pleasant, appealing. The kind of man any woman would find attractive. He dressed rapidly and set out to get what he wanted.

VII

Jane Bonner returned to the apartment. She was tired. Up late the night before and on her feet all day.

She opened the door and called Holly's name. There was no answer and she remembered that Holly had her Tuesday class. She slid a TV dinner into the oven, showered, donned a pink terry-cloth robe. She ate and watched television. At midnight she lost interest in the late movie and switched over to Johnny Carson. But the show failed to hold her attention and she turned the set off. Since Holly was still out, she left the safety chain off and went to bed.

She turned her attention to Leo Diamond. Sooner or later she was going to have to make it with him. He would insist on it.

All that mattered was that he might be able to help her. Jane hungered to escape the strictures and rigors of

A-1. She had dreams of television stardom, the movies. She had yet to see a girl on the box who was better-looking than she was, or had a better figure.

There was no reason why she couldn't become an actress, a star. All she needed was a little help. Leo Diamond would provide that. Public relations was his game and that meant he came in contact with all kinds of people in show business. He could do it for her.

She made up her mind. She'd phone him in the morning, arrange a meeting in New York. During the day. Late nights were getting her down. She'd plead sick at the market; Miller never fussed. Not as long as he got his occasional grope.

She'd make Diamond promise to help, then give him a matinée in one of those expensive hotels, something better than that old place he took her to the first time. She'd never been laid in New York.

Satisfied with her plan, she closed her eyes and was soon asleep. The sound of a car woke her. Footsteps climbing the stairs. Holly, bringing home a date. Who was it this time?

There was a scraping at the latch. Holly, stoned out of her skull most likely, and unable to get the key into the lock.

Jane went to the door. "Holly," she said sleepily, opening the door at the same time.

A shadowed figure stepped inside, the door swinging shut behind him. Jane tried to sweep the sleep away, to see clearly.

"Who is it?" she said.

She never saw the fist that hit her. She went over onto her back on the floor. He came after her, fists pumping. She fought back, clawing at him. "Get out of here!"

She heard her nightgown rip, the nightgown that had cost sixty dollars at Lord & Taylor's in Stamford. For the first time she grew really angry.

"Let me alone, mother fucker!"

"Dirty cunt!"

He hit her again and again. All strength drained out of her and she felt herself sinking into a gray void. She protested weakly. Suddenly she understood who he was, what he had come for, that he was killing her. And she was afraid. She wanted to scream but it was too late. She dropped down into a deep, warm darkness where everything was safe and still. And felt nothing.

CHAPTER EIGHTEEN

I

LOUKAS SAT AT HIS DESK in the Bureau and stared at the paper cup partly filled with cold coffee, struggling to make sense of what was happening.

Jeanine Stafford. First the daughter had accused Arthur Slater falsely; and now the mother had been attacked, but unable—no, unwilling—to identify her attacker. Though he had questioned Jeanine Stafford for a long time, had virtually accused her of lying, Loukas had been unable to make a dent in her story. The Staffords, mother and daughter, troubled him. They drew trouble to them; they caused trouble.

He ticked off the names. Horn, Spratt, Keyes; all raped and killed. Slater, a suicide. Ruth Diamond raped. Judith May murdered by Carl Johnson. Jeanine Stafford attacked. And now Jane Bonner.

Loukas blamed himself for Jane. If he'd followed through, gotten to her before the killer had, she might still be alive. He'd put it off, telling himself that she had nothing to say that mattered. That Virgil had lied in claiming her as his girl friend he had learned from Jane's roommate, Holly. What else could Jane have told him?

Maybe he might have warned her, impressed her with the seriousness of the situation. But he'd never gotten around to Jane Bonner. A really good cop would have done so.

Guilt had been building in Loukas for some time. The guilt of failure. The guilt imposed on him by people in the street. Imposed by their sidelong accusatory glances,

240

the way their eyes followed him as he went. His presence
stirred them. He was on their minds, their tongues. He
made them uneasy.

Victor Fellows marched into the Bureau as if it were
his private club and positioned himself carefully in a
chair opposite Loukas. He crossed his legs, adjusted his
trousers, placed his hands delicately on his thighs.

"Tell me about this one."

Loukas lowered his eyes. "Victim's name was Jane
Bonner. Twenty years of age. Check-out girl at the A-1
Market. Roommate's name is Holly Mason, twenty-one.
Same M.O. as the others. Beaten, raped, strangled. M.E.
puts the time at between two and four in the A.M."

"No witnesses?"

"No witnesses. Nobody heard anything. No screams,
no noise, nothing. Our hero is very good at what he does.
Very good."

"What about the roommate?"

"Out with a guy all night. We've checked; she was
there."

"Who knew Holly would be away?"

"Holly says nobody. It was a last-minute thing. She's
been seeing this fellow on and off over a period of time.
Right now it's on. She went to his place directly from the
high school. Takes a class in American poetry at night.
Holly just plain forgot to mention it to Jane."

"That sounds peculiar to me."

"The girls operated on different wavelengths. Each
one out for herself. They didn't share boy friends or bedrooms or secrets, apparently. Anyway, that's Holly's
story."

"You believe it?"

"I believe everything everybody tells me. Only not so
much anymore."

Fellows frowned. It gave him the look of a schoolboy
mulling over an examination question. "How did he get
inside? What is it, a house or an apartment?"

"Apartment. No break. Lock not picked. The safety
chain was intact. I'm guessing that Jane Bonner let
him in."

"She knew him."

"Not necessarily."

"But likely."

"Worth considering. Henderson is going over it all again with Holly."

"The A-1 Market," Fellows said. "It keeps coming back to that. Isn't that where the delivery boy works?"

"Virgil Reiser," Loukas said.

"Yes. I'm beginning to have very strong feelings about our Mr. Reiser. Let's pull him in."

"Tom Petersen went after him ten minutes ago. They'll be along." Loukas spoke grudgingly, not wanting to tell Fellows everything, annoyed by his own pettiness.

"We'll see."

The phone rang and Loukas answered. He listened and hung up. "Petersen's got Virgil next door. He'll keep. I'm going to see how Henderson's making out with Holly."

"I'll come along."

In Captain Henderson's office, Holly Mason sat curled in over herself, face drooping. Her fingers plucked at one another, and her knees were locked, as if to ward off danger. Her eyes were discolored.

"Well?" Loukas said.

Henderson grimaced. "Holly has to have the world's worst memory, or else she's holding out on us."

"You wouldn't do that, would you, Holly?" Loukas said.

"I'm the Circuit Prosecutor," Victor Fellows said, stepping forward. "I must warn you that you are liable to be charged with complicity and the obstruction of justice if you fail to tell us everything you know."

"Hold on a minute," Loukas said. He smiled encouragingly at the girl. "Maybe Holly is just trying to protect Jane. After all, they were roommates. Friends. A girl's reputation can mean a lot, especially under such circumstances as these. Isn't that right, Holly?"

Holly wet her lips, looking from one man to the others.

Loukas went on easily. "Holly, you have to believe

we are after only one thing—to catch the guy who did this to Jane. Her killer."

"I don't know anything," she protested.

"We need all the help we can get, Holly. Four women are dead. A fifth just got away with her life. He's going to hit again unless we stop him. You might have some small fragment of information we could use."

Holly shook her head.

Henderson made his voice harsh. "We are going to find out whatever there is to find out. With you or without. Hold out on us and it will surely go hard on you."

"Jane was my friend."

"Then help us find the man who killed her," Henderson said. "Hell, it could just as easily have been you."

"Give us some names, Holly," Loukas said. A phantom thought fluttered around his head, then was gone. He swore silently. "Did Jane see anybody regularly?"

"She didn't want to be tied up. She kept talking about being free."

"Jane liked men," Loukas said, not unkindly. "She wasn't going to do without."

Holly hugged herself. "Sometimes she went to the Sweet Dreams."

"A pickup place," Henderson growled.

"You went with her?" Victor Fellows said. Disapproval scored his manner.

"Sometimes," Holly said. "Chicks can go crazy in this town at night. There's nothing to do if you're young."

"Jane met men at the Sweet Dreams?"

"It's a place for meeting people."

"You must remember some names?"

"No, no. It wasn't like that. We didn't stay together. One of us would make a score, we'd split up. No competition that way."

"Miss Bonner slept with these men?" Victor Fellows said.

Holly spread her hands. "How would I know?"

"Did she bring them home?" Loukas said quietly.

"Maybe. When I was asleep. I can't be sure."

"Holly," Loukas cautioned, "I've been in the apartment. Those walls are thin. Anything goes on in one bedroom you hear it in the other."

Holly looked off into space. "Oh, I guess I knew when she had somebody in there."

"Many men?"

"Some."

"Are you sure you don't know any names?"

"I'm sure."

"Let's circulate a photograph of Jane around Sweet Dreams," Fellows said. "Somebody will know somebody who was with her. I think we're on to something this time."

"We'd do that automatically," Henderson said, annoyed.

Fellows gave no sign that he'd heard. "I can't believe that Jane never mentioned any name, Miss Mason. It doesn't seem logical, two girls living in such close proximity. I want you to consider the seriousness of this situation. I will not hesitate to bring charges against you or anyone else hindering our investigation. You understand that?"

Holly shuddered. "I don't want to cause anybody any trouble."

"Who?" Fellows said.

The tension seemed to go out of her. "There was a guy who was after her. But they never really got it on together."

"Who?"

"He's married."

"There's our motive," Fellows said cheerfully.

Loukas measured the prosecutor. "You figure he was sleeping with all of them, killed them to protect himself in every case?"

"Maybe not."

"What's his name, Holly?" Loukas asked.

"Leo Diamond."

II

Diamond was in Captain Henderson's office. In the hallway outside, Henderson, Fellows, and Loukas were talking in hushed tones.

"He doesn't know a thing, not even about Jane," Henderson said.

"I don't like it."

"Dammit, Theo, why not? He had the hots for the girl, we know that. She held him off. It got to be too much. He went after her just the way he went after the others."

"Including his own wife? He beat her and raped her in his own garage?"

"Stranger things have happened."

"And she didn't recognize him?"

"Maybe she wants to protect him. Stranger things have—" He broke off and swore. "Nothing but blind alleys."

"He might tell us something," Fellows said. "After all, he was involved with two victims—Mrs. Diamond and Jane. Something might come of this."

"You two guys work on him," Henderson said. "This fucking case is screwing up my whole department. Nothing's going right. I got important work to do." He marched down the hall, relieved to be out of it for a while.

Loukas led the way into the office. Diamond was at the window, looking out. He came around, hand extended, smiling. It was what he liked to call his Bullshit Grin. Warm, welcoming, open.

Loukas pointed to a chair. "Sit down, Mr. Diamond."

"I'd just as soon stand," Diamond answered. "If you don't mind."

"Sit." Loukas made his voice thin and hard.

Diamond obeyed, suddenly puzzled. "What's this all about? Thought about your call all the way out from the city. This is costing me a great deal of time and time is what I have to sell in my business. I suppose you've finally found the man who attacked my wife, is that it? You want

Ruth to identify him and figured my presence would make things easier. Ruth's in New York. I have a number you can call. Or would you rather I do it?"

Loukas bent from the waist, the normally lambent eyes glinting. "When did you sleep with Jane Bonner for the first time, Diamond?"

Diamond started out of the chair. Loukas dropped his hand on Diamond's shoulder and pushed. Diamond sat back down.

"When?"

Diamond's face began to disintegrate. The pale skin became mottled. The washed-blue eyes grew dull and gray. His mouth trembled.

"I don't know the young lady."

"Cut the crap," Loukas snapped. "You knew her."

"Yes," Diamond said. "I knew her." He made an effort to rouse himself. "I don't see what this has to do with— This doesn't have to come out, does it? I mean, we're all men of the world here."

"When did you see Jane last?"

"A couple of nights ago. In New York. She spent some time with me."

"Where?"

Diamond hesitated. "Does it matter?"

"Where?"

"A hotel."

"What hotel?"

"The Plaza. I wanted to impress her." He made a sound that began as laughter and ended as a sob. "She said I could not think much of her if I'd take her to an old beat-up fleabag like that. The Plaza, a fleabag!"

"Where were you last night?"

"In New York."

"You slept there?"

"Yes. What difference does that make?"

"Where?"

"What do you mean?"

"Where did you sleep?"

"At the Plaza."

"We'll check. Who were you with?"

"My God, I was by myself. What kind of a man do you take me for?"

"You spend a great deal of your time in the city?"

"Well, yes."

"What does Mrs. Diamond think about that?"

Diamond felt his strength seeping back. "Is that relevant to any of this?"

"Answer the question."

"My wife and I, well, we're having some difficulties. It will all straighten itself out."

Victor Fellows gazed down at Diamond. "This morning, at approximately two o'clock, you went to see Jane Bonner."

"Two o'clock in the morning! I told you, I was in the city."

"At her apartment, here in Arcadia. On Duncan Road. She was asleep, you woke her. She probably tried to keep you out, but you talked your way inside."

"No, no."

"She let you in and you attacked her."

"Attacked! I attacked Jane! Why would I do that?"

"Because you had the hots for her," Loukas supplied without enthusiasm. "Because she was holding out on you. Because you lost your head."

"That's crazy. I don't know what this is all about, but ask Jane. She'll tell you that I've never been near her apartment. You think I'd take a chance like that?"

"You raped her," Fellows said.

Diamond's eyes widened.

"Then choked her to death."

Fear appeared on Diamond's face. Loukas imagined he could see the workings of the other man's mind, already constructing barricades behind which to secure himself.

"Jane is . . . dead?"

"No one is any deader," Loukas said crossly. He felt no sympathy for Diamond, would have enjoyed charging him.

"Raped and murdered. Just like the others."

Diamond began to feel sick. His throat was parched,

painful, and his eyes were aching. Every avenue open to him was marked Danger!

"Gentlemen," he said in a placating manner, "we are all men of the world here."

"You said that before," Loukas said. He didn't want to be coupled with Diamond. Or Victor Fellows, for that matter. It occurred to him that in some way he had never explored, he was a snob. A moral snob; perhaps that was why he had become a cop. It was something to consider.

"We," Diamond was saying, "understand how life is lived in the real world."

"We are talking about homicide, Mr. Diamond," Fellows said coldly.

"Can you prove you were in New York last night?" Loukas said.

Diamond hesitated before answering. "I think so."

"You have a name for us?" Victor Fellows seemed disappointed.

"Yes." Diamond's voice was almost inaudible. "Her name is Michele." He looked around as if pleading. "She's a professional."

"All night?" Loukas said.

Diamond answered slowly. "She was in the room when I went to my office this morning. A very nice woman, I want you to understand. I wouldn't want to cause her any trouble."

"Full name, address, phone number," Loukas said. Diamond pulled out an address book, handed it over. Loukas wrote down the information. "Be sure you're available when I want you, Mr. Diamond."

"Does that mean I can go?"

"Yes."

Diamond stood up. "Please, this doesn't have to get out, does it? About Jane and me, or Michele. I mean, it comes at a bad time. I'm trying for a reconciliation with Ruth, you see."

"Thank you for coming in," Loukas said. Diamond left, closing the door behind him.

"I don't understand that kind of man," Victor Fellows

said. "His wife has been raped, their marriage is in trouble, and he sleeps with a prostitute. I find that kind of behavior reprehensible."

"If you want pat answers, Mr. Fellows, find someone else. The older I get, the less I know."

"We don't seem to be getting any closer," Fellows said. "We need a break. A change of luck. Sooner or later, something's got to go our way."

Loukas knew better than that.

III

The telephone was a squat symbol of his destruction. It would ring, he would answer, and life would blow up in his hands. He moaned as if in mortal pain.

Dark impulses had always driven him. Impulses that he had examined and understood, kept under control. His energy, his passion, his needs. He fed them as carefully as other men fed their pets. With loving concern.

Only three times in all these years had he allowed the beast to crawl out of its hiding place. Three times he had catered to its black craving. He remembered them all. The first one had been thirteen years old. With faded-blue eyes and honey-colored hair. Her skin creamy and her flesh smooth. So young and unspoiled. So willing to please him. She was a fan, desperate for an autograph, for a picture of him, for a moment in his shining presence. He had taken her into his office and used her. He had explored every crease, every crevice, every tender opening. She had cried out in pure ecstasy and begged him to go on.

The second time was four years later. A darkly Latin girl. She had been a year younger than the first one. Younger but taller, more developed physically. He had assured himself that it was perfectly acceptable with this one, that she would know what it was all about, she would be experienced.

He was wrong. When he touched her, she had cried out, protested. When he exposed himself she had shrunk back, begun to whimper. When he went on his knees in front of her, burying his face between her thighs, she panicked, tried to run.

What choice did he have? He brought her down to the floor, clamped one hand over her mouth, fighting to subdue her. She lashed out with her feet. An unexpected blow sent him rolling away. She ran for the door. He caught her from behind, smashed her down. A blinding wildness caused him to hit her again. More than once. Blood seeped from her nose and her eyes swelled. He saw none of it, ripping at her clothes.

He forced her legs apart, pounded at her, not hearing her cries of anguish and fear. Not hearing her rising wail as he ripped her open. Not hearing the door to his office open.

"Emmett!" Judith had cried out in revulsion and womanly pain. "Emmett, stop it!"

He obeyed. But it was too late. Judith May, star of Broadway and Hollywood. His wife. Mother of his children. The only woman he had ever loved had discovered his terrible secret, his awful weakness. And there was no way of going back. She hated him after that.

They worked out an arrangement. Each of them would do as he or she wished. Go with whom he or she pleased. But he had wanted nobody. Except Judith. And she had wanted a succession of men, but not him.

He thrust himself into his career. Worked endless hours and earned immense sums of money. And kept away from women. It changed nothing. Judith refused to live with him as man and wife. She kept her own apartment in the house and he kept his. They were civil to each other, went to parties together, presented a harmonious front to the world. But they lived separate lives.

Now Judith was dead. Destroyed by the existence he had forced upon her. And he waited for the telephone to ring to learn what further punishment awaited him.

"*Jesus . . .*"

At last it rang. And rang; would not stop. The caller knew he was there, knew he had no other place to go. He reached out.

"Yes . . ."

"Oh, Emmett," she began, "you must be very ashamed of yourself."

She made him feel like a small boy, chastised and guilty. "What did you tell them, Jeanine?" he said.

"The police? They gave me a hard time, Emmett. Insisted that I must have recognized the man who attacked me. A Sergeant Loukas, Emmett. I don't think he believed me. But there was nothing he could do. Perhaps he believes it was the town rapist who attacked me. That's what you wanted people to believe, isn't it, Emmett?"

"Why didn't you get in touch with me sooner, instead of letting me hang like this for days?"

"What you did was evil, Emmett. I thought I'd let you sweat for a while."

"I went crazy, Jeanine."

"Would you actually have gone through with it, Emmett? Killed me?"

"I don't know."

"And raped me?"

"I don't know."

"Oh, Emmett, you worry me."

"It was a stupid mistake, I admit it."

"We are going to make another adjustment in our relationship, Emmett."

"I understand."

"Up until now you have been paying only for the pleasure you had with Belle three years ago. You are a pervert, Emmett."

"Please." He spoke with some indignation.

"Now," she said with tight satisfaction, "you must pay for trying to kill me."

"And if I refuse?"

"Don't be silly. All I have to do is accuse you. Attempted rape, Emmett. No conviction is necessary, no proof. Just an accusation and there goes your precious career. Consider how your sponsors would react. Oh, you'll pay, all right, because it's the only way to keep your dirty little secret to ourselves."

"How much?"

"Five thousand dollars a month."

"That's insane!"

"Not at all. You make plenty. Five, ten times as much. It's only fair."

"I should have killed you."

"That kind of talk will get you into more trouble. Anyway, I am writing a letter, Emmett. All about you and that time with Belle, and about what you tried to do to me. I'm going to send one copy to my lawyer, another to my sister in Jacksonville, and put the third in my safety-deposit box. Just in case some sudden accident should befall me. But that doesn't seem likely, does it, Emmett?"

"No," he said, after a while. "You'll undoubtedly live a long, long time."

"Mail the payments each month, Emmett. I'll miss our little meetings, but I can't afford the risk anymore."

"Whatever you say, Jeanine."

"Yes, whatever I say."

CHAPTER NINETEEN

I

GROUP OF MEN CLUSTERED around the piano in Jerry's
ool Hall. They were singing "The Sidewalks of New
ork," making it sound like a hymn.

In the back booth, Loukas and Sandy Felton ate lobster
ils and some of Jerry's coleslaw, and drank Miller's out
f chilled glass mugs. Loukas, preoccupied all evening,
cused on his food. Sandy took the opportunity to study
im. His face, quirky in detail, was strangely appealing—
e blunt features, the grooves and ruts and puffs of skin,
ose soft brown eyes.

Still a stranger, still a cop, an official person. She was
able to separate him from his job or from the gun on
s belt. Any man who toted a gun around had to be
gressive, tough, dangerous. The gentle appearance that
e presented to her had to be an assumed façade, she
cided.

"You enjoy being a cop, don't you, Theo?"

He thought about Chief Wakeman warning him to stay
vay from the Morrison family, about all the political
essures, and then swallowed the complaint. You didn't
are such things with civilians.

He wanted her respect, wanted her to admire the work
e did. He wanted her to like him. But the vast social
If that separated them seemed unbridgeable.

"In a small town like this one," he said, "you put in
ur time, take the pension."

"That's what it amounts to?"

"Mostly. There's not much excitement."

253

"You want to retire?"

"I think about it a lot nowadays."

"It's the case you're on."

"Probably."

"Everybody is upset."

"I hate him," he said, the words out before he realize
what he was saying.

"The rapist?"

"For what he's doing to this town, for what he's do
to those women, for what he's done to me."

She touched his hand briefly. "Does it bother you th
much?"

He turned away. "I'm just not used to it. But nobo
ever ordered me to become a cop."

"You'll catch him, Theo."

"A lot of time is passing. The odds are in his fav
more each day."

"You must have some idea—"

"Nothing that matters. If there were clues, they've be
lost, wiped out."

"How will you ever find the right man?"

"By getting to know him better, by figuring out wh
he isn't. Who he isn't."

"Do you think he actually knew each of his victims?"

"Everything points to it. Not friends, but he had
come in contact with them somehow. That's what's lousi
me up. The guy who this all fits refuses to stay in th
mold."

"Then it must be someone else."

"Seems that way."

"Why must he kill the women? Rape is bad enoug
but murder—"

II

They left Jerry's Pool Hall, drove to the beach and s
in his car looking across the sand at the wintry water
Long Island Sound.

"Do you enjoy living in Arcadia?" she said, breaking a long silence.

"Enjoy? I guess so." It wasn't something he thought about. This was where he'd been born, raised, always lived. He was part of the town, the town part of him. Just like the Fort or the Town Hall or the mallard ducks that came to his house every spring expecting to be fed whole-wheat bread. "It's my home," he said.

"All that talk about retiring, did you mean it? You're too young not to do anything."

"I'm a couple of years short of my twenty. I could go early, I guess. Pick up on the pension when it comes due. I've got enough aside to make it for a few years. My brother likes it a lot in North Carolina and wants me to come down."

"What would you do?"

"Grow vegetables, play golf."

"Ah, Loukas, I don't see you on a golf course. Or piddling around in a garden."

He grinned. "I could watch birds. They must have a million different varieties in Carolina."

"Sure, you could do that. But I don't see it."

"What do you see, Sandy?"

"I think you were supposed to be a cop."

"The Big Chief in the sky made me that way, right?"

"Right." Now she was grinning, too. "You wouldn't feel right without that thing on your belt."

"Could be. Seems like I've always been on the job."

"You love it."

"Not the blood and pain and violence."

Without warning, she kissed his cheek. Nothing showed on his face. He said nothing, did nothing. She grew apprehensive. She didn't want to offend him, or deprive him of one of those precious prerogatives men were so concerned about.

Then, without speaking, he bent toward her. His lips were firm, and much too dry. She placed her hand at the back of his neck and extended her tongue. He drew back.

"I want you to know," he said very formally, "that I like you very much."

Relief surged through her. "I thought you didn't
want to kiss me."

"Some guys say there are women who turn on to cops,
the way kids do to rock singers."

"Ah, maybe. But I like *you*, Loukas."

"That's good."

"Yes. Let's kiss some more. It's something I could get
to enjoy."

"I'm not very good at this."

"Well, then, practice, Sergeant. Practice."

After a while they separated.

"You're improving," she said.

"Thanks."

"You pick up on things quickly."

"I'm glad you approve."

"More?" she said.

"Unless it's getting too late for you?"

"Do you suppose we could go somewhere?"

"Anywhere you say."

She spoke into his ear. "Your place would be just fine,
I believe."

He started the Valiant without speaking. She put her
head back and closed her eyes. "Drive carefully, please.
We don't want to get stopped by a cop."

A sound of satisfaction rumbled in her throat. She
changed her position, arranging one leg across his middle.
He felt the round, firm thigh, rested his hand on her hip.

"You're not much of a talker," she murmured, without
complaint.

"What can I say!"

"Is that a compliment?"

"You're unbelievable."

She breathed deeply, setting herself against the tension.
"It was good, wasn't it, Theo?"

"Yes."

"Will it keep on being good?"

"Why not? Sure, it will. All we have to do is let it."

"I think you're a very nice man, Theo."

"You're the one who is nice, very nice."

She smelled him and was pleased. He wore no cologne, no after-shave lotion, no scent but that of his own body, a very distinctive male smell. She licked his skin and he shivered.

"Don't you like it?"

"It makes me jump."

She moved and her leg came against his thickening penis. "It does more than make you jump. Theo, you can't be more than eighteen."

"I used to be forty-two, but I'm shedding years rapidly."

"Is that good?"

"You tell me."

"Very good for me." She spread herself on top of him. "Am I too heavy for you?"

"You're perfect."

"I could lose twenty pounds."

"Just my style, the way you are."

"You say it, but do you mean it?"

"I mean it."

"Absolutely?"

"Absolutely."

"Prove it."

"How?"

She rotated her middle against him. "You think of a way."

"Give me a minute."

It didn't take that long.

"I've been thinking," she said in the still darkness of his bedroom.

"Hmmm." He made an effort to listen. But not much of an effort.

"Couldn't you set a trap?"

"What do you want to catch?"

"The murderer, the man you're after."

"Entrapment's against the law."

"Don't cops ever break the law to uphold the law?"

He thought about Arthur Slater, his entry into the teacher's home. "It's been done."

"There, you see. The way I figure it, you set somebody up, somebody the killer would be attracted to."

"A beautiful woman."

"Yes! And when the killer comes after her, you've got him."

"I know just the woman."

"Who?"

"You."

"Ah, Theo, I'm not beautiful."

"You're beautiful."

"You're prejudiced."

"That's true."

After a while, she spoke hesitantly. "If you want me to I'll do it."

"What are you talking about?"

"Put myself up as a decoy. As long as you were close by, I'd be okay, wouldn't I?"

"I don't think so."

"I'd be willing to try, if you say so."

"Forget it."

"You're sure?"

"Sure."

They stirred as one and came slowly awake in the darkness and made love again. When they were done, Loukas found himself saying, "I love you."

The words echoed and she tested them for glibness, for a hint of the easy promise; she found none.

Shocked at his own daring, he expected to be mocked, put in his place. He did love her. Loved her without really knowing her, and the strangeness and newness of it frightened him. And made him happy.

"You don't have to say it," she told him.

"I mean it. I love you."

There was an ingenuousness about him that put her on edge, made her distrust her reactions. He was very different from most of the men she had known.

"I like you," she heard herself say tentatively. "I like to be with you. In bed and out." She laughed nervously. Love! The word distressed her. It represented some childhood fantasy, romantic nonsense she had long since put aside. Love, and its awesome demands, frightened her. Love extracted a price she had never been able or willing to pay. Love left you naked and vulnerable.

"Don't depend on me," she told him.

"But I trust you."

"Can't we just enjoy what there is, what we're doing?"

"I've been alone for a long time."

"Then you can be alone for a while longer." When he made no response, she knew that she'd hurt him and she didn't want to do that. "Ah, Theo," she said, reaching out. "I've been thinking about leaving Arcadia. I could use a fresh start."

"You have a place picked out?"

"I'm after some dull town without any wise guys, without sophisticated people. A warm and easy place."

"Spring will be here soon," Loukas said hopefully.

"That's not what I mean."

"The birds will be coming back."

She said nothing.

"Robins come to my place every April. And ducks."

"Maybe you'll see an eagle, the way your father did."

"No more eagles. I don't think so. Once they're gone, they don't come back."

She wanted to comfort him, but there was nothing to do. Or say.

"Sandy," he said after a while, "in a couple of years my pension will come through. I've got some money put away, enough . . . I could buy a Winnebago. We could travel."

"Theo, are you proposing to me?"

"I guess I am."

"What about Carolina, about learning to play golf?"

"Who am I kidding? That's not my style. Anywhere you want to go, it would be all right with me."

"Ah, Theo."

"You don't have to decide this minute. Think about it. I can wait."

"Don't plan on me, Theo."

"Think about it."

"You're just too damned sweet for your own good Theo. Now go to sleep. It's a couple of hours till morning."

He tried but his mind kept turning over, asking questions, finding no answers.

III

Loukas arrived at the Fort and found the entrance blocked by television camera crews, photographers, reporters. Microphones were shoved in his face, shutter clicked and questions were hurled at him.

"All right, boys," he said, pushing forward. "I've go nothing to tell you."

A TV reporter shouted: "The Circuit Prosecutor say, he can get a conviction. Do you agree?"

Loukas felt himself grow cold and wary. "Why don' you boys go back where you came from? Let us do what we have to do."

"Hey, Loukas, give us a statement. What led you t the guy?"

Loukas manufactured a grin and shook his head worked his way closer to the entrance of the building.

"This collar, Sergeant, did you make it yourself?"

"No comment."

"Has there been a confession yet?"

Loukas warned himself not to say anything. A spread ing restlessness gripped him and his hands closed an opened.

"Can you make it stick?" a reporter from the *Banne* called over the heads of his colleagues. "This arrest o Reiser?"

Loukas felt cold suddenly. He reminded himself tha he was past forty, that it was time to begin wearing a overcoat.

"Any further information will come from the office c the Circuit Prosecutor, boys. Or from my superiors. have nothing to say at this time. Let me through, please I have to earn my pay . . ."

Once inside, he headed for Captain Henderson's office. "What's going on!" he began as he entered. "What's this about Virgil?" Only then did he see Victor Fellows and Tom Petersen. Petersen avoided his gaze but Fellows turned to him, a pleasant smile curving his fine red mouth.

"Virgil was arrested and charged about an hour ago."

"Charged with what?" Loukas made no effort to conceal his scorn for the other man.

"Homicide One, Rape One."

"You made the collar, Petersen?"

Victor Fellows answered, "On my instructions."

Loukas addressed Henderson. "This stinks, John. Fellows here needs those cameras out there. And Tom is hungry to make a score for himself. Okay. But what are you after, letting this happen this way?"

"Knock it off, Theo." Henderson's voice was heavy with warning.

"This is a shit way to handle it, John, and you know it."

"His alibis won't stand up, Theo," Petersen said. There was a plea for understanding in his voice.

Loukas ignored him. "Any decent defense attorney will get him off."

"I don't agree," Fellows said blandly. "I have a fairly substantial case against Virgil. It will get better. A confession may be forthcoming. It wouldn't at all surprise me. Do you know what Petersen found hidden in Virgil's room? Hard-core pornographic materials. Sadomasochistic magazines and books. *Sex Through Pain,* that kind of thing. A black snake whip. Chains. Virgil isn't going to fool a jury with that baby-faced innocent act of his when that evidence is introduced. Not only that; he lied about Jane Bonner, about her being his girl friend. Why'd he do that if not to cover up? I'm going to put that sonofabitch away."

"Does the Chief know about this?" Loukas said.

Henderson answered, "He ordered the arrest."

Loukas blew air out of his lungs. "It's his department. I only work here."

"Easy does it, men," Fellows said smoothly. "The

people of Arcadia want a conviction. I will give it to them. That's what counts ultimately."

"Oh," Loukas said flatly, "I had the idea we were supposed to catch the guilty party. Tell you what we ought to do, let's drag Willy Morrison in here. He makes a much more likely suspect than Virgil Reiser."

Fellows snapped back, "Don't lecture me on how to administer justice, Sergeant. I know my job."

Henderson broke in. "The flak is getting pretty heavy, Theo. Right down the line. The phones don't stop ringing. Somebody's got to go, why not Virgil?"

"It's all there in front of us," Fellows said. "Virgil was after Bonner. He says he was in bed. He says his mother will vouch for him. Not much of a defense there."

"You figure he went up to Bonner's apartment at two in the morning?" Loukas said. "Raped her, killed her?"

"That's the way it happened."

The phantom infiltrated the crevices of Loukas' consciousness once more. This time, thick and syrupy, the mist held, gave him time to examine it. All his thinking had been in a straight line. *"Virgil was after Bonner. . . ."* Fellows had said it and all of them had accepted his reasoning.

But Loukas was unable to accept it. He inspected the phantom again. Very slowly it came back to him, Henderson's casual remark to Holly Mason: *"Hell, it could just as easily have been you. . . ."*

What if the killer had been aiming at Holly? In the darkness of that small apartment, he might have failed to realize his target was absent. Mistaken Jane Bonner for Holly.

If so, if Jane's death was an awful accident . . .

But who was after Holly? He would be the same man who had plotted and schemed and worked so hard and waited so patiently to attack each of the other women. Did Holly know him? Perhaps without realizing it she possessed the answer. Loukas opened his mouth to speak, thought better of it.

"It's the pressure, Theo," Henderson was saying. "We all feel it."

"Then you go along with this?"

"I have no choice."

"I do. I'm taking myself off the case."

"That seems like a reasonable thing to do," Fellows said.

"It's up to you, Theo," Henderson said.

"Petersen can handle any follow-up necessary," Fellows said.

Loukas returned to his desk in the Bureau. He went through the case files. Thick folders filled with photographs, laboratory reports, coroner's reports, transcripts of every interview made, measurements, theories, false starts. He struggled to make sense out of it, to arrange the separate pieces into a coherent pattern.

It was then that he remembered that meeting. The accidental coming together at A-1 Market. And the fragment of information that had come out of it, almost lost, only now recalled. Remembering it he knew, *knew* that Holly Mason was the key piece in the puzzle.

He almost laughed aloud. All of it was so simple, so obvious, had been there all the time to see. If you could see. But obscured by the cloud of detail, cast aside by the need to proceed in orderly fashion, in that damned logical, bureaucratic straight line. The line, he reminded himself grimly, had simply been cut short. Now Loukas extended it to its full length.

IV

"The guy who this all fits refuses to stay in the mold," Loukas had once said to Sandy Felton.

She had answered sensibly, *"Then it must be someone else."*

So simple, but like everyone else attached to the case, he had resisted simplicity. As much as Petersen or Fellows, he had wanted it to be Virgil, had wanted the damn case ended.

But it wasn't Virgil. Couldn't be. After every assault he was the one they considered. He had been sought out, questioned, his alibis checked. And all of it had appeared valid. Nevertheless, the line of logic had continued to point at Virgil, and not having a better suspect, Loukas had bulled ahead, hoping for that one break that would open the case for him.

He went over it once more. The old trail, the old questions. With one basic difference. This time inserting an alien element. The answers came as they had before, but now the pieces of the puzzle fell into place without strain. An image of a man loomed up, the figure fully fleshed out this time. And now a name attached itself to the face and form.

Loukas phoned Ned Bookman. An answering service responded. He left his name and number, said it was urgent. Eighteen minutes later, Bookman called back.

"Doctor," Loukas began without preliminary, "I did you a favor in keeping things quiet. Now I need some information from you."

"That's fair enough."

"It seems our killer had to function at least part of the time in the orbit of his victims. Well, supposing he had been in that orbit in the past. Is it psychologically possible that he picked his victims then and returned now for revenge?"

"Oh, yes." Bookman sounded relieved.

"A year ago, maybe more?"

"Entirely feasible. Such a man might nurse his desire for the women in question for a long time, his resentment building toward them, raging because they failed to recognize his existence."

"As a psychiatrist, what do you think the killer would do if a woman made herself available to him? Indicated some interest. Flirted, maybe. Would he make legitimate overtures, ask her for a date, try to seduce her?"

"I doubt it. More likely he'd follow the same pattern. Come skulking around, attempt assault on her. He probably possesses very little self-esteem and would not believe that a woman might actually be interested in him. More likely, he would view any show of interest as a sexual taunt and would try to gain revenge."

"I see."

"Is there anything else?"

Loukas understood that Bookman wanted to prolong the conversation. "Nothing, Doctor."

"Are you on to something?" Bookman said quickly. "To someone? I mean— Listen, Loukas, you comprehend my position. Obviously you no longer suspect me. Man to man, you'll keep my little secret? I can depend on you, can't I?"

"You've got nothing to worry about, Doctor," Loukas said coldly. "Not from me, anyway."

"Ah, Loukas, you're a good man. I knew it."

But Loukas had already hung up.

Certain he knew who the killer was, Loukas still needed evidence enough to send the prosecutor into court and gain a conviction.

He went to see Holly Mason. "Just a few more questions, Holly," he began.

"Oh, sure. If you think it will help."

"I do. Is anybody after you, Holly?"

"After me?" She frowned.

"Somebody trying to seduce you?"

She laughed. "Oh, that. There's always somebody. I mean, I'm not a bad looking chick, wouldn't you say?"

"One special man, Holly?"

"I meet a lot of guys."

"Someone you keep putting off, turning down? Someone you're not really interested in?"

"Well, I don't make it with everybody."

"This would be a particular kind of man. He wouldn't approach you directly. As a matter of fact, he might not approach you at all. Maybe just look at you. From a distance. Maybe he never even spoke to you."

She hugged herself. "Sounds spooky."

"Is there someone like that?"

"I can't think of anybody . . ."

"Take your time."

"I can't think of anybody."

"This class you take, at night, at the high school—"

"Oh," she said, "now that you mention it, there is somebody like that, sniffing around, watching kind of . . ."

Loukas waited for her to go on.

Back in the Bureau, Loukas started to phone the A-1 Market, decided against it. Instead he put a call in to Ruth Diamond in New York. He gave her the name Holly had given him.

"Does it ring a bell, Mrs. Diamond?"

"I'm not very good about names."

"Suppose I provide a face to go with the name?"

"You mean you've caught him?" There was fear in her voice. She was reluctant to be drawn back into the life from which she'd escaped.

"We'll have him soon, I think."

"It was so dark that night. I was afraid."

"Will you try to make an identification when the time comes?"

He heard her sigh. "I'll try."

Loukas had not expected more from her. He would have to find some way to build a case without her help. He would have to act himself and act soon.

Virgil Reiser sat frightened and alone in the cage of the Fort. He deserved to be freed.

And there was Victor Fellows. Lusting to propel himself onto the political stage. A man without moral roots, no sense of right or wrong, concerned with only one question: Will it work?

That he could gloat over his certain triumph over Victor Fellows made Loukas ashamed. He had allowed this to become a contest between himself and the prosecutor.

Oh, shit, he told himself.

"Don't cops ever break the law to uphold the law?" Sandy had asked the question.

Well, Fellows was not alone in twisting the rules. An illegal entry had taken Loukas into Arthur Slater's home —had shown the teacher to be innocent of all charges, he reminded himself defensively. And now Slater was dead. How much had Loukas' efforts in his behalf driven the teacher to the point of suicide?

Now he was about to repeat the pattern. There was no time to get a warrant. The killer might strike again; he had to act. Was this how it began? How a cop first justified breaking the law? The shame returned, but not for long.

V

Loukas stood inside the closed door of the apartment until his eyes grew accustomed to the dark. Each time was easier, forcing a locked door, entering alien premises. Working without sanction.

He flashed his light around. Books were on shelves or scattered on the floor: *Pain and Love. Sexual Agony; A Manual for Today. S-M; The Real Man's Way.* Some were open to passages recently read; pages marked with strips of cloth. Passages were underscored, words circled, photographs given marginal attention.

There were stacks of magazines showing muscular men in leather jerkins and breeches, in loincloths, or naked. They brandished clubs and maces and whips over nude women who prostrated themselves in mock terror and subjugation.

Loukas went into the back room. A heavy worktable stood in the center of the floor. Under his moving light, weird and frightening figures seemed to shift and leap in the darkness. A grotesquely large penis carved of wood, wearing a crown of thorns; a clay breast, cleaved by a woodsman's ax; a female head, shaved clean, the nose broken, hammer scars in the skull, an ear smashed away; a gray clay vagina with a knife rising out of it, daring to be withdrawn.

Loukas went back into the living room and sat down. Mixed emotions took hold of him. Relief because it was almost ended and a fierce anger that a man so clearly ill and consumed with hatred could roam free to damage and destroy innocent human beings.

Loukas had no doubt he was seated in the killer's chair. But he had uncovered no legal evidence; his very presence was a violation of the suspect's civil rights. Loukas meant to see that those rights were fully protected. He meant also to make this arrest stick before someone else was victimized.

CHAPTER TWENTY

I

VICTOR FELLOWS SAT propped up in bed studying the
Schor-Matheson contract. One hundred thousand dollars
a year; retainer plus costs. It was the most lucrative contract his law firm had ever had. Add to it the fact that
Harold L. Matheson was a man with considerable political clout, the kind who put his money where his political
interests lay, and the deal became doubly exciting.

Yet it was not Matheson who was primary, a situation
that unloosed considerable discontent in Fellows. With
Virgil Reiser locked away, with Petersen out collecting
evidence, Fellows had every reason to be satisfied. Yet
he felt neither satisfaction nor optimism.

A worm of doubt gnawed at his innards.

Loukas.

Petersen was hungry, desperate to advance himself,
willing to take risks in order to ride Fellows' coattails
to the top. First Selectman DaCosta, a man anxious to
retain his political head above water, was easily manipulated. Chief Wakeman vacillated, a weak man. Henderson, a good cop, was too much the Establishment man
to stand alone for very long.

Only Loukas craved nothing from this case. Correc-
tion: He wanted only to find the guilty man. To end
the trouble. Fellows had to admire Loukas, even to like
him. It was just unfortunate that Loukas owned no
greater ambition than to be what he already was—a cop.
It distressed Fellows that he had not been able to work
out an accord with the detective.

A car drew up in the driveway, interrupting hi
thoughts. A door slammed and there were familiar foot
steps on the stairs. Pauline had come home. The cloc
on the night table read one-thirty-five. Fellows put th
contract aside and arranged himself in a more uprigh
position.

"Well," he said in greeting, "I'd about given up o
you."

"I was in the city." She took off her dress. "You knev
that."

"That's twice this week."

"Friday will make three times. The gallery demand
a great deal of work." She removed her brassiere an
panties. Her body was neat, surprisingly well conditione
for a woman who'd had a child, was lax in her eatin
and drinking habits, who never did any exercise.

"We need you here," he said.

She disappeared into the bathroom and soon wa
splashing around in the shower. He waited patiently.

She returned, wearing a long cotton-flannel gown
ruffles at the wrists and the throat. "I'm terribly tired,"
she announced, taking her place in the bed. She lay o
her side, back toward him.

He touched an exposed patch of skin on her neck
She shivered.

"It's been a long time," he said in a restrained manner

"What brought this about?"

"Watching you undress, Pauline. Seeing you naked
You have a lovely figure."

"Victor, you are a surprise at times. Up till now you'v
always been a man of the dark.

"People change."

"Not my Victor."

He reached under the gown, caressed her bottom
"You feel absolutely marvelous, Pauline."

"I must get some sleep."

"There are such things as conjugal rights." He laughe
briefly. "Any judge in the world would say—"

"Not tonight, Victor."

"Isn't that why you showered?"

She heaved herself around, eyes burrowing into him
if trying to fix the state of his mind. "Very well," she
id. "You have a right to know."

"Know? Know what?"

"That there are other men in my life."

He frowned. "Would you mind explaining that?"

"Victor," she said patiently, "I am telling you that
go to bed with other men."

"You admit to committing adultery!"

"In some circles they refer to it as screwing around."

"Try to keep your natural vulgarity under control,
y dear. You said other *men*. Plural. Was it merely a
p of the tongue?"

"A fact. More than one. Plural as hell. A number of
en."

He took that under consideration. "How many?"

"What difference does it make?"

"It makes a difference to me. How many?"

"The number varies. Three men with some regularity.
oes that help?"

"Why?" he cried. "Why?"

"Because I need what I don't get here. What you have
ever been able to give me, Victor."

"You're a mother and a wife."

"And a human being with her own private needs.
ou'd prefer me to continue to exist in your reflected
lory. I can't do that. I'm not equipped to go on accept-
ag physical and emotional handouts. I want my own life.
need it. I'm entitled to it. Men are part of that life."
he sat up. "The gallery is a success, Victor. Oh, not
early the biggest or the best, but moving along. It
ill become even better, more successful. I am good at
hat I do. I meet rewarding, attractive people in my
vork. They like me. I am in demand. Socially and
exually. I intend to go wherever I want to go, do what-
ver I want to do. Should you try to stop me, Victor,
will leave you."

He stared at her, unable to immediately respond. Then
e said, "That's absurd."

"Perhaps. But crowd me, Victor, and you'll discove that I mean what I say."

"You've got to stop it, what you're doing. There's n way to keep it secret. . . . Those men—"

"Victor, in all the years of our marriage, I accepte blame for the failures that occurred in this bed. I fe inadequate, emotionally pinched and starved, and guil for feeling that way. Now I know better. Men assure n that I'm uncommonly good in bed, that I possess ver and imagination."

"Don't you care about your reputation?"

"Oh, poor, poor Victor. My reputation is very soun thank you. It does very well for me."

"I'll divorce you."

"As you wish, Victor."

"You don't care! Very well, but you might consid James."

"I've considered him at length. James will go wher ever I go."

"No court would award you custody."

Her smile was thin, her eyes flinty. "Victor, fight n on this and it will mean the end of your political dream The publicity generated by a nasty divorce would ru you."

"You'd do that to me?"

"If necessary."

He weighed what she had said and decided to tal her at her word. He slumped slightly. "What do yo expect of me, Pauline?"

"Just leave me alone, Victor. I'll be a proper wife public; we'll be a proper family. As long as you do interfere. With your material assistance and enthusiast backing, I shall, in the not too distant future, open gallery in Manhattan. I will also rent a small but ve pleasant apartment in town. Commuting is such a dra as they say. Mondays through Fridays I'll remain in t city. Weekends I shall return to Arcadia and assume n wifely duties."

"And if I refuse?"

"Can you afford to refuse?"

"I'll consider it," he answered petulantly.

She shifted onto her stomach, head on the pillow. er eyes closed. "Do that, Victor."

She was almost asleep when he spoke again, his voice nall, almost pleading. "Pauline, I've never been very ood at chasing women. I don't think I'd like to do it ow. On weekends, would we still live as a married ouple? You understand what I mean?"

"What an interesting suggestion!" she said lazily. "We n discuss it. In the morning."

Satisfied with her reply, he turned off the light and ade himself comfortable. In a few minutes, both of em were asleep. Side by side in the bed. But not uching.

CHAPTER TWENTY-ONE

I

THE AMERICAN WOMAN: Romance and Roles.

The course was part of the Adult Education Divisi
at Arcadia High School, the title exuding suburban se
importance and cuteness. She disliked both qualities.

The class was held one night a week in the Lit
Theater, a bowl-like chamber with seats rising alme
to the ceiling. Each week a different lecturer, each co
petent in a discipline of concern to women. The cour
had become known as Lib Lab.

Loukas had asked her to come. And when he had, s
had responded with a mixture of disappointment a
anticipation. He apologized, said he would never ha
come to her had she not raised the possibility herse

She acknowledged her mistake.

He said he'd understand if she refused.

She said of course she wouldn't refuse. If he thoug
there was no danger.

There was always *some* danger, he told her. Son
chance that matters would not work out according
plan.

She conceded that. But the odds were long in the
favor?

Oh, yes. But he didn't want to mislead her.

They discussed it. They planned it. They went over
a number of times until it seemed foolproof. Or almost s

"What if it isn't him?" she asked finally.

"It must be. It must be."

But she knew from the sound of his voice that he
asn't certain. Not even about that.

Now, entering the school building, the anxiety intensi-
ed. This was no game of tennis in which losing caused
nly minimal and transient distress. The stakes in this
ame were pain, and possibly death.

They had talked for a long time, rehearsed everything
e was to say. Loukas had chosen her clothes, told her
ow to walk, how to stand, detailing her every move.

And as soon as she set foot in the main entrance
bby, all of it fled her mind.

A man in crisp, starched khakis sat in a chair not
r from the doors. He was reading a magazine. Seeing
r, he tucked the magazine into his pocket and came
rward. The night watchman. Loukas had told her his
ame; what was it?

"Can I help you, ma'am?"

Her mind functioned sluggishly, finally throwing up
ne of Loukas' commands. "Take your coat off as soon
s you enter the building. . . ."

It seemed to take forever, undoing the oversized
uttons, tugging at the sleeves, draping it over one arm.
he felt exposed. The slacks she wore were too tight,
ought when she was ten pounds lighter. They hugged
er hips, outlined her panties. A thin white nylon sweater
ung to her breasts; no bra, Loukas had insisted. Her
.outh was dry and she touched her tongue to her lips,
s if to summon up moisture.

"I'm Mrs. Felton," she said. "I'm here for the Lib
ab. Can you tell me where I go?" Her voice was sur-
isingly steady.

"Started about five minutes ago. It's back near the
ym building. Just follow the corridor, you can't miss it."

"Thank you," she said, lifting a hand. She turned back.
've seen you before, I think." She breathed deeply and
emembered that a last look in the mirror had shown
er brown nipples revealed through the white nylon. She
aw his eyes flicker, lift up again.

"Here at school, Mrs. Felton. Parent-Teacher meetings.
m always here."

"Somewhere else."

He nodded solemnly. "Used to work at A-1. M[...] deliveries."

Her smile was wide, pleasant. "Of course. That's [...] You used to deliver to my house."

"That's right," he said.

"Ralph, isn't it? Ralph Burleigh."

He seemed startled that she knew his name. "You[...] got a good memory, Mrs. Felton."

"I remember you, Ralph," she said.

Not too much, Loukas had warned. Don't alarm h[...] Just lay it out and wait for him to nibble.

Sandy strode down the corridor. For the first time[...] her life she wished she were bony and flat, that her fl[...] provoked no man. She didn't dare look back.

When she returned two hours later, he was still at [...] door. She paused to put on her coat, smiled in [...] direction.

"An interesting class," she offered.

"Never get a chance to listen to any of them mys[...] There's rounds to make."

"Well," she said cheerfully, "good night, Ralph."

"Good night, Mrs. Felton."

Maybe, she thought, hurrying to her car. May[...] Loukas was wrong.

"Do everything the way you always do," Loukas h[...] said. She considered every move. She drove into [...] garage. Pulled the overhead door into place, locked [...] went inside.

After a long, hot shower, she donned a flimsy nig[...] gown, then drew the drapes across the picture wind[...] in her bedroom. Was someone besides Loukas watchi[...] The possibility made her shiver. Suddenly she gr[...] afraid for Loukas, considered calling out to him, invit[...] him into the house to wait out the night with her.

Instead, she went back downstairs, made some De[...] and watched an old movie on television. Robert Ry[...] and Robert Mitchum. A bad picture, but the stars pleas[...] her. They looked the way men ought to look, not [...]

pretty, not too delicate, as if each had lived a life that had nothing to do with being an actor. It occurred to her that Loukas might have filled either role; he had the same kind of appeal, one of experience and native wisdom. When the picture was over, she went to bed, first taking a Valium.

In the morning, she woke rested and strangely calm. She lay in bed for a while, then went to the window and opened the draperies. It was a grim day, gray and chilly, the ground covered with snow. She filled her lungs with air and in one swift movement lifted the nightgown over her head, letting it fall to the floor. She forced herself to stand there, ticking off five silent counts before turning away.

Watching her from his hiding place, what had Loukas thought? Had he been revolted, shamed, by that impulsive, unplanned action on her part? She understood that in some strange and disturbing way she had wanted to expose herself to Loukas, as if to display some heretofore unrevealed portion of her private self.

She dressed quickly, anxious now to get on with it— sweater, jeans, tennis shoes. There was a limit to how available she could make herself.

She went through her morning routine. Open the garage; carry the garbage cans outside, to be emptied later by the service she employed. Her eyes flicked over the white expanse to the tree line, nearly forty feet away. Bushes and hedges, the stand of trees, formed an obscuring wall. Loukas was out there somewhere, had been all night, by now probably frozen solid, incapable of any quick movements. It was a stupid plan, she told herself with a surprising flash of anger and resentment.

She circled toward the kitchen door, moving without haste. Her heart began to beat faster and the dryness returned to her throat. No plan was perfect. People were an unstable element in every situation.

Behind her, a shuffling noise. The unmistakable sound of feet crossing the gravel driveway. Her joints stiffened and she had to force herself to go on. Loukas' voice sounded in her head—"*Stay calm, let him make the first move, then react.*" She kept moving.

His breathing was audible, harsh, irregular, and she imagined she heard bestial grunting as he came nearer. Nothing had prepared her for this, the animal sound of him, or the enormity of her own fear. It was too much! She started to turn. Too late. His fist landed on her cheek and she stumbled backward.

Loukas . . . ! she cried silently.

Ralph Burleigh was neither attractive nor boyish in the dull light of morning. His eyes bulged and his mouth worked without sound, his skin was mottled. He hit her again and she went down on her back.

Loukas . . . ! No sound came out of her.

She rolled, knees anticipating him as Loukas had instructed her to do. He dove forward and she summoned all her available power into the thrust of her legs. Burleigh fell away.

Sandy ran. He came after her, closing fast. His fingers hooked into the neckline of the sweater and she felt herself thrown off balance, flung to the ground. He began kicking her as she tried to spin away.

"Loukas!" she screamed.

Her own helplessness made her wild and weak and she was aware of her strength fading, knew that she could not hold him off much longer. *Where* was Loukas? Had the night been too long for him? As if in answer, she heard a distant voice . . .

"Police! Stand up and put your hands in the air! Now!"

Burleigh came up into a crouch, hands lifted as if to obey. Then he broke for the woods.

Loukas brought his pistol to bear on the fleeing man, bracing his wrist. "Stop or I'll shoot!" The service revolver was heavy in his hand, but not unpleasantly so, a solid extension of his flesh, and he perceived Ralph Burleigh distinctly across the sight.

His fingers tightened in place and a sense of power rippled along his nerves. There was no way he could miss.

Shoot, he commanded himself. Shoot and return peace

and tranquillity to Arcadia, to all its inhabitants. Shoot and kill Ralph Burleigh.

A cry of revulsion lodged in his throat. His gun hand jerked up and he fired into the air.

"Stop!" he shouted. "You're under arrest!"

Ralph Burleigh disappeared into the woods.

Loukas followed. His legs stretched and pulled; his stomach muscles set against the effort of the chase. He tried to breathe in more of the cold morning air. There was a relief and satisfaction in the use of his body. The stiffness left his joints and he felt an almost forgotten joy in being a purely physical creature.

He wanted to caution Ralph Burleigh. Don't run, there is no safe haven. Not in Arcadia, not anywhere else.

A low-hanging branch sent him ducking, tripping, going down on hands and knees. He lost his pistol, spent time searching for it, went on.

Burleigh's lead had increased. He circled north toward the Old Mill, sliced down toward Seven Mile River. Loukas projected an imaginary line to a point on the river where Burleigh had to emerge. He ran toward that point.

Branches whipped at his face. He tripped, bounced off the trunk of a tree. Weariness settled into his thighs. All that exercise in the basement of the Fort had failed to prepare him for this. And Ralph Burleigh was almost twenty years younger.

His knees began to wobble. The pistol grew heavier in his hand. What if Burleigh put up a fight? Younger, stronger probably, and in much better shape. He might be forced to use his gun. The memory of the earlier killing urge returned and he shuddered. He knew he would not shoot the other man. He couldn't.

At the point where Loukas broke out of the woods, he was less than ten yards from the river. A line of slippery rocks provided an uncertain path across the gushing water. As a boy he'd crossed here many times. But now he hesitated.

Some late leaves fluttered to the ground. A squirrel

scurried across the forest floor. Some mourning doves. But no Ralph Burleigh.

Loukas started back up the hill. The car. Ralph Burleigh would be heading back to his car. Loukas had checked it out. A 1965 Ford which Burleigh had purchased less than a year ago. He had worked on it diligently ever since, almost rebuilding the motor. It was a car that Ralph was proud of. Yet strangely, he had ignored its exterior. Paint peeled in spots and it was stained, dusty. Just another old machine that no one would pay much notice to.

Loukas felt acute pain. Lungs burned. Thighs ached. A stab of agony struck his gut. Why not let it go? Send out an A.P.B. Burleigh wouldn't get far. But Loukas couldn't stop.

Back past the Old Mill, onto a narrow path that led up to Brooks Drive. Fifty feet from the road he came out into the open. There was no car in sight.

He tried to hear over his rasping breath. Nothing. Had Burleigh outfoxed him, not doubled back at all? Or had he taken a more circuitous route, hoping to increase his lead time?

Brooks Drive opened onto Hightstown Turnpike, which was little more than a dirt road leading west. Loukas went along the Turnpike to where it bent, just prior to dipping under the Parkway. There, parked on the shoulder, in full view, stood the old Ford.

Loukas took up a position behind the wide trunk of an old red maple, working to bring his body under control. Soon the trembling ceased and some of the weakness departed. He strapped the Police Special back in its holster. Soon he hear footsteps.

As if at the end of an innocent morning stroll, Ralph Burleigh came out of the woods. His youthful face was serene, pleasant, attractive. He advanced without anxiety. He was less than twenty feet away when Loukas stepped out from behind the red maple.

"Ralph," Loukas said.

Burleigh accepted Loukas' presence with apparent equanimity. "Sergeant Loukas," he said. He lifted his right hand and Loukas saw that he held a rock the size of a baseball.

Burleigh heaved the rock and Loukas dove for the ground. He came up running. Burleigh picked up a thick branch and swung. In full stride, Loukas twisted, but was unable to avoid the branch completely. It glanced off his left shoulder, knocking him down.

Loukas kept himself moving, putting distance between Burleigh and himself. He came up, aware that his left arm was already growing numb. Burleigh came forward.

"I'll kill you, Sergeant," he cried. "I mean it!"

Loukas rose slowly. His shoulder pulsed with pain and he knew his left arm was useless.

"Put it down, Ralph."

"Don't come near me! I'm warning you!"

"Enough people have been hurt, Ralph. We don't want any more."

"Let me alone!"

Loukas charged and Burleigh swung. Loukas went under the branch, made contact with Burleigh at the knees. They went down together. Pain stabbed deep into Loukas' left shoulder and he almost cried out. He rose up, his fist cocked.

Burleigh recoiled, protecting his face with his hands. "Don't." His voice was thin, childish, almost a whine. "Don't hurt me, please. Please don't hurt me."

EPILOGUE

LOUKAS ARRIVED EARLY at the train station. He took up a position that allowed him to see the track until it bent out of sight in the general direction of New York City. He shuffled around uneasily, paced back and forth. Then the train swung into sight, almost on time.

She appeared looking slightly disheveled but tan and healthy. Her face lit up when she saw him and she waved. He went forward. They shook hands briefly and he lifted her bags.

"Ah, Theo. It's nice of you to meet me. It's been a long time."

"Nearly a year. You look terrific, Sandy."

"A quiet beach. Sunlight. Lots of time alone. Good food. All great for the health. I'm afraid I put on nearly five pounds."

"You look okay to me."

He led the way to his car. "I was afraid you might change your mind, not come back."

"I thought about it. I spent some time in Los Angeles. People I know live there. Even looked at a couple of apartments. But it was no go. I decided that I belong here."

"Good."

She shifted around to face him. "Theo, I wanted to run away, to get away from a lot of bad memories."

"I understand."

She hesitated. "There was something else. You, Theo. I was angry with you. Very angry."

"Why?"

"Because you set me up for Ralph Burleigh."

"You volunteered."

"Yes, but you weren't supposed to accept the offer. Crazy, isn't it? I wanted to do it, to be a part of your work, but I wanted you to refuse to let me. To protect me. Shield me from that filth. I tried to convince myself that you were no different from every other man I've ever known. That you used me, too."

"You came back anyway."

"Most of the anger is gone."

"But not all?"

"Not all."

"I'm sorry."

She grinned. "Don't worry, it'll go away. I can tell."

"How can you tell?"

"I told you it was crazy. Helping you is what did it, actually. Made me begin to like myself again. What the hell, I did pretty well for myself under pressure. I wasn't just a lump of useless meat. You needed help and I was able to give it. You depended on me to do a job. You trusted me and I learned I could trust myself. When I figured that one out, I decided that I'd come back."

He drove on without speaking.

"Once you said you loved me," she said softly. "Is it still that way for you?"

"Yes." He kept his eyes on the road.

"I have a lot of feeling for you, Theo. But don't go too fast. Let's get to know each other. Really know each other."

"That's all right with me."

"There's so much to talk about."

"We'll sort everything out."

"Maybe you'd like to buy this lady a drink."

"Jerry's okay with you?"

"Is there any other place?"

LOOK FOR THESE GREAT POCKET 🦘 BOOK BESTSELLERS AT YOUR FAVORITE BOOKSTORE

LOOKING FOR MR. GOODBAR • Judith Rossner
TOTAL FITNESS IN 30 MINUTES A WEEK • Laurence E. Morehouse, Ph.D. & Leonard Gross
THE TOTAL WOMAN • Marabel Morgan
DARK DESIRES • Parley J. Cooper
THE STONEWALL BRIGADE • Frank G. Slaughter
THE PIRATE • Harold Robbins
THE HAVERSHAM LEGACY • Daoma Winston
HARLEQUIN • Morris West
HOW TO BECOME AN ASSERTIVE WOMAN • Bryna Taubman
EVERYTHING YOU WANT TO KNOW ABOUT TM—INCLUDING HOW TO DO IT • John White
BABY AND CHILD CARE (New Revised Edition) • Dr. Benjamin Spock
MESSAGE FROM ABSALOM • Anne Armstrong Thompson
THE BOTTOM LINE • Fletcher Knebel
HOW TO LIVE WITH ANOTHER PERSON • David Viscott, M.D.
JACKIE AND ARI • Lester David & Jhan Robbins